The Sleepy Hollow Incident

Incident

Book Two

PD Alleva

Chamber Door Publishing, LLC

Chamber Door Publishing
Delray Beach, Fl

ISBN(s): Paperback: 979-8-9938039-0-6
          Hardback: 979-8-9938039-1-3

Cover: Cherie Foxley
Editor: Chamber Door Publishing
Interior design: Chamber Door Publishing

Printed in the USA

"All the love gone bad turned my world to black
Tattooed all I see, all that I am
All I'll be.
~ Pearl Jam (*Black*)

Part III

January 26, 1997

"It's an ode to Poe," declared the man in black. "One of the great minds of your species." He pulled the strap tight around his victim's wrist, tying him to the stone slab.

A whimpering groan escaped from the victim's throat. His eyelids fluttered as his head drifted from left to right. He'd yet to realize his predicament. His thick dark hair was moist with sweat- it was damn hot in the dungeon despite the frigid cold of winter outside-and his naked body dripped with perspiration, his skin tinged with the color of red heat, reflecting the many torches pinned across the walls.

"Now he showed promise." The man in black stood tall, staring at his victim. "He had the ability to see past the ether into the darkness existing within the human heart." He turned to Wren, standing by the wall beside the thick wooden lever that disappeared into the stone. "For which there is no end to such darkness."

Wren couldn't help but smile. To smile for his master. Today marked the first moment of the stars' alignment, beginning the celestial connection to the master's home and officially beginning their work. The sacrifice was already on the slab. But the opening would not last, and there was so much to accomplish before the celestial bodies closed on their venture.

Their victim-Michael Tedesco-groaned once again. Michael was a college student attending Fordham University. He was a stellar student, close to graduating with an MBA. His devious nature was what first attracted the master. It was always good to torture the sinful-those whose egos drove their wretchedness-and Michael would rather witness someone's demise than offer a helping hand.

Michael's continued sedation was troubling. Wren knew his master wanted Michael to be fully awake when the torture came. Wanted him coherent, alert and orientated. How else could they elicit the fear necessary to drive the portal open? The portal fed on fear energy, growing stronger with every vibration that buzzed with a fear frequency. It was this very frequency that was the key to strengthening the ether and opening the astral plane that would connect the master's home to Sleepy Hollow.

"Miiichaellll," his master sang, sinister and goading. But all Michael did was groan, his head lolling to the side, his eyes closed.

"Perhaps we gave him too much?" said Wren, lifting his gaze from Michael to the master.

The man in black looked at the firepit to the left of the stone slab and the burning coals within. He turned to Wren. "Perhaps we should wake him from his slumber?"

Wren turned to the firepit and the steel rod that was gathering heat from the coals. The master gripped the rod then carried it to the slab, its sharp pointed tip glowing bright orange with heat.

"Miiiichaaaaeeelllll," groaned the master. "Time to wake up." He pressed the tip on Michael's stomach. Wren heard the hiss when his skin bubbled and welted, drawing blood to the surface that was enveloped inside the wound, turning the infected skin into a shade of dark purple. Michael's eyes snapped open as a scream erupted from his throat.

"Ahh, I see you're awake." The master grinned then laughed, pressing the rod to Michael's chest as another holler screeched from Michael's throat. The master held the rod in place. Michael's skin bubbled, seared from the heat.

Gurgling in Michael's throat as if his scream returned to choke the air from his lungs. The master pulled the rod from Michael's chest, holding the heated tip close to Michael's wide-open eyes.

"What the fuck…" Michael whined, writhing in anguish. His mouth opened to a slit; a stare filled with wretched pain plastered across his scrunched face.

The master craned his head, glaring at Michael with a stoic stare, holding the rod for him to see. "Perhaps your eye should go next?" Michael's eyes widened, staring at the cherry burning on the rod. "Or your scrotum. It makes no difference to me what part of you burns, but should you drift off once again I promise you, either your eye or your scrote will be gone a second later. Do you understand? *Michael.*"

With gritted teeth, Michael nodded, his eyes darting around the dungeon. Wren always found it humorous when the victim realized their predicament. Michael yanked his arms and legs, but the restraints held. The master gripped his jaw, squeezing as Michael cringed, staring fearfully at the master.

"And don't move, Michael. Should you pull on those restraints one more time, I'll cut out your liver and eat it in front of your dying eyes."

Michael seemed to settle down with the master's gaze. His body went slack, and the master released his jaw. "Where am I?" Michael whined as the master stepped in front of the firepit, returning the rod to the coals. "Who are you people?" He turned his head to see Wren, who couldn't help but grin for the man.

The master stood over the fire, staring at the burning coals. "We are the harbingers of fear, Michael. And considering your dark heart, your fear is a necessity. For what fear truly has more essence than the fear spawned from a nefarious heart?" The master stepped to the slab, craning his head and glaring at Michael. He placed his hand on Michael's forehead. Michael scanned his dark, calloused hand and Wren was certain that if Michael could melt into the stone to avoid that hand he would. Tears pricked in his eyes, dripping down the side of his face to his ears. Whimpers in his throat, it was obvious to Wren he was attempting to squelch a full out bellow and cry. The fear plastered across his face was priceless.

"You are the first, Michael. The first in a long line of souls that will spill an ocean of blood in this room. We need fear, Michael." He paused and craned his head. "Can you provide us with what we need?"

10

Michael seemed to cringe within himself, staring confused at the master. "I want to go home," he whined to the frustration of the master, who turned to Wren. "Whatever I did, I can make up for it. Please, just let me go."

"He doesn't get it, does he Wren?" The master glared at Michael. "You're only good to us if you're dead, Michael. Allowing you to return home is not in our best interest. And you know more than your share of someone's own best interest now, don't you?"

Again, Michael receded into himself, cringing as the master dipped his head closer to Michael's eyes. Michael turned from the master's gaze and shut his eyes as if he could disappear.

"No, no, no, Michael." The master gripped Michael's jaw and forehead, forcing his head straight. "I need for you to see Michael. To watch death's decent as it comes to claim your soul."

Michael started mumbling.

Is he praying? thought Wren.

"Little late for God, Michael. You shouldn't have let him go all those years ago." The master tilted his head, listening to Michael whispering the Lord's Prayer beneath his breath. "Open your eyes, Michael. Or should I cut off your eyelids?"

Michael snapped his eyes open, no longer whispering.

The master grinned. "Good, Michael. Very good. Shall we begin?"

"Begin what?" asked Michael with a crack in his voice.

The master craned his neck, looking up, all the way to the ceiling.

11

Michael followed his gaze to the pendulum hanging from the rafters. "My god what is this?" He started thrashing, attempting to remove his restraints.

The master looked at Wren, closed his eyes and nodded. Wren pulled the lever that clicked with a wooden thump followed by a screech from above as if the bowels of hell had suddenly awakened. Chains rattled as the master took his position, standing in front of the slab by Michael's feet. The master liked to watch. He enjoyed it when the victim squirmed, petrified as the torture arrived in full swing. Enjoyed watching the light leap from their eyes. Wren stepped to the opposite side, across from his master.

"Get me outta here," Michael screamed, pulling on his restraints, wriggling across the slab as the wooden creak slapped across the chamber and the swing from the pendulum whooshed across the air. "Jesus Christ!"

The pendulum dipped down with a wooden creak and a rattling chain. Closer to Michael's navel.

"Death comes for us all," said the man in black. "It truly is a wonder to witness firsthand."

Thrashing. Wriggling. Pulling. Yanking. Michael did all he could to free himself, his eyes wide, grunting and groaning. Panicked and huffing. The pendulum dipped closer.

"Oh, Michael, just let it happen. Take your medicine with the same pride you use to advance your own interests."

"This is fucking insane!" Michael screamed.

And the pendulum dipped closer with a wooden crunch, the blade swiping empty air but ready to strike. To nip at Michael's skin.

"Fuck you," he screamed at the man in black. "Fuck alllll of youuuuuuu."

The first cut across his navel cringed his body. His eyes bulged from their sockets as if they could explode from his skull. Blood bubbled from the wound as the pendulum swiped again. Deeper. His scream caught in his throat; his head thrashed from right to left. Another swipe from the blade, and Wren saw blood and skin leap into the air. He turned to his master and his wide staring eyes, seething and gritting his teeth as Michael yelped and yawped, hollering as the blade cut again, deeper, tearing into his innards.

Michael's tongue extended over his lips with a scream that leapt off his wriggling tongue when the pendulum swung back with vengeance, slicing deeper and this time Wren was certain his organs were diced in half as blood coughed over Michael's lips. Gurgling now. Drowning in his own blood.

"Thank you, Michael," said the man in black. "Thank you."

The last swing from the blade severed his body in half, his innards draped across the slab as blood pooled across the stone, raining to the floor. The man in black gave a nod to Wren. He stepped to the wall then lifted the lever just as the last swipe chinked against the stone before the wooden creak groaned, lifting the pendulum to the ceiling.

The man in black stood, unwavering, wide eyed, watching the ground absorb the blood when a loud thump barreled into the ancient wooden doors. Wren twitched when he heard it, the sound was a loud boom that echoed across the dungeon. The doors buckled, as if someone behind the door was squeezing the wood. The doors creaked and groaned, clicking, on the verge of splintering. Behind the doors a rickety growl erupted, clicking and clucking.

"Come," said the man in black. "Breathe with new life received through fresh blood."

The doors then stretched, ballooning into the dungeon with a loud creak followed by several snapping pops, returning to normal a second after. The creaking and growl ceased and the man in black gritted his teeth.

Wren felt his heart drop into his stomach. He turned to his master.

"The portal has been dormant for so long. What must be done for it to thrive once again?" He could see his master's hands were clenched into fists. "What human can construct such a door?"

"Those doors were not created by any human, Wren, but from the servants of hell. Fortified by Baphomet and sealed from the inside by the King himself. Even our priming sacrifices have done little to aid in our endeavor."

The master turned to the slab, gazing over Michael before lifting his gaze to the entrances then continued towards the sky. He ran his tongue across his teeth then returned his stare to Michael

14

when he stepped over to the body and placed his hand on Michael's forehead. With his free hand he reached into the severed corpse, all the way past his elbow. His arm moved within the body, inching his fingers further into the chest until he clutched the heart then tore it from the severed corpse. His arm came away slick with blood and little pieces of Michael's innards. The master gripped the heart tight then dropped it onto the hot coals.

"Let it burn, Wren. Let it sit and simmer and burn into the coals as an offering to the ether. The more hearts we capture, the stronger our hold in Xibalba." He clucked his tongue before he stepped to the side, taking his cane that was leaning against the slab. He twisted the cap then thrust the hidden blade from it.

"But what must be done?" asked Wren. "What task will open the portal?"

Staring at the blade, the master answered Wren's question. "It's going to take a bloodbath." He eyeballed Wren. "Sleepy Hollow will never be the same... Not after we are done. Let us introduce them... to medieval torture."

The Super Bowl party was in full effect. The Hampton mansion was shoulder to shoulder with guests and waitstaff attending to their every need. A new large screen television captured the game with a host of guests sitting on couches and chairs. Mostly teenagers, the son of the owner and his friends, waiting for the game to start, as the adult guests mingled and drank and consorted over the next big venture.

A social event if there ever was one. Lori arrived with Elena. Despite Lori's protest, Elena had coaxed her into attending the party.

"It's good to get out," Elena had said. "I think it's time to put the past to bed."

Lori was under the impression that Elena had an ulterior motive waiting at the party. Lori couldn't care less about social gatherings. Since she arrived home in September, she spent most of her time in her bedroom. Her body ached with a hollow pain, a depression she believed she would never shake, as if a part of her soul had been amputated. Staring out her window for days on end, watching summer recede into autumn, then autumn succumb to winter. Holidays passed by in a blink of weary mindlessness. No matter how much time had passed, the wound that Marc had brought to her heart remained fresh and unhealing.

But maybe Elena was right. Perhaps it was time to start over because the alternative was death, either slow or in a rush of depression and self-loathing, although always inevitable. There comes a point where you either give in and give up or give in and get up. There's no two ways about it, and Lori couldn't shake the notion burning in her gut that she had unfinished business. As if she was being kept alive by some phantom belief that life could return to laughter and gratitude. Somewhere in the future, after the dark veil was lifted.

Elena introduced Lori to the owners-Jordan and Constance Bellinger-who offered their hospitality and a graceful welcome. But Lori had no use for small talk, and quickly excused herself, grabbing a drink from the bar before she made her way outside to the cold frigid air, staring at the ocean waves glimmering under the crescent moon. She enjoyed the quiet of the ocean over the hollers and chatter erupting in the house.

Elena was wrong though. It wasn't the right time, and all Lori wanted was to go home and return to her hovel of darkness and torture. She couldn't care less about the game and even less about the people getting juiced and congratulating each other for a life well done. She longed for simplicity, because simplicity catered to a larger care for the world, without judgment or ridicule. Sleepy Hollow had cultured her, cultured Lori in a way that snapped the façade brought on by wealth.

She looked over her shoulder at the people inside. Most would cut off their mother's head if their riches were in question.

They seemed like plastic, all of them, with their pearls, and diamonds, and dresses and suits she was certain were worn in some warped decision to keep up with the elite and maintain the façade that they could never break free from. It turned her gut knowing these were her people. She wanted nothing to do with them.

Now here comes Elena.

Shit! Lori gritted her teeth, turning back to the ocean. She wasn't just coming out by herself. There was a man following closely on her heels. Lori gulped down her drink as the sliding glass door opened.

"Lori, darling," said Elena and Lori cringed, shaking her head. She despised that whining, fucking voice. "Let me introduce you to Henry Clavell. He works for the FBI."

"Marc will return come morning, Wren," said the man in black. He was sitting in the living room, staring through the window. A single lit candle sat on the table beside him, his cane in his right hand. "In the darkness, while I sleep, his shall be the eyes that greet you come morning." He shifted in his seat-a dark red leather high-back-and leaned his head against it, staring into the cold dark outside the mansion. "Light the bonfire and toss Michael into it. The blood should be fully absorbed by now. It is best to toss away the rest of the garbage."

Wren, standing beside his master, said, "The stars are aligning in our favor, my master. What does this mean for our host?"

"As we draw closer to the celestial constellation, Marc will have less time in the host body."

"Does he remember? Is it possible he sings about our work here?"

The man in black waved his hand through the candle's flame, cupping the smoke then drifting the scent to his nose. "Not at all," the man in black whispered. "He chooses not to know, to recede into himself when our deeds are done. With every moment he remains in the cemetery's ether he grows more confused, incapable of deciphering between what is real and what is delusion. And the ghosts surrounding him keep him in a state of panic."

"I do as you wish, my master. What are your instructions during your rest?"

To which the man in black responded, "It is time to ramp up our efforts and for our efforts to play to an audience. To conjure fear in abundance and spill an ocean of blood...." He paused, staring at the flame. "The celestial bodies are approaching their full alignment, and we have only this window to open the astral plane to my home. There is much work to be done. And I must be prepared. I must bring myself to full strength."

"As you wish, my master."

"Continue to provide the absinthe during sunset to our host. It is true that I require more time in the ether to gather my strength. I shall rest during the day and awaken with the sunset." He looked around, gathering his thoughts. "This dimension taps my power more than I had expected. Perhaps too much time in the cemetery has affected my cells more than I was aware. I grow tired so quickly." His head down, he closed his eyes and breathed deeply before lifting his head and gazing into the darkness. "We have five days before the constellation is in full view and close enough to open the astral highway. There is so much to do. After the absinthe is provided, I will return to the body." He looked at Wren. "But worry not. During the day I'll be listening... watching from my slumber." And he laughed, a slight chuckle, amused by himself. "Although I will not be at full strength when our host has taken the

20

mantle, I'll be able to provide the necessary confusion for Marc to assist you in your endeavors. In the event of an unforeseen circumstance… I'll be listening and providing instructions. You have no cause for concern about it. During such times I'll be the consciousness for our host while my cells regenerate. I'll feed off his life energy to save my own." He looked over his shoulder at Wren. "I'm always listening, Wren. Always. We've come too far to falter now." And he paused, thinking. He squeezed the top of his cane, placed it over his lap then pinched the green rope around his right wrist, rolling the rope between his fingertips. "The next five days are crucial to our existence *and* our purpose. They must be executed with precision if we are to attain our ultimate goal."

Wren bowed to his master. "As you wish," he said. "As you wish."

Henry wasn't like the others. He was calm and sincere and had learned to enjoy simplicity. Lori breathed a sigh of relief that she didn't have to listen to the egocentric ramblings of another rich prick. Henry was poised and intelligent, but a bit on the boring side- Lori didn't care about the secret society behind the CIA-although he seemed harmless enough.

Plus, it was good to have someone to talk to. Even if the conversation consisted mainly of the trivial notions that life has to offer. Sometimes those trivial moments are all we need to break free from the chains that bind the heart. And since she was talking with Henry, her mother was nowhere in sight. Although Lori was certain Elena was watching from somewhere in the house, pretending not to be eavesdropping and stealing glances from the corner of her eye.

An awkward silence split the air between them. They could hear that the game was about to begin. Introductions were ongoing and the chatter from inside rose a few levels to compete with the game beaming from the surround sound system.

"Not into football?" Henry cupped his hands together, blowing into his fists. It was damn cold, but Lori preferred the frigid air and icy winds erupting from the ocean. They helped to cleanse the mind.

She leaned against the wall separating the patio from the beach. Lori shrugged. "It's okay. But I prefer baseball."

"Ah, Yankees fan?"

"Of course. Greatest team in sports history. You?"

"I'm a Mets fan." Henry rolled his eyes.

"Should I offer my condolences now, or wait until you've successfully mourned your team?" Lori cocked a smile in the corner of her mouth.

"Damn, you're brutal."

"Call em like I see em."

"I can't argue with that."

Lori drifted then, thinking about the last time she attended a Yankee game with Marc. She could see him, sitting, cheering, having the time of their lives. Saw his eyes, those beaming blues and how his smile lit up those eyes and cut into Lori's heart with a stab of frustration.

"You, okay?" Lori turned to Henry. "You seemed to have drifted for a moment."

Lori clenched her jaw and pressed her lips tight together. "I was just thinking about someone."

Henry nodded. "Understood. Your mother said you had a nasty accident and break up not too long ago."

"She did, did she?"

Henry nodded again. "That she did."

Lori looked back into the house, seeing her mother in the kitchen, talking and jabbering when she stole a glance outside and locked eyes with Lori.

"She has an uncanny knack of putting her nose where it doesn't belong." She turned to Henry.

"I think she's just concerned."

"Oh, she's concerned all right. Just not about what she pretends to be concerned about."

Henry cocked his head and clucked his tongue. "Damn, you're brutal."

"I like honesty."

"Brutal honesty at that."

"Is there any other kind?" And she laughed, as did Henry.

"Listen, do you want to get out of here? Go hit a bar or something?"

Lori paused, looking him over, assessing his intention.

Henry put his hands up. "Listen, I just went through a divorce. As I told Elena, I don't need any romantic entanglements and it seems you're in the same boat, so at least we can enjoy misery together. It's up to you."

Lori narrowed her eyes then looked at her mother again. Elena's stare was glued to Lori and Henry like some wild animal seething over an anticipatory feeding. Lori turned to Henry.

"Sure," she said, "I'd love to."

John Hardwood sat by the bay window overlooking the western woods. He could feel the chill from outside. The window was like a pane of ice and when he touched it, his hand turned numb from the cold. He could hear the big game on the television in the living room where his grandpa, Claude, sat watching the game. An event that brought with it a semblance of order and hope. John had learned a new word over the last few months: Depression. Grandpa Claude was suffering from depression and, according to the research he'd read on the internet, he may never be the same. Not after what happened. Not after the events that unfolded a few months ago. So, the fact that he was watching the game may be a sign that life was becoming normal once again.

John breathed against the glass, his breath fogging the window. He used his finger to streak letters into the glass.

The other kids at school wanted nothing to do with him. *Heart Eater* is what they called him.

Heart Eater. Heart Eater, come and take your soul. Heart Eater. Heart Eater, eating hearts… all night long.

That's the damn rhyme he heard every day during recess. And all because his father was in an upstate hospital where Grandpa Claude said he would live the rest of his days. John was well aware his sister was never coming home. The boys at school told him so. And why? Because her heart was eaten. Eaten by his father. Which made no sense whatsoever. Why would anyone eat someone's heart?

He heard Grandpa Claude move in his chair-it always crinkled and creaked when he got up-and John quickly wiped off the steam from the window. He knew grandpa didn't like it when he wrote those letters, Initium Novum. He'd gotten so angry with John when he added those letters to one of his drawings, but John couldn't help it. They were the letters that followed him into his nightmares. When he was able to sleep, that is.

John studied his reflection in the window and the thick heavy bags beneath his tired eyes. Grandpa said it was because he only slept a few hours every night and the nightmares didn't help either. Stress bags are how grandpa referred to them. Stress over losing his family. His father, his sister, and his mother.

But John was confused about that last one. Sure, he heard the gunshot and was aware of all the police and ambulance people that came to his house that night. For Pete's sake, he could still hear grandpa's high-pitched scream every time he closed his eyes, although he didn't understand why he screamed like that.

Momma hadn't gone too far. In fact, he could see her at night in the western woods, standing at the edge of the woods and watching the house. She was still watching him and still looking after him. From the ether, she had told him, she would wait to guide him.

26

"You okay, John?" This was grandpa. John could see his reflection in the window. He was holding a glass filled with ice and that brown liquid John thought he drank too much of.

John nodded, crossing his arms and leaning his head against the window.

"You've been standing there for a while now. Why not come and watch the game with me? I'll explain how the game works if you want. Might be a pleasant distraction."

John looked over his shoulder at Claude. "It's a mindless game, grandpa. Nothing to it, really." He turned to the window. "I prefer baseball."

Grandpa Claude shrugged. John was hoping he would leave, but he didn't. He just stood there, dumbfounded, not knowing what to say. He never knew what to say. Always choked up and emotional, and John wanted him to return to the game because he knew it was a good distraction for grandpa and then John could go back to searching the woods for his mother.

Instead, Grandpa Claude joined him by the window. He stood next to John with his drink that he sipped every so often, baring his teeth after each swallow.

"You're always staring into the woods," Claude said. "What's so interesting about it? Just dead trees and darkness."

Now, John knew he could not tell grandpa about mother living in the woods. It would sound crazy and everyone-grandpa, his teachers and all his doctors-would be very concerned if he said such things. He knew it was true. Knew it was true because that's what his mother told him.

He could hear her speak to him in whispers.

So, he said what his mother told him to say when he was asked about the western woods. "I find it peaceful."

To which grandpa Claude cocked an eyebrow before belting out a laughing cackle, then downed the rest of his drink.

"That was funny," Claude said, putting his hand on John's shoulder. "I'll be watching the game, buddy. Would love for you to join me, even if it's just for a few minutes."

John looked at him and said, "Okay. I'll be in soon."

Grandpa nodded and tightened his jaw. "Good. I'll make some popcorn." And with that he left and went into the kitchen where John could hear him dropping ice into his glass while John returned his gaze to the western woods.

Momma said to be on the lookout tonight. That there will be something for him to see. No amount of popcorn was going to tear him away from his window. Those trees had become his friends. Like brothers and sisters he could confide in. Brothers and sisters who protected his mother.

And he knew his mother was protecting him too.

60

Lori took her seat in the crowded bar. They were lucky to get a high-top table, considering the bar was shoulder to shoulder and six people deep from the bar. Everyone was watching the halftime show, mostly laughing at the ongoing stage act with the Blues Brothers Bash. Lori froze when she saw them. *The Blues Brothers* was one of Marc's favorite movies.

He was probably having the time of his life watching Dan Aykroyd reprise his old role. She sat and ordered a beer while Henry looked over the menu, her attention glued to the television, but not seeing the television. Her thoughts were with Marc, wondering where he was watching the game and if he was at the Sleepy Hollow Tavern, sipping on a stiff scotch, hollering at Mr. Aykroyd and singing along. Her love for Marc was like a fire, and all she wanted to do was burn. He was in her thoughts and in her dreams, whispering to her from the dark recesses of her mind.

She couldn't shake his memory. All she wanted was to see him again. To look in his eyes one last time, even if it was to put the past to bed and walk away. His letter was scathing, but she knew Marc. Knew he was scared and that he'd rather live alone than risk another broken heart brought on by tragedy. His entire life could be summed up in one word: *tragic,* to say the least, and Lori's brush with death was enough to put him over the edge. But in the end, in his fear of death, he abandoned Lori. He never fought for her, and this simple fact crushed Lori's heart more than anything else. It made her feel useless, a thing to be pitied. Insignificant was the word she used.

"Lori?"

She looked at Henry, his brow raised in an inquisitive, although skeptical, stare.

"You, ok?"

"Yeah, just thinking of someone." She took a sip from her pint glass.

"I notice you tend to drift a lot."

She shrugged. "Good observation, detective." Her voice came off a little more curt than she wanted.

Henry put his hands up. "I apologize. Just looking after the person I'm spending time with. I meant no ill will."

Who the hell talks like that?

Lori cleared her throat. "I'm sorry too. Some breakups are harder to get over than others and you're right, I do drift off a lot. Especially lately."

"Not sleeping well?" He cradled his drink in his hand-a vodka tonic. "It took me close to a year to finally get a full night's sleep. The mind just kept racing, second-guessing every decision I ever made. Second-guessing myself, as if there was something inherently wrong with me. Not that every human being doesn't have something to work on, but in the end, matters concerning the heart are often too deep to fathom. It's best to just accept the situation as it is, do what you have to to change what is necessary and make the turn back into society."

"Honestly, all I do is sleep. I just can't seem to drag myself out of bed. Doesn't seem like there's any reason to do so." She sipped her beer again, feeling herself turning inward, receding into herself. Her heart was racing, pounding against her chest.

"Ahh, the depressive phase," said Henry. "Everyone responds to tragedy in their own unique way, but there is a common thread towards absolution. We either live the rest of our days broken or mend the tear in our hearts and move forward, but always with the scar as a reminder of the past to help us identify the red flags as we trek forward. Either way, we are undoubtedly changed, but here's my honest evaluation of the response to tragedy. It's a choice. A choice to either wallow in pity and allow that pity to turn us into jaded, vengeful people, or accept what has happened and reach into the darkness to pull out the light. Remember, life happens for you, not to you, so figure out how you can grow from the experience and be grateful for the tragedy because it has been a great teacher for the soul to evolve." He sipped his drink, but all Lori could do was stare.

She wasn't sure if she should slap him across the face or give in and accept his advice.

He's just trying to help, Lori thought and cleared her throat once again. She was certain he could feel her tension. She could feel it herself, like a thick ball of energy suppressing her thoughts.

"You sound more like a philosopher or psychologist than an FBI agent."

"I studied psychology in college. It's a mindless practice with few exceptions. I find it interesting how the more widespread psychological interventions are quite brutal in their execution. Those interventions are so mundane and only scratch the surface of the human mind. It's like the entire school of thought is still in the dark ages while scoffing at the more viable and successful therapies like NLP or science of mind concepts that drive everlasting change." He shook his head. "It's like the industry just wants to keep people in therapy for a lifetime when they should provide the knowledge necessary so their patients can learn to cope without attending weekly sessions for the rest of their days."

"Well, if they went around curing everyone, no one would need therapy."

"Exactly." He shook his finger. "All part of a system that consistently remains inside the problem and not the solution. It's rampant in the medical industry."

The restaurant erupted in a collective gasp, then cheers and applause. The sound was so loud, Lori cringed. She turned to the television where players were celebrating in the end zone. She sipped her beer then turned to Henry.

"Touchdown," he said with a smile and a cock of his head.

And she smiled too. Couldn't help herself. She didn't know what got into her. It was the first time she had genuinely smiled since the last time she saw Marc.

Maybe Henry was right. Maybe it was time to put the past to bed.

The only problem was, sometimes the past refuses to die.

The fire started small but quickly twisted into a bonfire. John saw the first flicker of the flame. It caught his eye, all the way from the darkness. A quick spark of blue that erupted a moment later. He stood tall, wide-eyed and mesmerized by the fire burning bright in the middle of the western woods.

His mother said something would happen tonight, and she was right because here it was, a bonfire in the middle of the western woods. The house lights flickered, casting John in a battle between light and dark like a signal from his mother that he was right and the fire was exactly what she wanted him to see.

But did he dare risk taking a better look? Did he dare risk the wrath from his grandfather and sneak out of the house to travel through the woods to the source?

The lights flickered once again, and John heard the television cut out.

"God damn it," Claude muttered from the living room. John heard his chair creak and the cushion crinkle but then the lights returned and remained on. A second later, the game returned and Claude settled back into his chair.

John looked up at the lights while gnawing on his bottom lip, then craned his head around, assessing if Claude was going to get up to determine the cause of the electrical concern. There was no cause that he would find, of course. At least none that would make sense to anyone who was confined to the third dimension of reality. John knew all too well that his mother caused the lights to flicker because that's where she was, in the ether, where invisible electrical waves existed within the folds of earthly matter. At least that's how his mother had explained it to him.

She said he would see something tonight and here it was, a bonfire in the western woods. John believed his mother flickered the lights to confirm his suspicion. He also took it as a sign that she wanted him to investigate. Now that Claude was once again mesmerized by his television, John took it upon himself to begin his inquiry. He went to the back door, quiet and meticulous, and carefully twisted the dead bolt from its locked position to open. He then turned over the lock on the doorknob, then eased the door open so it wouldn't creak and alert Claude to his whereabouts. The icy wind brushed across his skin from the open door. The chill cringed his spine, nipping his cheeks and nose.

He stepped outside, turning around to the door to pull it closed but left it open a crack. He noticed the door sometimes locked from the inside when it closed, so why take the chance? After all, he needed to return sometime before the end of the night. Satisfied, he turned around, standing on the top step of the three stairs that led down to the property. The backyard was large and open with an entrance to the western woods at the end of the property. The pool was covered for the winter. The patio furniture sat covered in dead leaves and snow and the rocking chair swayed slightly in the icy wind as if some phantom sat in the chair, watching John while rocking back and forth.

He gazed into the woods; his stare fixed on the fire in the distance. Noticed how quiet it was and there wasn't a cloud in the sky to cover the slivered moon hanging in the night sky, just a range of twinkling stars watching his every move. He looked around, then took the steps to the snow-covered yard as his breath plumed across his lips. It had snowed earlier that day, blanketing the Hollow in a sheet of white. Snow that was fresh and packed tight across the earth, beamed bright under the light of the moon, turning the night into perpetual twilight.

He could hear the fire crackling. It was so far away, but he could hear it as if the fire was right here in the yard with him. He wanted to run to it. To warm his hands by the fire. It seemed like the fire was calling him, summoning him to its warm embrace. John eyeballed the woods as he approached the end of the property. Trees creaked under the cold gale that rippled across the yard through the trees. His hands were hooked beneath his armpits, so cold they had turned since he stepped outside. He was almost there, close to the woods, when he heard Grandpa Claude raise his voice to the heavens.

"What the hell are you doing out there?"

John stopped in his tracks, staring at the fire in the distance.

"John, get back in here right now."

John turned around to his grandfather, his eyes growing wide as the house lights flickered in a mad fever.

Wren watched the first flicker from the fire rage into a bonfire. He stood under the cover of night, watching the flames lick the dead wood he had piled high over the last few days.

The master was sleeping, and soon the host will return, and Wren will have to placate Marc. The task was a difficult one, considering the forever state of anxiety and confusion Marc experienced when he returned. It was as if Marc understood what was happening but he either didn't care to confront what was right in front of him, or his mind had become so warped by the cemetery ether that he didn't know what was real and what was fiction.

Marc had come willingly when Wren first arrived at his apartment all those months ago. The master was always with Marc, some special part of the master that was on alert to Marc's thoughts and actions. He lived in the subconscious, driving those thoughts and actions to keep Marc confused and guessing over the real and the sane. But there was also a dark side to Marc that Wren found rather intriguing, as if he secretly enjoyed the torture they inflicted on their victims as he sat in the shadows, waiting for his time to return to the host body.

Of course there was. The master required not just a host body, but a host body with a similar dark frequency was required for the ether in both souls to match perfectly. Like matching two identical pictures that are always different because they are individual in their construction.

Marc was told he inherited the house, which came with a personal servant-Wren obviously-who would tend to his needs like a dutiful parent. Wren knew at the time that Marc would not challenge the notion. He was all too eager to leave the past behind. His broken heart being the catalyst that drove him to accept what he normally would not. Plus, the confusion that impeded his mind kept his assertiveness at bay. Marc was the vessel for the master to manifest into flesh and bone in this world. His participation was paramount, his destruction necessary, but did the master possess the strength required to conquer Marc's beloved?

Wren grinned while staring at the bonfire. "Of course he does."

Now that the fire was burning bright, it was time to add Michael to the flame. And then he will rest. Rest until Marc opens his eyes in the morning.

"Five days," Wren whispered.

There was so much to do in those five days.

"Here, use this if you want to get a better look." Claude spread the tripod legs in front of the bay window, then turned the telescope towards the window. "But I'm telling you, it's just teenagers having a party in the woods. I've seen them happening for decades. There are always teenagers in the woods."

John squinted while looking at the telescope. He raised his stare to his grandfather. "Can I bring it to my room?"

Claude thrust his head back. It looked like he was expecting a different reaction. He nodded, tightlipped, with a smug smile. "Sure. Just be careful with it." He pinched the eyepiece. "They're very fragile."

With a big smile across his lips, John said, "Thank you, grandpa," before wrapping his arms around the telescope and lifting the tripod legs, scraping against the carpet as he trekked to the staircase. Those same legs flopped against the steps as he stomped up the stairs, rounded the platform and then dragged the telescope down the hall to his bedroom where he closed the door.

He'll have a better view of the western woods from his room and why he hadn't thought about that simple fact before eluded him. It didn't matter though; he was set up with the right equipment thanks to good old Grandpa Claude. He stretched the tripod legs to the carpet, then turned the telescope towards his window. He could see the fire raging in the distance, and he dipped his head to the eyepiece, adjusting the focus until the fire was in clear view. It looked like the quiet burning of the sun from this far away.

John looked up, biting his lip and thinking. Thinking about the lights and how they were flickering like carnival lights when Claude called him from the porch. Now John may be young, but he was a very intelligent boy, deducing that his mother was flickering those lights in some riddled anxiety over him about to trek through the western woods. The lights flickering alerted Claude to John's quest, which meant his mother did *not* want him to go into the western woods.

She just wanted him to see.

To see *what* was the question. Obviously, the fire, yes, but something else too, because he was already aware of the fire. He looked into the eyepiece, seeing the fire burning bright. He moved the telescope, scanning the perimeter around the fire. Mostly a dead and barren opening in the woods. But then the house came into view. Dark and foreboding, he could see it creak and sway in the wind. He scanned the windows. Nothing but darkness greeted him. Scanned across all three levels. The house seemed abandoned. But then who started the fire?

John ran his tongue across the inside of his mouth, scanning the perimeter again, then back to the...

There was a man pushing a wheelbarrow from the house to the fire.

Now, where did he come from?

40

John zoomed in on the man and his limbs tensed. He looked like an evil character from a black and white movie he once saw on television. He looked like a vampire with his pointed nose, thin face, and smooth round head. Plus, he was dressed in all black. He definitely looked like a vampire.

But vampires don't exist.

Or maybe they do, because John was certain he was staring at a vampire. A vampire who now stood by the fire and reached into his pockets, pulling out a pair of work gloves.

"What's he got in that wheelbarrow?"

John dipped the telescope down and immediately pulled his head back. He stood frozen.

Was that?

He couldn't be certain, but he believed there was a dead body in the wheelbarrow. He stood, unmoving, staring. Staring at nothing. No thoughts. No movement, just a freeze-framed image of the dead body in the wheelbarrow that stained the back of his eyes. The torso was stacked on top of the lower half of the body. Intestines hung from the cut torso. From the corner of his eye, he could see the fire gained strength through the western woods, as if something big was added to the fire. He pursed his lips and forced a swallow down his throat.

He dipped his head to the telescope, widening his eye to the eyepiece. And the vampire who was staring directly at him. John cringed from his head to his toes then beelined for his bed, racing beneath the covers that he stretched and held over his head, leaving his face uncovered.

A million thoughts raced through his mind all at once. So many thoughts, but no thought at all. He felt paralyzed, shaken with fear. He wasn't expecting the man to know he was watching.

John pictured him trekking across grandpa's lawn to his bedroom. Saw him rise to the window. Saw him outside, scraping his nails against the glass.

It's just my imagination. Just imagination.

Started shaking his head.

He's not really outside the window.

But he refused to look. Refused to go there.

Instead, he clamped his eyes shut.

One thing was certain: the telescope was going back to the basement.

Lori stumbled out of Henry's car, laughing as she did, and gripped the door to steady herself. She was pleasantly buzzed. A few shots downed by a few beers hit her harder than she thought it would, considering when she was with Marc she'd drink that much before they even went out for the night.

"You, ok?" asked Henry from the driver's seat. He was laughing with her, his arms on the steering wheel of his BMW, parked outside the Francon Mansion that was lit up like a Christmas tree.

"Just fine," she said, stretching her eyelids in the cold to relieve the pleasant buzz.

"Do you need me to walk you to the door?"

Lori looked over her shoulder at her home. She could hear the ocean waves behind the house, faint, however profound. All else was quiet. The house beckoned her to enter. She craved her bed and sleep. Saw Elena in her bedroom window on the second floor. She disappeared a moment later.

Lori felt the energy drop. The last thing she needed was an Elena inquiry into how the night had gone.

She turned to Henry. "I'm good. You get home safe, please."

Henry looked through the windshield before he answered. "Of course. I'll be happy to hit the pillow tonight."

Lori thanked him for a pleasant evening. And it was pleasant. The fact that there was no romantic entanglement allowed the night to go off without a hitch, and it was a relief to talk to someone who was going through a similar situation. They bonded as friends and as friends they will remain. She closed the door and watched Henry drive down the long winding driveway then through the gates to the street before she walked to the front door.

A wave of warmth greeted her the moment she walked inside. Directly opposite the front door was a hall that led to the dining room and the sliding glass doors that led to the patio outside and the beach beyond the patio. She noticed a stack of boxes next to the dining room table. On her right was a wide-open living and sitting room with a fireplace and a wide expansive staircase that led to the second floor. She took off her gloves and hat and placed them on the credenza by the front door, then peeled off her jacket and hung it on the coat hanger. She was about to go to the kitchen for a glass of water when she saw her mother walking to the steps on the second floor.

"How did it go?" Elena asked, her hand on the banister, standing on the second floor. She looked tired, and Lori could hear it in her voice.

"I had a great time. Henry is quite the gentleman."

Elena closed her eyes and nodded as if relief had washed over her and she could finally get some sleep. "Good. I was hoping you would have a good time. It's time to get back into the world, Lori. Life's too short to waste it mourning the past."

She knew Elena was right, but there was always that nagging feeling that Elena had ulterior motives behind her kindness. Lori had no response, but she forced herself to respond. All she wanted was for the inquiry to be over as soon as possible. It was best to placate the situation and shuffle Elena back to bed. "Agreed. I do believe the time is right."

Elena nodded again, then yawned with her hand over her mouth. "I'm so tired. I'm going to bed. Get some sleep. Tomorrow's a new day."

"I will. Get some sleep yourself."

Elena nodded, turning to her room, holding the banister on her way when Lori inquired about the boxes in the dining room.

Elena stopped in her tracks and paused as if she were attempting to recollect her thoughts or deter the current situation. "I forgot to tell you. The hospital dropped off your belongings. I guess they held onto everything for so long they needed to either throw it all away or send it back." She looked at Lori. "You don't have to go through it. Honestly, I was going to have Gerard toss them in the garbage but figured it was your decision."

Gerard was the groundskeeper. Lori had known him since the family moved in. Lori's stare was fixed on those boxes.

"I'll take care of it," she said, then added, "It's a good idea to just get rid of it." She locked eyes with Elena. "Put the past to bed, right?"

Elena's lips tightened into a smug smile. Her eyes widened when she said, "Agreed."

Lori watched her walk to her room. She waited to hear the door close before she went into the dining room. There were six medium-sized boxes stacked into three columns, all with Lori's name written on the sides.

Memory lane, she thought. But was she ready to open a doorway to the past? She knew what those boxes contained: heartache and the memory of what she lost. Her attention was caught by the rattling wind chimes on the patio. The wind buckled against the glass doors as an empty pit grew in her stomach. Those boxes represented a foreboding she didn't want to cross. She didn't realize it at first, but there were tears in her eyes. She wiped them away. The wind chimes continued to rattle, the wind howling across the patio with the snow drifting in the wind.

"Fuck you too Marc Saduj." Her voice was a muttered whisper. She looked at the boxes again. "Put the past to bed." Now she was crying, thinking about Marc.

This was the last thing she needed.

Put the past to bed.

Lori left the dining room and went to the stairs.

But don't just put it to rest. Kill it and be done with it. Strangle the past so it never rears its ugly head again.

She took the stairs to her room. Lori couldn't wait to get to bed. Her decision was made. She'll have Gerard toss the boxes in the garbage in the morning.

65

When Marc was in the cemetery, all he felt was anguish, as if those ghosts projected their pain into his cells.

Every moment was a grinding of emotion into pain. Physical pain. His innards squeezed with emotion filled with fear and a profound sadness. His bones ached, so tired he just wanted to rest, but there was no rest for the weary in the cemetery ether. Aside from the ghosts-for which there was plenty-there was another presence in the cemetery. An evil Marc wished to avoid, in the mausoleum he had entered on the very first day he became trapped in the cemetery. The presence with the jaws that liked to snap and bite. Bite into the soul and turn his ether into dense matter.

When he was in the cemetery, the real world he'd come from seemed like a dream. And when he was in the dream world of reality, the etheric cemetery seemed distant, wavering in his consciousness like a nightmare from the past. But the dream reality also brought confusion. As if he'd lost the ability for rational thought. As if he were a puppet with evil holding his strings. The real seemed like the dream, living in that mansion with his servant at his behest.

Sometimes he felt like it was all a dream and that he died in the accident. Sometimes he would just scream and howl in the night, the forever night of the cemetery. All the time, the ghosts would watch him, as if he were some specter to their ethereal presence. A conundrum, an enigma they had yet to decipher. He could feel them always, as if they were in his bones and a part of his ether. Demons come to tear him apart.

The cemetery gave way to the western woods, but Marc did not dare to enter the woods. There was pain in the woods, the pain of living and dying. At the very least, the cemetery brought with it a knowing. Knowing where he was, familiar like an old friend. He spent his time there, sometimes standing at the edge of the western woods, listening to the bloodcurdling screams wrought from centuries of suffering that rifled off the trees in a mad fever.

Birds gawked in the trees, and owls screeched and hissed as he walked by. He felt like he'd been walking for a century, trampling over gravesites and past mausoleums. Sometimes all he would do was sit and tangle that green rope around his left wrist. Sometimes he'd talk to his parents, although they never returned his conversation. And then there was the barrier.

He discovered it a month ago. Like a towering curtain that was draped around the cemetery's perimeter. It was so difficult to see, translucent as it was, but it was there. Without a doubt, it was there, guarding the cemetery. The barrier pulsed every so often with an electrical current, and it was this very current that first caught Marc's attention, requiring further inquiry. Sometimes he would stand and stare into it, waiting for the current to ripple through.

He didn't know why, but he believed Lori was inside the barrier. Lori, whose letter stung like a bee every time he thought about it. How her words had cut him to the core. Nevertheless, he longed to see her. To feel her skin against his. A notion he believed would never happen, but if he could just see her, he knew he'd be justified in his actions. He knew he'd be free.

The time had come, and Marc stepped closer to the barrier. Upon closer inspection, he noticed that the barrier was fluttering, moving like waves in the ocean, but subtle, and hard to see. He reached his hand out, feeling the electrical energy that rippled through his hand from the barrier.

He heard steps in the grass over his shoulder and when he craned his head around, he could see the cemetery ghosts were all watching him. A horde of ghosts standing at attention. Their eyes beamed in the darkness, licking their chops for a taste of him, waiting and watching, anticipating Marc's next move.

Marc, the lovesick uninvited guest they all sought to torture like a plaything for cannibals. He could feel their presence, weighing on his shoulders and filtering into his blood with noxious poison. He wondered if they'd tear him apart before he had a chance to look inside the barrier. He couldn't trust any of them.

Marc turned to the barrier, knowing they all took a step closer, as if they were playing some ghostly game of red light, green light.

"So be it," he muttered, grinding his jaw. He thought about Lori when he dipped his head into the barrier. It was like submerging his head in water. The scene wavered and rippled, but he could see a dark bedroom with a bed beneath him. He looked down and saw Lori sleeping peacefully.

"I wouldn't do such things if I were you."

The voice startled him, and Marc jumped back into the cemetery, whipping his head around so fast he stumbled against the rock wall, fumbling on his feet to catch his bearings and when he did, he laid eyes on the most unassuming woman he'd ever seen. Thick blonde hair dipped past thin shoulders. Eyes as blue as the sea, with a confidence that was both endearing and fierce. She wore a white cloak tied with a golden rope. Marc craned his head, assessing her fair features and how her skin, after careful inspection, seemed translucent, as if she was projecting herself from another world. She looked like her skin was made from porcelain, so smooth and yet he could see right through it.

She gestured to the barrier. "It taps our energy," she said, turning around and walking away. Even her walk was confident.

Marc looked at the barrier, then turned to her when he noticed there were no more ghosts in the cemetery. No wind or cold, but with a silence that invaded the soul. He watched as she walked further into the cemetery, seeming as if she were looking for something, reading headstones and mausoleums and moving between them and the trees. Marc followed cautiously. This was the first ghost who talked to him, other than the dark-haired woman who lived in the mausoleum that seemed to stretch into some unknown dimension. The one who talked in tongues and who wanted his heart. Marc did everything he could to avoid that

50

particular mausoleum, although on some occasions he'd wake up there with the ghosts and that woman hunting him.

He followed until she stopped outside another mausoleum. She stood, holding one hand over the door and the other over her heart. Marc craned his head to see that her eyes were closed.

He looked over the cemetery when the most god-awful wail rattled in the woman's throat. Marc studied the mausoleum when the woman gave out a guffaw, followed by a whine that died in the back of her throat. Her head down, her hand slid off the mausoleum.

Her breath stuttered across her lips. "On those days and nights when the heart is broken and the cells are depleted, come to this final resting place and you shall find a profound rest to aid in your endeavor."

He wasn't certain if she was talking to him or to herself. Marc looked at the mausoleum. "I've had enough with mausoleums and what exists beyond those doors. There are devils and witches in those places." He shook his head. "I think I'll just stay with the headstones."

She nodded, wrapping her arms around her shoulders. "So cold," she whispered when across the cemetery a red glow beamed bright from the western woods. She raised her head to look at it, as did Marc. Behind the light existed a subtle rickety groan that cringed Marc's bones as fog raced across the cemetery from the red glow.

"Whatever you do, stay away from the mausoleum with the black volcanic rock across the door that looks like glass."

Marc snapped his attention to her, watching as she shifted, then turned around to the mausoleum. He knew exactly which mausoleum she was referring to. It was the same one with the witch in it.

"It leads into hell."

Marc stepped forward when she disappeared through the door.

Lori was sleeping when the shriek awakened her. She heard a scream; she was certain of it. Like someone was being tortured to death.

Awakened her from as deep a sleep as she'd ever had. As if all the pain from the past had been filtered from her cells in a gush of relief and all she needed was sleep to squeeze those last remnants away. An empty pit grew in her stomach as she sat up in bed, listening in the dark night for the scream to come again.

"Marc?" His name whispered off her lips as if it had come from another. She could feel him as if he were in the room; his scent was in her nostrils. She could feel him in her cells and across her skin. For the briefest moment, a grin spread across her lips before her stomach raged with pain, her face pinched in anguish as the pain rolled into her heart. She felt hollow, as if her soul was torn from her body, leaving a cavernous space that bled into her heart.

Her eyes flitted from one corner of the room to the other, looking for him as if he were in the house. In her room, hiding in the shadows. She could hear the wind chimes rattling in the wind from the patio on the first floor. A stabbing pain twisted in her gut, and she hunched forward, her hands over her stomach. Her eyes were closed, but she could see the sliding glass door in the dining room with Marc standing outside the door, looking in.

"Marc?" she whispered, although she knew it couldn't be true. There was no way he would be here.

Lori shot out of bed, raced into the hall and immediately froze. There were red eyes in her mother's doorway. They disappeared the moment she laid eyes on them. She stepped back into the wall when on her right a bright white light beamed through the darkness.

Her breath stuttered over her lips. Her heart was pounding in her chest. She saw Marc standing, watching her. He looked dead, his eyeballs all black, like two black holes in a sea of darkness.

I think I'm… having… a… night terror.

Her eyes wandered, wide open and drifting over Marc. He seemed so scared, frightened to his core.

"Initium Novum," a sinister voice growled from behind Marc, echoing in her bones.

Now she heard a noise on her left, as if someone had stepped onto the landing by the stairs. She craned her head around to the demon standing in her mother's doorway, glaring at Lori. Its red, beaming eyes glowed in the dark hall. He was dressed in all black, his skull smooth with black horns like a goat that curved around his head. His skin was ashen gray with veins that swelled across his face like spiderwebs. His nose was a button, and his mouth bared small pointy teeth.

Lori was paralyzed with fear, standing wide eyed with her jaw hung open. She couldn't feel her heart beating in her chest any longer. Hadn't taken a breath either. The demon's presence seemed to suck all the life from her bones.

The demon craned his head, glaring at Lori. "Holler," he said.

He stepped closer, just one step, but it was enough. Lori's entire body cringed, and she stepped further into the wall as if she could fade into her room.

The demon grinned; his arms stretched as if he welcomed Lori into his embrace.

"Holler," he said again and took a second step.

When he moved, it was as if the air moved with him, projecting energetic ripples of nefarious energy that washed over Lori with a suffocating strangulation of rampant heat. He stopped and craned his head again, staring at her, staring through her. He dipped his fingernail into the wooden banister, and as he walked, he dragged that nail across it, splintering the wood. A thin, toothless smile crossed his lips as he approached.

He started speaking in tongues, driving Lori into a frenzy. His voice pierced her eardrums with a cringe that raced down her spine. He stopped a few feet from Lori.

"Seek your beloved and all you will find is me."

Lori's breath caught in her throat. She couldn't breathe, couldn't get air into her lungs as her head shook with quick strokes, her vision blurring as the man in black stepped closer. She could feel his presence barreling down on her. It was hypnotic and suffocating.

"Holler," he said with a snap of his jaws towards her face.

And Lori did just that, hollered at the top of her lungs.

The morning sun stretched its first glorious rays across the Hollow, turning the snow-covered grounds into a blanket of white light.

Wren climbed the steps from the dungeon to the yard. The earthy chamber door made the hidden passage invisible. Unless you were standing on top of the door, you'd never know there was a door there, and it served Wren's purpose perfectly. He could go in and out of the dungeon without being seen by the host. And there was so much to do in the dungeon. He planned for many sleepless nights.

He still had tasks to complete before tonight. There were so many volunteers required to gather in the dungeon. The master said it best: the blood they spill and the fear they cause are necessary commodities to strengthen the astral plane.

Wren looked up to the early morning sun rising beyond the woods, its orange-red glow burning bright across Sleepy Hollow. He raised his head to the last few stars still twinkling in the twilight's last gleaming. The moon was a sliver that hung by a string in the sky. Wren closed his eyes, thinking about the moon, the stars, and the constellations. They were a few days away from the alignment to the earth and with it, the portal to Xibalba will see its greatest strength in over a century. The house was constructed as a beacon to Xibalba, the dungeon and third floor pointed directly to the celestial location across the universe, and when the celestial bodies were aligned, the astral plane was strengthened, creating a pathway to Xibalba.

And then the master can unleash an army of devils upon humanity.

Wren grinned just thinking about it. Grinned even more, thinking about the torture he and the master were about to unleash on the Hollow. Five days, he thought. Five days until the constellations align and open a cosmic highway to Xibalba. Five days required thirteen victims, and thirteen unique tortures. He wondered which device the master will choose tonight.

The master had said that to strengthen the astral plane, not a day could go by without a sacrifice. The portal has been dormant for so long, the suffering and fear that was required to open the portal were abundant. The energy that fear and torture create is like a stain that bathes the air in evil.

And what better evil exists than the calculated desolation of hope?

What he knew above all was that he had a very busy day ahead of him. He'd spent the last six months perfecting and rebuilding the master's torture devices. The work was laborious, but Wren didn't mind. He was grateful to be working with the medieval antiquities, and now that the devices were ready, his next project was polishing the chains and locks, the shackles, across the dungeon's walls.

And then-tonight, in fact-it was time to add fresh bodies to the fold and provide those shackles with a purpose.

Abduction was never easy, but he had an ace in the hole to assist him in his venture. His master will be with him tonight. He looked up at the house and smiled. Smiled because he knew all the house brought was death.

Many of the citizens in Sleepy Hollow were about to go missing. Their destruction was necessary. Necessary to drive fear into the heart of every citizen in the Hollow, altering the atmosphere so that it's suitable for the master's minions.

The master promised him eternal life should their little ruse become a success. In charge of his own horde of demons and devils. He rolled his tongue inside his mouth, thinking about it as he walked around the house, his footsteps scrunching in the snow. Walked around to the front porch when he stopped in his tracks.

The host, Marc, was already up, standing outside in a pair of shorts and a T-shirt, staring mindlessly into the western woods. He looked worse for the wear. His eyes were sunken and dark-the ether did that, turned those eyes tired and weary-and his skin was worn, ghostly, and thinned. He looked like a toothpick standing in his shorts. Food had gone by the wayside. Marc barely ate a thing, always choosing a drink over a meal, his stomach a cesspool of alcohol and mixers that rejected most solid substances. And that scar on his head had never completely healed. It looked raw and beamed bright red with beads of green pus that broke through the scar when he pushed on the itch the scar caused.

Disfigured is how Wren described it. Marc was disfigured. His hair had grown back, except over the scar that was prominently displayed beneath his hairline. The scar that crawled across his forehead to his eyeball. His left eye a forever stain of yellow and red.

Marc hadn't noticed Wren was standing and watching him. He hugged himself, and Wren could see that the skin across his arms was pimpled with gooseflesh, cold and pale, deathly pale. Marc's jaw quivered in the morning cold. His hands stretched up higher, holding his shoulders. Marc pursed his lips and swallowed. Wren craned his head to see Marc's eyes closer. The eyes that bred tears cascading down his cheeks.

Eyes that seemed as if they were circling in his skull, mesmerized by the western woods. Wren wondered what monstrosities Marc had witnessed during his time in the ether. What devils and ghosts did he befriend in the western woods? Has he spent time with the master's ghost demons? Has he come face to face with the witch protecting the master's dominion, guiding Marc away from absolution?

The master explained it the best. The cemetery held power-similar to the astral plane in the dungeon-and that power opened portals for the master to reach his home to regenerate his cells. The same home where the master kept the most important part of the host. His heart. Tied up and imprisoned in the maser's home. But it was a one-way ticket, the cemetery had been cursed with a spell that doomed the cemetery ghosts to a perpetual limbo where absence burrowed into the heart and soul, creating a cavern filled with anguish. This is the reason the master required a host to complete his duties outside the cemetery. The same reason his ghost demons could not leave. Not until the astral portal is strengthened, allowing him to conjure their spirits from the ether.

Wren's eyes drifted, his thoughts on Marc and the agony Wren knew he was suffering. When the heart is lost, all that remains is pain. Now a creak from the front porch and Wren looked back at Marc as he quietly turned and walked into the house, his arms still draped over his shoulders.

Wren thought about calling him, but his voice caught in his throat and the words melted off his lips. He watched Marc disappear into the home. Wren closed his eyes, thinking about Marc.

The depression was necessary. The master told him so. It kept Marc in a state of confusion where isolation was his best friend and inactivity was his only activity. Plus, the drink kept him sedated.

The master will return come dusk with the help of the Absinthe accelerant. Until then, Wren will need to be at his most optimal level, protecting the master while he slept and placating Marc to the extreme. He looked up to the sun, now higher in the clear sky.

There was so much to do. He'll deal with Marc later, but for now, he had to prepare.

Abduction always went better when you had all your wits in check.

Especially with the way he presented.

People usually thought he was a vampire.

John didn't sleep well last night. The vampire was tapping on his window all night. Not that he looked. Panicked and frightened the entire time, he kept his eyes closed. As if closing his eyes made him invisible to the vampire outside his window.

And then there were the whispers.

The ones that breathed against his ear.

Initium Novum!

Humanity's end as a new beginning.

We need hearts for the master.

The whispers were relentless, as if their purpose was to drive him into a frenzy of madness and frustration. His mother's voice was among them, like a beacon of hope in a sea of darkness. It was her voice that graced his ear when he finally drifted off to sleep, awakening to the fresh morning light and the smell of coffee drifting from downstairs.

He climbed out of bed and went to the window. Stared wide-eyed at the footprints in the snow. Two sets, one coming and one going. And they were just below his window. The tracks came from and returned to the woods. He followed the tracks into the woods, squinting to see further. He could see the house in the distance.

"Morning buddy."

John froze, his body constricted, startled. He turned to see Grandpa standing in his doorway.

Grandpa threw his head back. "You, ok?"

John turned to the window, his jaw agape. "I'm fine," he said, staring into the woods. Staring at the house.

He felt as if the house was calling him.

Heard grandpa over his shoulder. "Good. Get dressed and brush your teeth. I've got oatmeal downstairs."

In all his wondering and assessment, John had forgotten.

He's got school today.

When Lori opened her eyes, she was not in her bed. Not even in her bedroom. The demon's red eyes, his horns and devilish grin awakened with her. Staring into those bloodied eyes was mesmerizing, captivating. As if they refused to allow her to turn away. She could feel her bones creak and rattle, willing herself to turn. To wake up and force her eyes away from the demon's stare. She couldn't breathe. Couldn't speak. But she could hear her heart beating in her chest, racing in her throat. Behind her ears. Suffocating, she struggled to bring air into her lungs.

Trapped!

Get up… NOW!

She shot up in her mother's bed in her mother's room. The same place where the demon had been hiding when she came out of her bedroom last night. Wide-eyed, she looked around the room, breathing hard, catching her breath with a loud gasp. Heard shuffling outside, footsteps scrunching in the snow.

Lori clutched her chest, calming her breath. Her hands were trembling. A stutter in her throat. On the verge of tears.

The footsteps outside were receding away from the house.

She looked around. No Elena in the bedroom. No Elena at all. Maybe she was the one walking outside? Lori scoffed at the notion. The woman never walked outside except to the car waiting to drive her to whatever destination she chose.

Her breathing calmed, and she rubbed her eyes when she heard the demon speak in her head. "Holler," it said. That's what the demon said last night.

"Holler," he'd said several times. "Holler."

The word was unmistakable. She could hear the demon's voice fading from her mind.

But there was something more to it. The way he pronounced the word and how his voice floated across his lips was peculiar. Not holler, but ho-lair. *What was that? Holer. Holair.* Her eyes narrowed; brow scrunched in confusion. Where had she heard the same pronunciation?

The enigma tickled her memory. Her head bent; she raced to catch the memory. Someone said the word with the same pronunciation. Who was it? She could see them, hear them. See their mouth move, the name on their tongue, projected across their lips.

She saw Marc then. Marc in the cottage last summer. In the bathroom. It was the same name as the demon he said was in his dream. The same he'd written about in his book. *Why is this memory surfacing now?* Just when she was ready to take a turn and step away from the past. Why, after such a long time, had the memory surfaced as if calling her back to the past?

But was the demon's name revealed in his dream, or did Marc conjure the name in his book?

She remembered finding his notebook in the cottage. Remembered Marc had dropped it in the backseat.

The hospital dropped off your belongings. I guess they held onto everything for so long they needed to either throw it all away or send it back.

Elena's voice rang through Lori's mind. Maybe Marc's notebook was included in the boxes?

She scurried out of bed and hurried to the staircase, then stomped down the steps. Elena was sitting on the couch, a magazine in her hands.

"Lori, dear. Are you all right?"

Lori paid her no mind and rounded the steps to the dining room.

"Lori?"

She heard the couch scrunch and knew Elena had gotten up, a sense of urgency in her step. Lori's heart dropped when she saw the corner was empty. There were no boxes in the dining room.

Lori turned to her mother. "Where are the boxes?"

"Boxes?" she said, as if she didn't know.

"Yes, mom. The boxes from the hospital. Where are they?"

"I had Gerard put them out with the trash."

"You what?"

The look on Elena's face revealed both shock and awe.

"Why would you do that?"

"You said to put the past to bed. That's what you said. I was just following what you said."

67

Lori ignored her, her attention on the front door, listening for the garbage truck.

"Lori? What's gotten into you? Between what happened last night and..."

Lori's gaze darted to her mother. "What happened last night?"

Elena shook her head, left and right, with slight movement. Her brow pinched with concern. "What *has* gotten into you?"

She looked over Elena's shoulder again, listening to the footsteps outside approaching the front door. Gerard was returning. Lori beelined past Elena to the front door.

"Lori?"

She tossed the front door open to Gerard's surprise. He jumped when he saw her, but Lori kept going, out the front door to the driveway.

"Lori, get back in here. You're not even dressed. You'll freeze to death," Elena called from the front door.

Heard Gerard ask, "What's all the fuss about?"

"No idea. She got up like a woman possessed."

The air was freezing. The sun glimmered in the morning sky, beaming off the snow to squint Lori's eyes. The still quiet of the moment seeped into her skin and clutched her heart. She could see the boxes just outside the gate.

Heard her mother call her name again but again she ignored the inquiry. Lori pulled the gate open then stepped to the boxes, tearing the closet one open. Clothes mostly. Lori's old makeup bag.

Hairdryer. She moved the box to the side then opened the flaps on the second. Marc's notebook was on top. Beneath it were several items from the car. She swallowed her breath. Her fingers trembled as they hovered over the blue cover and the word written across it: Holer, spelled with one 'L.' Her blood curdled then turned to ice in her veins.

Now the sound over her shoulder, the garbage truck squealed to a stop in front of the neighbor's house.

Lori looked away from the notebook. She turned to see her mother and Gerard still standing at the front door, watching her with perplexed stares. Lori understood what it meant if she took the notebook. Knew it was breaking open the past with another chance for heartache, but it seemed like the notebook was staring at her, watching her, willing her to take it. As if life depended on her reading the story contained within its pages. She could feel Marc's presence as if he'd imprinted his essence into the notebook. She could smell him in the air and feel his touch. His gentle touch on her skin.

She had an uncanny sensation that Marc was attempting to communicate with her. Why, she did not know, but she understood that such a notion was insane. If he wanted to see her, why not just call? Maybe he can't call? Maybe something was wrong and he couldn't pick up a phone.

Such ludicrous thoughts and notions these were. Marc had ended their romance and tucked tail and ran. He couldn't handle the situation and left her in the hospital to fend for herself. Her admiration was now replaced by rage. The garbage truck motored closer.

"To hell with this," she whispered, turning to the driveway when she locked eyes with her mother. The look in Elena's eyes was revealing. It was anticipatory, as if she was licking her chops for Lori to leave those boxes right where they were. As if she would kill if it meant Lori would never read what was on those pages.

The garbage truck stopped behind her. Lori turned, scooped up the notebook and held it close to her chest as she made the slow walk up the driveway to the house that waited to swallow her whole.

Marc was standing in his bedroom, biting his thumbnail and staring at the empty canvas on the easel in front of him. He hadn't written a word since the accident. He'd stare at a blank page for hours before getting up and abandoning the project. It seemed like the words had dried up. Dried up along with his wit. Marc understood his thoughts hit a brick wall on more than a few occasions, as if confusion had become his normal mode of thought. As if there was a second person in his head, catching his thoughts before they could manifest then tossing them off a ledge into the unknown.

As if there was someone else behind the wheel of his mind.

He looked at all the paintings scattered across the room. Some were hung up, while others were leaning against the walls, and some were on the floor. There had to be at least thirty paintings. The lot of them depicted scenes from a graveyard, or scenes portraying carnal appetites associated with debauchery, slavery, and horror. Most of the paintings revealed a dark-haired woman manipulating the scene. She was always set inside the background as if watching and waiting, biding her time before taking center stage. There were a few paintings that featured a woman dressed in white, standing beside a crypt that beamed with golden light. But no matter what the painting revealed, the red, beaming eyes were always a part of it. No painting created by Marc Saduj was complete until the red eyes were there.

Marc's eyes burned in his skull. The paint fumes were irritating. At least, that's what he told himself. He understood that his left eye would be red and disfigured for the rest of his days, but it was easier to blame the paint fumes than accept the inevitable.

The floor was covered from wall to wall with a drop cloth with scattered blotches of mixed paint stained across it. The only window in the room was wide open, allowing the icy sting of winter morn to freeze his skin. He preferred the bitter winter chill to the summer heat. The sun beamed through the window. Dormant candles stood on three shelves on the wall across from the window. Marc used them when he was working at night. Below those shelves was a tattered mattress. No box spring or rails, just the mattress on the floor. This was his room, a place where he was free to recede into himself and create. A place where he could leave the past behind and move forward, a task he'd learned was more difficult than he imagined.

After the letter, Marc didn't know what to do. So much had changed so quickly. It was hard to take it all in, although he tried. Tried to move on, which to Marc consisted of nightly drinking binges at the local tavern, followed by sleeping it off for long hours. He was heartbroken and often found himself in the arms of another woman, hoping she would fill the void and mend his shattered heart. But those were futile efforts, and Marc was grateful to Wren for taking the women home before he rose the next morning. Wren was good like that, disposing of his weakness and wrapping up loose ends that Marc was too drunk or too kind to do himself. Those women were always gone before he woke up the next morning.

Then there were the bar fights he'd gotten into on a close to nightly basis while at the tavern. His anger had boiled into rage and Marc was quick with a punch to the face or a bottle across the skull. Although the violence never took the hurt away, and after a while he stopped going out, turned in his social badge of honor and confined himself to the hermit life where the drink was always available and the pain was kept at bay, hiding behind a subconscious wall thanks to the joy of purpose through creativity. And alcohol of course.

However, in all that time Marc could feel something beneath the surface, stewing and conjuring and mixing, sprinting to a finality he knew was inevitable and over the last week he could feel that the end was coming to a head. His confusion was getting worse. Most of the time, he didn't know what day of the week it was and had to coach himself to remember what month he was in. His past seemed like it belonged to someone else, or that it belonged to a past life, or rooted in a movie he had once watched, and he had difficulty remembering all the fine details. Marc also felt sick, as if his organs were rotting, sucked dry and wrung out. Dying. He felt like he was dying. Fading away one minute at a time.

When Marc first decided to set up an art studio, he wanted to take the third floor, but Wren advised against it. The circular room with windows facing north, south, east, and west would have been the perfect setting to provide the muse he was looking for. Nonetheless, according to Wren, there was too much to do on the third floor, so Wren set him up here, on the second floor with the window facing the east for appropriate morning light. Wren came with the house that Marc inherited from a great uncle twice removed on his mother's side who he never knew he had. Something about probate and attaining appropriate family records caused the delay in the property's transfer.

Marc didn't question it. Considering his state of mind when Wren knocked on his door, he just went with it, but whenever Marc inquired about the house Wren's answers were vague and cryptic. Not that Marc cared too much. Wren was a loyal servant, affording Marc his alone time while Wren took care of the house. There was so much to do, and Marc had once asked Wren about hiring a contractor to update the home. Wren had scoffed at the notion as if Marc's suggestion was insulting.

"Give me until spring," Wren had said. "When the snow melts and the flowers bloom, I'm more than certain you'll feel differently."

And then he grinned. So strange was Wren. Marc concluded he'd seen his share of ridicule over the years. Considering his appearance, Marc was certain the kids on the playground had been cruel, but Marc didn't care about how the man looked. Wren was at his beck and call and who the hell wouldn't want some servant feeding them drinks on the fly?

Marc wiped his hands across his shorts, then bent down to pick up his palette and paintbrushes. He eyeballed the empty canvas, seeing the scene he was about to paint take form in his mind's eye as he stepped closer to the canvas. Dipped his brush into the paint and made the first stroke, the paint a mix of dark green and violet, when he heard a knock on the door.

"Master," said Wren.

"Come," Marc called, maintaining his focus on the canvas and another stroke of his brush. He was keyed in on the canvas now, mesmerized by it. Focused, as if everything that existed in the universe was contained within the canvas. He heard the door slide open, buckling the drop cloth, but kept his gaze on the canvas, listening as Wren walked across the drop cloth to Marc's left. He was holding a tray with Marc's morning pick me up, a bloody red eye, on top of it.

"What masterpiece are you working on today?" asked Wren, as he placed Marc's drink on the table beside the canvas.

Marc took a small paintbrush off his palette, dipped it into the dark green paint, then applied gentle strokes to the canvas. Small strokes with fine green detail. "Another cemetery." He stood tall arching his back, then regarded Wren standing next to him and holding the serving tray. "But this one will have an additional element. I call it the heart of the past." He pointed to the small green brush strokes. "This will become a heart, and this…" He pointed to the larger brush stroke. "The trees of the western woods."

His scar started itching, and he pushed on it, gritting his teeth as he did so. The itch was one thing, but when he pushed on the scar, pain pressed against his skull and his eye felt as if a hand had wrapped around the eyeball and squeezed.

"Oh my," said Wren. Marc looked at him. "The scar is infected again."

But his words landed on deaf ears. Marc was well aware of the burn in his skull from the scar. It was puffy and hurt when he touched it. He could feel it burning. Feel it burning always. Itching. And the wet drip that cascaded from the scar across his temple told him the wound had broken open again, certain that blood was dripping from his scar along with a good amount of pus. He stared into Wren's compassionate eyes.

"Allow me to take care of that for you."

Marc returned his gaze to the canvas. "Later. I just got into the groove." He took the larger paintbrush.

"Very well," said Wren. "Later it is. Don't forget your drink."

Marc eyeballed his red eye and the celery stalk drowning in the dark red liquid. A green olive sat on the top of the drink with the raw egg yolk beneath it. He returned to his painting. "I won't."

Of course he won't. Marc spent his days getting all liquored up because what else was there to do? Paint and drink. Drink and paint. Fuel that burning desire to create and unleash his creativity across the canvas. That's all he wanted to do. His passion for social interaction had died along with his writing.

76

Wren stepped closer to the wall with all the paintings. "Some of these are so disturbing, master." He looked at Marc from over his shoulder. "What do they mean?"

Marc regarded the paintings Wren was referring to. One was a depiction of a labyrinth with upside-down stairs and multiple levels. The second featured black roses, some as tall as a redwood with crystalized thorns on the stems. The third looked like an underwater scene with ghostly visions floating in the water.

Marc's answer was abrupt. He didn't have time to explain things. "The labyrinth houses our fears and evil deeds." He pointed to the next painting. "The roses represent our nefarious thoughts. The thorns are the tears that those thoughts brought to others and the tallness is how far those thoughts affected humanity over time." He craned his head to look at the third painting. "That's the sea of regret. It shows scenes from what did not happen, or what could have been if another decision had been made." He returned to his painting.

Wren continued to study the paintings before addressing Marc. "I'll leave you to it then. I have a mountain of work to finish today, so please confirm, we are going out tonight, correct?"

Marc paused mid stroke. He remembered nothing about going out tonight. He looked at Wren, confused, but Wren said nothing. He just stood there, holding the tray against his chest.

"Yes," Marc said then returned to his painting.

"As you wish," said Wren. "I'll have the car ready by six."

Marc said nothing. His focus was on the canvas. He arched his back, listening to the door close behind him when he looked at his drink. Wren's statement echoed in his skull-*as you wish*-and his thoughts hit a wall.

Where had he heard those words before?

At the same time Marc was turning his canvas into a Picasso, John received a visitor at his school.

He was at recess at the time and although he couldn't believe they brought the kids outside because it was so cold, he was glad they did. John was eager to test his theory. He believed he could use his magnifier to reflect the sun and use it as a light beam to kill ants. Not that he wanted to kill ants with his theory. His thought was that he could reflect the sun onto his vampire and burn him to all bloody hell.

"What are you doing?" asked Mrs. Calloway, his seventh-grade English teacher.

John looked up at her. He wasn't expecting to be caught. Sitting in his snowbank, he had successfully shoveled a good amount of snow to get to the dirt below where he knew the ants would be. He had found none yet, but he was eager to do so.

"Just playing," he said, looking over the playground and the other kids who were watching the scene play out.

"Well, forget about it. You have a visitor."

Reluctantly, John stood up. "Where are we going?"

"To the principal's office. They're waiting for you."

"Who?"

"I don't know. But we'll find out soon."

The who was Detective Carver. John's immediate reaction was a smile-he'd come to know Detective Carver over the last six months although why the detective had an interest in him, he could never understand-but after seeing the concerned stare in Carver's eyes that smile melted into a tightlipped foreboding. John stood in the principal's doorway, holding the doorknob and staring at Carver and his principal, Mr. Shelby. Both were staring at him with concern.

Was it possible Detective Carver knew about the vampire living in the middle of the western woods? Maybe that's why he's here.

"Hello, John," said Mr. Shelby. "Come in. Close the door, please."

John stood motionless, staring at the two older men.

Carver sat up in his chair. "You're not in trouble or anything. I just wanted to speak with you for a minute." When John didn't answer, Carver reaffirmed, "You're not in trouble."

John nodded, staring at the older men, and closed the door. Principal Shelby provided some small talk about John's grades-all stellar, by the way-and his progress in school, but when the conversation turned awkward, he excused himself, allowing Carver to use his office. John was quiet the entire time, wondering how much trouble he was in, and for what. Carver took a seat beside the principle's desk so they could talk face to face.

Maybe they know about the magnifying theory. But he was only going to use it to kill a vampire, so what's the concern?

Carver got to the point real quick. "You're probably wondering why I'm here," he said, his arm on Shelby's desk with a toothpick between his lips. "I'll be quick with it. Your grandpa called me."

It seemed like the air went out of the room. John sat frozen, staring at Carver.

"What's with your interest in the western woods? He said he found you last night walking into the woods and that you brought a telescope to your bedroom to watch the woods." He shrugged. "Why?"

A million thoughts ran through John's mind at that moment. Should he tell Carver about the vampire? About the house? Should he tell him about the bonfire and the dead body he saw in the wheelbarrow? Would he be in trouble if he said nothing?

Carver must have registered the fear in John's reaction because he went into his all too serious mode, hunched over with his elbows on his knees and staring intently with his toothpick wedged between his lips.

"There was a fire in the woods. A big fire."

Carver nodded his head. "Happens all the time. Teenagers are always in the woods."

John's gaze drifted to the floor, and he heard Carver shift in his seat, craning his head in some attempt to force John to look at him. John didn't notice he was trembling.

"John?" said Carver. "Are you ok?"

"There's a vampire out there," John whispered, as if the vampire could hear him talking about him.

"What?" Carver just about laughed. He sat back in his chair, elbow back on the desk. "Where did you come up with that?"

"I saw him."

Carver's brow knitted in confusion. "You saw a vampire? Where?"

John was nodding. "In the western woods. He's the one that started the fire." The look on Carver's face revealed both disbelief and humor. "He's living in that house in the woods."

"The house that's been abandoned for more than a hundred years? Come on John. Maybe it's some homeless guy. That happens every once in a while. People fall on hard times and need a place to go. It won't be the first time someone's taken occupancy in that house over the years."

Now John was shaking his head. "It's not a homeless person. He's a vampire. I know he is."

He must have used the correct tone because Carver paused and the stare in his eyes changed. More sympathetic than skeptical. "How do you know?"

John's throat tightened; his body constricted. Did he dare tell Carver about the body? Tell him that the vampire was at his window last night? Should he tell him about his ghost mother and the whispers and the signs she was showing him? John may be young, but he knew his father was in a hospital for being insane and should he go down this path it might be him who ends up in a hospital for the rest of his days.

So, John responded in the only way he felt safe. "I don't know."

To which Carver twirled that toothpick between his lips, his stare barreling down on John. "I have a feeling you're lying to me right now. Or at the very least, withholding information and not telling me the whole story." His eyes narrowed as he stared at John, waiting for an answer.

John said, "I don't know. But I saw him, and he looked like a vampire?"

"What do vampires look like?"

John explained about the vampire he witnessed through his telescope.

"Are you sure you weren't watching old movies last night because you just described *Nosferatu* to a tee?"

"I don't know what Noserfto is?"

"Nosferatu is a term used to describe a vampire."

"Whatever." Silence then, as John waited for Carver to respond. When he received no reply, he asked, "You believe me, don't you?"

Carver sat up again, thinking.

"Detective?" John's voice was a defeated whisper.

"Guess I have to. I don't see any reason why you'd lie."

John shifted up in his seat. "Which means?"

83

"Which means I'll be spending my afternoon in the western woods."

John's eyes widened, his jaw agape. He started shaking his head. "But the vampire. He'll get you."

Carver laughed. "I'm not worried about it. Plus..." He gestured to the window. "It's daylight out, so I'll be fine." He stood up. "I'll stop by grandpa's later tonight with a full report."

"You can't go out there," John just about hollered. "He'll kill you if he finds you."

Carver put his hand on the boy's shoulder. "No, he won't. I'll be fine, John. I've been going out there for decades."

John's mind raced with possibilities. He saw the dead body in the wheelbarrow. Saw the vampire's eyes staring at him. Heard the scrape from the vampire's nails against his window. He had to tell Carver about the dead body. Maybe then he'll understand how serious the situation is. He knew Carver's bullets wouldn't help him. Vampires are already dead. Bullets don't work. What he needed was a wooden stake and a large knife to cut off the vampire's head. That, or expose him to sunlight.

"I'll bring in Principal Shelby. And I'll see you later tonight." Carver squeezed his shoulder. "I promise." And when John said nothing, Carver turned to the door.

But with his hand on the doorknob, John blurted, "He had a dead body last night."

And Detective Carver stopped in his tracks.

Lori was convinced Marc's story would shed some light on her nightmare. After she picked up the notebook, she went into the kitchen and fixed herself a cup of coffee. All the while, Gerard and Elena watched her every move. Elena remarked about the notebook, seeing it on the kitchen counter, and Lori knew the woman could not resist plugging in her two cents on the subject.

"What is that... that notebook you went and retrieved? It's garbage and you should keep it that way. What's gotten into you this morning? After last night, I thought you'd be more complacent."

Lori shot her head back. "What are you talking about?"

Elena, hands on her hips, glared at Lori. "You don't remember screaming at the top of your lungs in the hallway? I had to coax you awake. It took over thirty minutes. And now this..." She gestured to the notebook. "What has gotten into you?"

Lori thought about what Elena said. She had no memory of screaming in the hall. All she remembered was the nightmare and the demon in the nightmare. "I must have had a night terror." Which was the only logical conclusion. She crossed her arms, staring at Elena. "I've had them for decades. You should be used to them. And what does that have to do with anything?"

Elena said nothing. She regarded the book. Lori noticed Gerard was listening, standing outside the kitchen.

"This is his, isn't it? That Marc character." She looked at Lori. "I thought you said to put the past to bed?"

Lori gritted her teeth. She didn't appreciate the inquiry and said the only thing she believed would placate her mother. "It's part of the letting go process." She pointed to the book. "Reading it will help me put the past to bed." She went to the counter, took a spoon from the drawer and stirred creamer into her coffee while watching Elena from the corner of her eye. Elena stared at the notebook as if it were the devil himself. Lori dropped the spoon on the counter, gripped the mug then snatched the notebook from under Elena's nose, taking one last look at her mother and her angry, devilish stare before she walked away.

Elena was on her heels. "I don't believe this is a good idea. All you're doing is driving back into the past. When you're ready to move forward, what you don't do is look back."

"That's for me to decide, not you." Lori took the first few steps up.

"This is insane. What you're doing is insane. And not very becoming of a lady with pride."

Lori turned on her heels, looking down on her mother standing with one foot on the first step and her hand on the banister. "Now, what's gotten into you?"

Elena stiffened; Lori could see her bones contract, and her facial muscles tense. When she spoke, that gruff voice bellowed her words. "What are you referring to?"

"You. The way you watch me. Like you're trying to drive me to a conclusion that only you are aware of. And the things that happened in the hospital. The way everything went down."

"Are you accusing me of something, Lori?"

Lori paused while shaking her head. The stare across Elena's face was telling. Hiding something from Lori, she was certain. "There's something you're not telling me. You know something about Marc. What is it?"

Elena said nothing.

"Very well, I'll find out myself." She turned around and hurried up the steps.

"You'll regret your current actions, Lori. Don't forget I said it either. Opening the past the way you are…" She paused. "Not good. Not good at all."

Lori screamed from the second floor, "What are you so afraid of? What harm could possibly come from reading a book?"

"Is that what this is? To understand, or is it to find an excuse to go back to him?"

"If that's where the path leads, then so be it. Unless you want to tell me what you know, then maybe I won't have to read the notebook."

Elena glared at Lori through narrow eyes, her head moving left to right. Her jaw clenched. "I know nothing."

"Excellent. Then I'll be in my room. Reading." She stomped over to her room.

"This is wrong Lori," Elena hollered from the steps. "Leave the past alone. When we stir up the ghosts from the past, they come back to haunt us. Best to leave it alone and walk away. Don't do this to yourself."

Lori closed the door with a thud, then stood with her back against it.

Elena hollered, "Don't open the door, Lori! Leave it shut so the demon can never rear his ugly head again."

Lori's blood turned to ice. She thought it was peculiar, Elena's use of the word demon.

73

Carver was driving to the western woods, his conversation with John on his mind. Carver understood the boy had gone through one hell of a traumatic experience. His sister was dead by his father's hand, the same father who was doing time in a state mental institution where he'll live for the rest of his days. And his mother put a bullet in her head not more than fifty feet from where he sat in his bedroom. What these circumstances had done to the child's brain he'll never know, and he was more than certain the boy was seeing things.

But he seemed so sincere.

Carver shook his head. There was no such thing as vampires, and that was it. End of story. Close the book. Carver was certain there had to be another explanation, but was the boy developing signs of a schizophrenic mind? Was the entire situation a delusion brought on by severe stress? Was it wishful thinking? Conjuring a phantom vampire to explain all he'd been through. Carver understood it; fantasy is always better than reality.

He knew he could get into trouble for investigating any matter concerning the Hardwoods, but he couldn't care less. The boy had reported a murder, and investigating was what he needed to do. After Sheila put a bullet through her brain, Carver was put on leave for one month and when he returned, he was assigned to desk duty.

He couldn't believe it. For the first time in his long-standing career, he'd been sidelined, and he was required to attend weekly therapy sessions. Now that was a joke if there ever was one. One hour a week with some therapist half his age. What the hell did she know other than how to pass a test and now she's giving advice on adult issues she'd never experienced herself? Unrelatable, that's how Carver saw his therapist. Everything she said seemed to come right out of a book. Textbook Therapy is how Carver referred to it.

A big waste of time.

And shuffling papers across a desk was not doing the Sleepy Hollow citizens any good. His talents and investigative acumen were being reduced to nothing. If you don't use it, you lose it, type of scenario. Being in the field kept him sharp and on point, and he was losing his edge. Becoming complacent and losing his ability to care.

Carver rounded a bend in the road. Not really a road, but a deviation in the woods where a car could fit. He could see the house in the distance. It looked barren. But the deviation led to a copse of trees and bushes. He stopped the car, looking through the windshield. Carver couldn't find any other road to the house.

"Guess I'm walking from here." He cut off the engine. It looked like there was a half-mile trek to the house. Carver popped a toothpick between his teeth before he climbed out of the car.

And as he walked through the woods, he couldn't shake the sensation that the woods were watching him.

Marc took a gulp of his red eye. The salty, peppery fluid felt good on his tongue and warm in his stomach, buzzing his mind open with creativity. He had taken off his shirt, permitting the frosty morning air to litter his skin in gooseflesh. He enjoyed the cold across his frail and bony torso. He'd lost a considerable amount of weight since the accident. He looked sick and ghostly, as if he were fading away.

He downed the drink, then bit into the celery stalk, gnawing on it then swallowed. He'll leave the olive for later, after it's soaked up all the alcohol and spice. Marc placed the glass on the table, his mind buzzing with alcohol. He licked his lips with a gasp of goodness and stared at his painting. The heart he painted was green and was embedded into the trunk of an oak tree with gravestones surrounding the tree and the western woods in the distance. Apparitions lifted off the cemetery ground with their long limbs reaching for the heart.

He stood and stared for what seemed like an eternity, studying his painting and assessing flaws to determine what was missing. What must be added to complete his vision? His scar itched and burned, and he pushed against it, rubbing the scar feverishly as wet pus and blood spotted his fingertips. The same fingernails he deposited between his teeth, nipping at his nails and cuticles. His nails were bitten down to close to nothing.

Marc nipped a cuticle between his teeth, gnawing on his thumb, and tore that cuticle off as a sting ripped across his thumb. He looked down and saw he was bleeding. A thick stream of red pooled across his thumb, cascading to the knuckle. He looked at the painting. Looked at his thumb, then the painting again. His stomach trembled, feeling nauseous and sickly as if his blood had been tainted with venom. His hand shaking, Marc picked up the paintbrush from off the floor and with his forefinger pushing against his thumb, he deposited his blood onto the brush, squeezing with all his might.

And with his blood, he painted two red eyes in the top corner of his painting. The red eyes that beamed bright in his thoughts and visions. Noticed his breath was labored, as if his lungs were struggling to catch a breath. He clenched his jaw as he continued to paint those eyes. Those red beaming eyes in the darkness.

Where had he seen those eyes before? So familiar, yet so far out of reach. The eyes in the painting seemed to embed themselves into it, as if they were waiting to be created and took to their position with gratitude and conformity. And then, he dipped his brush into the smoky white paint he created from a mix of white and gray and weaved that brush across the canvas. It looked like the invisible body from the eyes had reached its long ethereal arm around the heart in the tree. Marc painted fingers around the heart as if that hand were squeezing the blood from it. Blood that he painted with his own blood-the dripping blood from the squeezed heart by the hand of the demon with red eyes.

He stared, stiff and wide eyed, at his creation. The perfect mix of darkness and heartache. Felt his scar pulsing and throbbing with an ache across his skull as he gritted his teeth. Felt tears swell in his eyes and cries crawl into his closing throat. His hands were trembling, his bones shuddering. In the cold. The cold winter breeze through his window. The drop cloth wavered; his scattered paintings dithered under its gale.

Marc looked through his window and saw a policeman emerge from the woods; his badge was secured to his belt buckle and glimmered in the sunlight.

So strange, he thought as he craned his head, staring through the window, watching the officer trek through the snow towards the burnt embers of what had been a bonfire. Marc stepped to the window, gripped the top pane and watched the policeman.

Now why is there a cop on my property?

75

Carver's instincts were on high alert. As if the energy pumping from the house turned up the dial on his instincts, sending them into overdrive. He noticed the change in the woods and as he inched closer to the house, it felt like he was walking through a thicket of closely packed atoms that sought to deter him from the house.

His limbs grew tired, as if the gravity in the woods had intensified and pulled down on his core. His eyes were heavy, and he fought to keep them open and not drop into an unconscious dream. He pushed through it, forcing himself to keep taking steps and when he saw the clearing in plain view, the knowledge that his journey was ending brought renewed strength to his limbs and he stepped across the threshold into the clearing and stopped.

Cold wrapped around him and squeezed. It seemed like the temperature dropped ten degrees the moment he stepped into the clearing.

And I thought hell was supposed to be hot.

It was like ice in his veins, freezing his bones with a burn. He scanned the yard, amazed how the woods formed a perfect circle around the property as if the woods refused to enter the grounds. The bonfire-or what had been a bonfire-stood with its burnt embers not more than twenty yards from him.

That's the fire John saw last night. Carver could smell the faintest trace of smoke. He looked at the house, so dark and ominous and ghostly and decayed. *How can anyone actually live in there?* If there was anyone in there, that is. More than likely, some vagrants took refuge from yesterday's storm and may be gone already.

Carver stepped towards the bonfire.

There's something peculiar about this place. Something off... I can't figure out what it is.

He scanned through the bonfire, looking for body parts or bones. But there was nothing. No skull or femur. No foot or fingers. Just burnt embers and ash.

Not enough for probable cause to get a warrant for a full search of the house. All he had was the overactive imagination of a traumatized child. He'll never get a warrant with that explanation, but as he stood on the property the thought entered his mind that the boy was telling the truth. Carver's gut was tingling, telling him he was correct in his assessment.

Trust your instincts. Trust your wit. The truth always hides in plain sight.

He looked up at the house and cringed when he saw someone on the second floor staring at him through the window. No shirt on, his hand above him probably gripping the windowsill. Carver squinted in the sunlight. Something was off about him. His face looked distorted, as if his features were consistently changing from one form to another. One moment he looked one way, the next,

96

different. Carver couldn't explain it; it was as if he had two distinct faces that wavered back and forth. And his energy was off. Sinister and nefarious barreled down from that window as if the man's stare could reach out and cripple Carver's heart.

But who is he? More than likely, some homeless guy taking occupancy in the dilapidated house.

"Guess I'll just have to ask him."

Carver turned on his heels, ready to go to the house when he stopped cold and his heart jumped in his chest. He came eye to eye with John's vampire.

And he wasn't melting in the afternoon sun either, but damn did he look like a vampire. His short stature meant nothing when Carver investigated his beady, dark eyes. They were hypnotizing, mesmerizing. Carver thought that if he stared for too long, he'd fall through a trapdoor and end up in hell.

"May I help you?" His brow furrowed with the question, and Carver could feel his energy. It was like a deterrent. As if the energy was thick, surrounding him in a veil of protection that Carver's instincts could never penetrate.

Carver rolled his toothpick from one corner of his mouth to the other. He could smell the evil in the man's veins and immediately Carver knew there was something sinister in the man's heart. And the way he stared at Carver, as if he were devouring him with his eyes, ready to cut his head off if given the chance. Quite obvious he was not happy with the police arriving unexpectedly on his doorstep.

Carver said, "Yes, I'm sure you can. I'm Detective Stephen Carver. Are you the owner of the property?"

The man seemed to stiffen. "What business is that of yours?"

Carver shot his head back. He wasn't expecting such a response. "Because I'm a police officer and I asked." The man stood with a stare that cut Carver to the bone. "And you are?"

He shot his head up, as if he was appalled by the question. Apparently, he did not wish to provide an answer. First sign of guilt.

"Listen…" Carver took a step closer, and the man stepped back as if Carver were the assailant in this scenario. "Things will go a lot easier if you cooperate. I'm not here to cause trouble or anything. Just investigating some strange occurrences in the area."

"Strange occurrences?" he repeated.

"Yes, like a bonfire in the woods…" He gestured to the burnt embers. "On a property that is supposed to be abandoned." He paused to allow his words to sink in. "So, may I ask you again, are you the owner of the property?"

"I am not," he said abruptly.

"Well then, now we're getting somewhere. Is there an owner?" He looked up at the house. "Couldn't imagine anyone actually living here." He turned back to the man. "Doesn't look like anyone's lived in that house for a very long time."

"There are levels to what is acceptable living for some people."

Another odd response and Carver noticed he didn't answer his question. Carver's grin was tightlipped and smug. "So, is there an owner? Perhaps that guy on the second floor is the owner of the property?" He gestured to the second-story window, but the person was no longer there.

"Correct."

"Well, can I speak to him? Just a few questions and I'll be on my way."

"He's working right now and doesn't like to be disturbed."

"I'm more than sure he can spare a few minutes for law enforcement. Plus, considering the situation, I'd say it's in your best interest to answer some questions."

"What is the situation?"

Again, Carver grinned that smug tightlipped smile. "Well, I received a report this morning on a possible murder taking place on the property."

"Murder?" The man's head shot back, appalled.

"Yes, murder. A witness claims to have seen a dead body last night and a man who looked like a vampire..." He paused to let the information sink in. "...dumped the body in the bonfire." He gestured with his thumb to the burnt embers. "Now, you wouldn't know anything about that, would you?"

"Not at all. Such ludicrous notions from simple minds." He shook his head. "All we wish for is to live in peace and now this. The accusation is insulting."

"Well, what were you burning last night?"

"Old paintings, knickknacks, and we *are* beginning renovations, so more than a few rotted floorboards and such. Perhaps that is what your witness saw last night."

"Perhaps, but it would be good if I could search the house." He gestured to the house again. "With the owner's permission, of course." The man paused, glaring at Carver. "I find nothing, then I got nothing, and I can go back to my desk and file my report that nothing was found." Carver stepped closer. "And your cooperation will be noted in the report." Now Carver was itching to get into that house. He knew something was wrong. He could smell it in the air.

The man's stare narrowed. "Follow me." He turned on his heels then started walking to the front of the house. Carver noticed he gave a quick glance to the second-story window. Carver did too, but still there was no one there.

"And I still haven't gotten your name," Carver said, following him around to the front of the house.

"My name is Wren. Wren Field. And I am the servant to the home and my proprietor."

Carver nodded, keeping his eyes open and his senses on high alert. When he knew Wren wasn't looking, he flicked the clip on his holstered weapon and the sheath attached to his belt buckle that housed a one-inch blade. Just in case. One never knows what's lurking around the corner.

And what was lurking around the corner was the owner of the property. Shirtless, he stood on the porch outside the front door as if he was waiting for them. Waiting and blocking the entrance to the house.

"Detective," the owner said, offering his hand. "So good to meet you."

Carver shook his hand. "And you are?"

"Marc Saduj," he said. "The owner of the property."

Carver couldn't be certain, but he thought he saw Marc's face flicker in the sunlight. It looked like a shadow tore across his eyes.

76

Marc had been right. His book *is* a horror story. Lori read words like demon and sat-appalled no less-while she read about eating human hearts and torture and murder by the most sadistic means she could ever fathom.

The worst were the ghost demons and how they used mind manipulation and hallucinations to drive their victims into insanity, forcing their worst fears to live and breathe.

Honestly, the more she read, the more she wondered if she had ever truly known Marc Saduj. She didn't know such horrible atrocities could come from a man so gentle and kind. But when she read the parts in the story where the main character-his name was John Ashton-made a deal with the devil to save his wife's life, she recognized the man she agreed to marry. Marc was a hopeless romantic. It's why he wrote romance novels. When someone is raised by a mother who provides continued torture in the absence of love, the recipient either indulges in the darkness-because it's comfortable and all they know-or they turn into the exact opposite, always seeking the love they never received and willing to do anything for it.

But what she had not come across yet was the name of the demon John Ashton sold his soul too. For some reason, Marc only refers to him in the story as the man in black. No name is ever given, at least not up until the selling of the soul happens. She still had a good amount of the book left to read so it could come up later in the story.

She realized she was staring out the window. How long had she been staring? The notebook on her chest, she could feel the icy chill outside her window as she gnawed on her bottom lip, thinking. Thinking about Marc Saduj. Where is he right now? What is he up to? Where did life take him after the accident? After he wrote Lori off like some damn mistake that he wanted to rectify as quickly as possible. Left her in that hospital bed, alone. Abandoned and on the brink of death. The doctors and nurses said her recovery was a miracle. A miracle. One in a Million. One in ten million, considering there were no repercussions. No lifelong side effects nor brain damage.

Nothing.

A miracle indeed.

A miracle.

Total recovery, as if…

Her thoughts trailed off, and Lori sat up placing the notebook on the bed face down. She stared at it, thinking about the plot and how the story reflected their life together.

Could it?

No, not a chance. Writers often use real circumstances to embolden their fictional worlds. The fact that Mr. and Mrs. Ashton were in a car accident after a romantic weekend getaway had no credence. Or did it? Considering Marc had written those pages the day before the accident...

Did he see it coming?

That's impossible.

She looked at the notebook lying flat on the bed. The word 'Holer' written across the cover in thick red letters. On the back cover was a red inverted pentagram with the words Initium Novum written beneath it. The demon from her night terror then flashed in her thoughts, his red beaming eyes glowing in the darkness. How he just stared, and his stare was enough to cringe the bones and curdle the blood. Left her in a frozen state of panic. Paralyzed and suffocating, as if the demon ripped the air from her lungs with his stare.

And then the words, the words that boomed from beyond the light where she had been certain Marc was waiting.

What were those words...

Init Novus or something like that.

She looked at the notebook from the corner of her eyes and stared at the back cover. The words were as clear as the snow outside her window. *That has to be it. That's what the voice said.*

Initium Novum.

"I think I'm having an existential crisis." Her voice was flat, monotone. The accident was a blur, but perhaps Marc told her more about his story than she remembered. Maybe the story exists deep in the subconscious and is spilling into her dreams?

"I know…" Lori slipped off the bed and stepped to her desk where she snatched a small notepad and pencil then brought them back to the bed where she sat with one foot on the floor and the other beneath her bottom. She wrote the word 'Similarities' across the top of the first page and started listing the similar instances between Marc's fictional story and Lori's real life.

The weekend getaway.

The accident.

One a writer, the other an antique dealer, although in the story their careers were beefed up to astronomical success.

Mrs. Ashton was from a prominent family. Mr. Ashton from poverty.

Another similarity. What else will she find?

She looked down at the notebook.

"What else, Marc?" she whispered. "Are you trying to tell me something? Did you see the future and now here it is… in this present?"

Lori put the pad and pencil down, then stretched her fingers over the cover and flipped the book over. She had a lot more to read. Lori leaned against the headboard and continued.

77

Carver knew he was being watched. So very carefully too. He could feel their eyes on him roaming across his body, assessing every move he was making as if they were attached to his heels, breathing down his neck.

Carver wasn't certain who was in charge. The owner, Marc, or his trusted servant, Wren. And when they took him up on his request to search the house, he wasn't surprised they agreed. People with nothing to hide offer information to prove their innocence, but the guilty do the same when they know there's nothing to see, at least not at that moment. It's the classic case of showing everything but telling nothing. Considering this, Carver was almost certain he wouldn't find anything in the house. If John was correct, the body he saw last night was burned in the bonfire and although Carver gave the bonfire a quick look through, he was certain that if a body had been burned between those logs there'd be some remnant of it. So, what Carver was hoping for was probable cause. Something he could find in the home that would allow him to bring in a closer search of the bonfire.

Then again, it could be a wild goose chase. Some kid's imagination that got Carver all hopped up and ready to search and investigate. Could be nothing at all. Sure, Marc and Wren were strange, but strange doesn't equate to guilt, although it was the boy's sincerity and downright fear-he'd been trembling when he told the story-that convinced Carver something had happened here last night. And it wasn't just that Marc and Wren were strange, there was more to them. Something beneath the surface that signaled to Carver that all was not right in this house and definitely not right with its occupants.

And who knows if they're telling the truth. Carver will need to verify that Marc is the true owner of the house and not just squatting. They could just be two homeless people who found paradise in an abandoned mansion.

Wren opened the door for Carver, who took his toothpick from between his lips. "After you, gentlemen." As if he'd allow one of these two to slip in behind him. Carver had a gut feeling his head would be cut off if he did. "I insist."

After exchanging a quick glance, Wren entered first, followed by Marc. Marc, who Carver was certain would be the one to do the cutting if given the chance. Although he had a solemn face, his eyes betrayed him. So much anger and rage existed behind those eyes. His attempts at humor and the haphazard way he dealt with Carver made Carver's skin crawl. It was as if he was placating the officer when all he wanted to do was see him in anguish.

Carver stepped in behind them, scanning across the room, gathering as much intel as possible. First thing he said was, "Seems like you've got a lot of work to do?"

The house seemed smaller on the inside than it looked from the outside. He'd stepped into a large, open room. Carver believed it could be a ballroom if needed, and he was certain the room was useful for both a ballroom and a living room. Just a wide-open space with a fireplace on the far wall to his right. To the right of the fireplace was a hallway with a staircase on the left. The hall led to what he could see were two doors, one on the right and the other on the left, with an open room on the right at the end of the hall. The kitchen was on his left. First glance told him the kitchen hadn't been used in a day's age.

Then again, the entire house looked just the way he thought it should look-abandoned! The floorboards were worn and weathered and looked like he could fall right through if he stepped in the wrong place. The walls were strange. A mix of stone and wood, as if the original owner wanted some of the exterior to bleed into the house. Carver noticed a few holes in the wood and the floorboards had a few layers of dirt and grime. Three blown out windows were on the wall across from the entrance, looking out over the bonfire that had been raging not twelve hours ago. The only furniture was a dilapidated red leather high-back chair with a side table next to it and a red cane leaning against the chair.

How anyone was living in this house was beyond Carver's understanding.

"Correct, officer," said Wren as he looked up to the ceiling. "We've got a lot of work to do." He turned to Carver. "Renovations will take some time, but this old house is worth it." He stomped on the floorboards, sending a wave of dust into the air. "The foundation is strong. And when the foundation is strong, everything else can be fixed." He smiled then, and Carver's gut turned over with Wren's devilish grin.

"They don't make em like they used to." Carver looked up and noticed the ceiling was marked with what he assumed were water stains. "I'm surprised you're not falling through the ceiling from the top floors." He scanned across the ceiling. "Doesn't look safe."

"But it is, officer." Wren again. Carver noticed Marc hadn't said a word. He just stood there with his fingers intertwined in front of him, although he could feel Marc's stare. It sent shivers racing down Carver's spine. "As you shall see… during your search."

Carver snapped his stare over to Wren. "That I will." Marc stepped towards the red leather chair. Carver watched him, his movements slow as if he were laboring towards the chair.

"Where would you like to begin?"

Carver took the toothpick from his lips. "I'll follow your lead," he said, noticing Marc gripped the rounded top of the red cane.

"Excellent," said Wren as a smile crossed his lips and Marc turned on his heels, red cane in hand. "I'd be honored to provide a tour of our home."

Carver stood, looking over the two of them. Wren with his vampire looks and Marc behind him with his red cane. They were a suspicious pair.

Hopefully just weird.

Marc's stare was burning a hole through Carver, his facial muscles tense. *Is he gritting his teeth?* Looks like he's fighting something. Some internal catastrophe.

"Enough with the chitchat." This was Marc, his voice shaky as if his internal battle brought rage to his lips. Carver noticed he stretched and rolled his fingers around the top of his cane then squeezed. "Let the game begin."

78

John was staring through the school bus window when the bus turned onto his block. He couldn't wait to get home.

Couldn't wait to see the woods. He told Detective Carver not to go there. Told him to bring the SWAT team and let them do their job, but Carver wouldn't listen. He said there were protocols to follow.

What the hell is a protocol?

Shouldn't it be simple? John saw the dead body. What other information did Detective Carver need?

The bus slowed to a stop down the street from his house. He'll need to walk from here. Not too far, just down the street but he was hoping-hope wasn't the right word, he was begging to God-that Michael Duprey, Chad Ryan, and Logan Reeves were all in good moods today, ready to dash home as soon as possible. Because if their attention was on someone or something else, it wouldn't be on John and then maybe he'll be able to make it home without those three dickheads following him all the way to his house, blaring ridicule the whole way there.

John despised those three jackasses. He wanted to avoid them entirely, if he could.

The tires squealed to a halt as the bus gasped, and the driver flung the doors open. John jumped up in his seat when something knocked him in the back, and he fell against the seat in front of him.

"Watch where you're going?" It was Michael Duprey. He never even looked back. Chad and Logan were behind him. John noticed Michael looked at him as he took the stairs down. Chad and Logan too, and Chad belted out a high-pitched cackle.

Chad was the runt of their little threesome. John was certain a punch in the nose to any of the three would have him on easy street for the rest of his school career. Grandpa told him, bullies are only like that because they're crippled inside. Usually, they come from a broken home and aren't wired right in their head to begin with. Plus, they've got low self-esteem and need to overcompensate for it.

Whatever the hell that means.

John gripped the straps on his backpack and took the long walk to the front of the bus, staring through the window from the corners of his eyes watching as the threesome took a left from the bus doors. Which meant they were headed to Logan's house, probably to play the new *Street Fighter* game he received for Christmas.

Which also meant John had a clean getaway from the bus since his house was in the opposite direction. And good for it because he had more dire concerns on his mind. Like checking up on Detective Carver. One look through his telescope and he was hoping to see the abandoned house swarming with police. And then he could watch the show from the privacy of his bedroom.

He stepped off the bus with a jump and walked hurriedly towards his house. His heart raced like a rabbit in his chest. Cold winter air across his brow, staring into the distant western woods, listening to the bus squeal as it drove away. His breath plumed off his lips in a mist of heated cold.

He didn't get more than a few feet when he felt the hit as if some linebacker from last night's losing team wanted revenge. He dropped with a thud on the street. His left shoulder hit the ground hard, and he flopped onto his backpack holding his shoulder and wincing.

Michael Duprey stood over him. Chad and Logan were behind him. Chad was laughing. He was always laughing when Michael acted like an ass. That kid will be following morons for the rest of his life. Logan stood back, shaking his head. Of the three, he was the least problematic.

"Where are you running to?" Michael goaded him. "Gotta cut out grandpa's heart?"

Another loud, bellowing laugh came from Chad and John's shoulder ached like a son of a bitch. And then Chad started in with that stupid fucking rhyme.

"Heart Eater. Heart Eater, come and take your soul. Heart Eater. Heart Eater, eating hearts... all night long." His eyes were wide with delight.

John said nothing. After all, what could he say? Any response he had would bring more of the same, and there were three of them and one of him. With gritted teeth, he clambered to his feet. Never looked back or responded and just started walking.

"Oh, that's it? Gotta walk away, asshole?" Michael's voice was filled with venom.

Heard Logan say, "Let's go guys. If you want to play, let's go."

And that fucking rhyme again, now from the lips of both Chad and Michael. "*Heart Eater. Heart Eater, come and take your soul. Heart Eater. Heart Eater, eating hearts... all night long.*"

It was such a stupid fucking rhyme, but then again bullies are stupid to begin with so he wasn't surprised that's all they could come up with. John held his shoulder as he walked, blinking away his tears. His shoulder hurt something awful.

"Hey heart eater?" This was Michael. "I'm watching you, heart eater. I'm always watching you and one day I promise, I'm going to kill you so you can't eat anyone's heart. Like your father and your loser mother. You won't get off that easy."

He was fucking insane. His brain was wired in the wrong direction.

And that rhyme again.

Heart Eater. Heart Eater, come and take your soul. Heart Eater. Heart Eater, eating hearts... all night long.

He hoped one day someone would eat their fucking hearts.

114

So far, the house was clean. Carver hadn't seen anything suspicious-other than the two residents-and nothing he could use to get a warrant. The house was, as he thought it should be, abandoned. Gutted. A shell of a ghost if there ever was one. Other than the red leather chair there was nothing in the house. No furniture, no art hanging on the walls, no television. Not even a radio. If it weren't for the two very suspicious people escorting him through the house there'd be nothing to tell.

He felt like he was on a wild goose chase. Wild ghost chase seemed more appropriate considering Carver couldn't shake the feeling that there was more to the house than he could see. It was a feeling, a nagging sensation thumping in his brain that something was not right in Sleepy Hollow and the two people he was looking at had everything to do with it.

They watched him with apt focus. Wren was the escort, while Marc stayed close to Carver, watching his every move from the corners of his eyes. He had that look in his eyes, telling Carver he'd rather see him in anguish than allow him to search his home. Or perhaps he just didn't like cops. And maybe he really didn't like cops snooping around his home.

Carver could understand. He sure as shit didn't want anyone to snoop around his house. Not that they'd find anything, but privacy was a good thing and who the hell wanted someone's nose up their ass, assessing every miniscule detail of their lives? It doesn't matter who you are, anyone can distort reality to feed their own narrative and shine a spotlight on a simple circumstance to prove their point even if that circumstance had a different context all together.

He was beginning to think that John's imagination and trauma had gotten to the boy. Other than confirming that Marc was the new owner of the house, his investigation was coming to a close.

And then he stepped into what Wren described was Marc's art studio. Now Carver wasn't some so-called art dealer, nor did he know what would be deemed as good art, but what he saw in that room turned his blood cold. Specifically, the newest creation sitting on the easel in the center of the room. The one with the heart carved into a tree trunk. The moment he laid eyes on it Jerry Hardwood's voice boomed in his head.

I need hearts for the master.

Followed by the image he still couldn't shake from his brain: Zoe Hardwood with her heart ripped out.

"This is interesting," Carver said, studying the painting. The mix of green and gray made the art appear like it was floating like dense fog in the glow of an emerald night. Wren stood by the window while Marc stood in the open doorway over Carver's shoulder. He looked at Marc. "Where do you get your inspiration from?"

The stare in Marc's eyes was evil and deadly. Standing while gritting his teeth with both hands wrapped around the top of his cane. He looked like he could destroy Carver right here and now and honestly, Carver was wondering why Marc displayed such restraint from doing so. It was quite apparent to the detective that Marc either didn't want to answer the question or-for some odd reason beyond Carver's comprehension-couldn't answer the question. As if he didn't know the answer.

"I don't have time to explain how it works, detective," said Marc, his voice cold and gritty. "Can we just get on with it? Or did you come here with the purpose to delay our work to feed your own needs?"

So much for the pleasantries, but Carver took the bait.

"You do understand the current predicament, don't you?" He took the toothpick from between his lips, pointing it at Marc. "A witness claims you've got a dead body on your hands and honestly, I find the situation odd."

"Odd, detective? Because we bought a house and now we're renovating a house? Last I checked there was no crime in doing so. Yet, here you are, to pass judgment on us and foil our day to your liking. There is much work to be concluded and this…" He shook his head while looking away from Carver, cane in his left hand, and he squeezed his right hand into a fist. "This intrusion is unwarranted *and* unnecessary." He locked eyes with Carver; his gaze filled with devilish hatred. Carver couldn't tell if Marc's eyes were blue or inky black. It seemed as if the iris was black with blue embedded in the pupils. He'd never seen such eyes before. "I wish for you to complete your search so I may go on with my day. As you can see, we have a lot to do and houses don't build themselves."

Carver gave a slight nod, depositing his toothpick between his lips. "Well, I guess I'll just do what I'm here to do, then." He turned to Wren as he spoke, needing to relinquish his gaze from Marc's stare. Thought that Wren was standing closer than he was before. Wren had been by the window. Now he was close to the painting in question.

"Please do, officer. This intrusion is insulting. Having to escort you through my home so you can scrutinize every aspect of it is not what I choose to do today. Have at it and be gone, detective." Marc's gaze was steady, with a stare that could cut Carver to the bone.

Carver heard a shift over his shoulder and turned to see Wren a little too close for comfort. Carver took two steps back. "Can you stay where you are, please? More than an arm's length away."

Wren's stare was unwavering and the look in his eyes sinister and nefarious, as if he wished to deliver his master's justice across Carver's skull.

"More insults." This was from Marc.

But Carver never took his eyes off Wren. Wren, who craned his head while glaring at Carver, pursed his lips then ran his tongue over his bottom lip before gritting his teeth.

Should have told them to wait outside, thought Carver. Although, at the time he didn't believe they would have stayed outside, and he didn't trust them. Carver believed there was a large possibility they would have attempted to sneak up on him during his search. It appeared he'd gotten himself into a bit of a nasty predicament. If these two are responsible for a murder, Carver knew he was outmanned and possibly outmatched.

The tension was thick, and Carver's heart was racing in his chest. His hand hovered above his holstered weapon with the slightest bit of a tremble. Wren's gaze was telling. Carver knew all Marc had to do was provide permission and then Carver would have one hell of a time wrestling with these two. Thank the heavens for his .45 Magnum. Putting a bullet between Wren's nefarious nosferatu eyes would settle this matter quickly.

Instead, he said, "Do you gentlemen mind waiting outside while I finish my search?" He noticed Wren's shoulders went slack, as if he was disappointed. Heard Marc shift his weight from one foot to the other. Watching him through his periphery, Marc stood tall with his hands on his cane.

Marc scoffed. "Inside. Outside. We've grown tired officer and want this completed immediately." His voice boomed in the room. "I'd request a search warrant if I had the time on my hands, which I don't."

Wren's gaze never wavered. His dark pupils were like black stones and Carver believed he was staring into Wren's soul, a thick ocean of darkness filled with rage and hate. If the man was a vampire Carver was certain he'd tip Carver's blood into a goblet and drink it down like a fine wine. Carver said nothing in response, shifting his gaze from Wren to Marc.

"Come Wren, let the officer conduct his business without our attendance. Seems we've ruffled his feathers a bit. I do believe the good detective is quite frightened at the moment." He stomped his cane twice against the floor. "Let us go. To the outside while the detective molests our home."

Marc turned around and walked to the stairs, disappearing down the steps. Wren took a step towards the door, watching Carver from the corner of his eye.

"And stand outside where I can see you," said Carver.

Wren took the stairs down. Carver watched the door, bracing himself for one of them to rush back in with hell in their eyes. Instead, he heard footsteps on the stairs and then more on the first floor, listening as they shuffled to the front door and then they were gone, as if the winter wind swept them away.

Carver released the breath he didn't know he'd been holding. Obviously, there was more going on with those two than what he'd seen. So far, he was on the side of the traumatized child with the wild imagination over these two freaks. He knew he would find nothing in the home. If these two were up to something, they went to great lengths to hide their deeds. Unless... unless there's something about the house he was unaware of. Something that was not clear to the eye.

Hidden rooms, he thought. These old houses were always built with hidden rooms and passages. He'll need to locate old blueprints. But the house was built so long ago. Would such a thing still exist? He wasn't certain, but the thought was worth further inquiry.

He looked at the painting on the easel.

I need hearts for the master.

Couldn't get that line out of his head. And something was telling him the master was close. So very close.

Marc was in an in-between dimension, aware of what was happening around him but unable to take part. Like a prisoner in his own body, only allowed to observe.

He could hear what was being said, but the words seemed to float to his ears, like listening to voices underwater. And everything looked different, as if all the vibrant colors had been drained from the earth. The air and the surrounding walls too, all bathed in an old black and white film where the black pigment dominated the heightened HD clarity. And then there was the wind, like a hurricane but with no sound, that made movement close to impossible, barreling and pressing down on him with relentless fury. Wind that carried the silent screaming of the dead as they lay tortured and beaten in some far-off version of hell. Pain. Unimaginable pain gripped every cell in his ethereal body. He saw eyes in the walls, and slithering apparitions darting from one corner to the next. Chattering, clattering teeth and howls from the hounds of hell barked in the corners.

He felt sick, as if he'd swallowed venom. His stomach was rumbling and unsettled. Felt weak, lethargic and stuck, struggling to connect his thoughts to his lips. Unable to speak.

He wanted to tell the detective to run.

And he was well aware of the man in black's presence, although he looked different from what Marc remembered. Looked different but Marc knew it was him. He could feel his essence, and that essence arrived with a state of knowing, confirming this person was the man in black. He could see him everywhere. In the corners with the hounds. Over his shoulder, breathing down his neck. In front of him. Behind him. Everywhere he looked a version of the man in black was there, blanketed in a darkness that revealed his crooked face with his red eyes and his dark skin. The smooth ebony horns that tore from his forehead, and the plump spiderlike veins across his face. Marc would have thought he was looking at a dead man had he not seen the hate in his eyes that proved there was life in the body.

He saw the police officer enter his property from the western woods and when he went to the window, he ended up here. Where was here? So different from the ether in the cemetery. At least in the cemetery, he could move. And think. But here, it was like passing over into a black hole, filled with confusion and pain. Everything hurt.

Everything hurt!

They're outside, greeting the cop. In the house, looking it over. Upstairs, staring at the heart trunk when a fierce pain slithered through his veins into his gut and all he knew then was pain. Anguish was more like it. He closed his eyes, his head weary, attempting to garner some semblance of order, to understand what

123

was happening. Trying to push past the pain. And when he opened his eyes, everything was light. Bright white light and he could see.

Could see the man in black was waiting. Watching him. Keeping him confined.

John was watching through his telescope. Staring at the two men standing in the yard. They sent shivers down his spine.

Standing in the cold, staring at the house. The vampire hovered just below the shoulder of the one with the cane. The one who John couldn't take his eyes from.

He is the master.

His mother's voice breathed against his ear and John froze, staring into the eyepiece at the man whose facial features seemed to change in front of John's eyes, as if some metaphysical wave rippled across his skin. And he was angry, that was for sure. His hateful, menacing stare confirmed John's suspicion. John noticed the man's scar was bleeding. A small trickle of blood beaded off the scar and dripped across his eyebrow. John watched as he blotted the blood with a handkerchief the vampire handed him.

John looked up at the sun.

"Ok, so maybe he's not a vampire."

John clucked his tongue, staring out the window.

No, he's something else. Something much worse than a vampire.

His mother's voice again. John turned around, hoping to see her, but with no such luck. He liked it when she was here, even if she was in ghost form.

He's the harbinger of fear. The black heart of humanity.

John dipped his head to the eyepiece, staring at the master with his red cane and hateful glare as he looked over the house. It was obvious to John they were concerned about what was happening in the house, and John was certain Detective Carver was in there.

"But the body wasn't in the house. It was dropped in the fire. Why isn't he searching the fire?"

He moved the telescope a bit, then adjusted the clarity in the eyepiece, wanting a better look at the cane.

There will be many bodies soon. I see the earth bathed in the dead bodies of humanity. Torn apart and eaten. A planet of bones and blood.

The cane was red and made of wood with gnarls that cascaded up and down the shaft that gave the appearance of souls caught in the moment of a torturous scream. Thick and strong and capped off with a round golden top.

Humanity's end as a new beginning.

He could feel his mother's forced swallow turn into a gasp.

The end of humanity. The beginning of hell. All achieved through the power of the cane.

John looked up, rolling his tongue inside his mouth. He looked over the room. Empty. Nothing but himself and his mother's voice.

The master must meet his fate from the cane. He must be destroyed. All of humanity is at risk if he survives.

He looked through the window at the sunlight beaming off the fresh snow.

126

The cane must be taken from them. It must be presented to the only person who can put an end to this tirade.

"Who?" John asked in a whisper and cracked voice.

No response. John looked around the room.

"Who?" he asked again.

In time, you will learn who. But it is you who must provide the cane to them.

John investigated the woods with his own eyes. Saw the house standing in the distance. If his mother is right-and mothers always are-than that would mean *he* would have to go inside the house.

It is your birthright. It is… your destiny.

And that was something John wanted nothing to do with.

Carver stepped onto the front porch. He had enough of the house and had searched every room with the hope he would find something that would allow him to bring in the cavalry for a more thorough search. But there was nothing. Literally nothing in the house. If someone had been murdered, there was no evidence of it. At least not in the house and maybe the murder never took place inside but outside, considering John had seen the body thrown into the fire.

The fire!

Carver turned to the burnt and charred embers of the bonfire and the odd pair standing beside it. Wren was holding a lit torch. Carver craned his head.

He's not…

Wren touched the torch to the logs, reigniting the bonfire when the sunlight dissipated and Carver looked up. Looked up to the dark cloud that slithered across the sky, shielding the sunlight and bathing the property in an overcast shade of dark.

The bonfire now raging with life, Carver stepped towards his strange pair. Their backs to him, staring into the flames as a heavy gale rippled across the property. Carver hadn't expected a storm this afternoon; the weatherman had predicted a clear day. Guess there were a lot of unexpected surprises today.

His boots scrunched across the snow-covered land, his eyes narrowed from the wind, listening to the crackling logs burning in the fire as he gnawed on his toothpick. Considering the bonfire was exactly what he wanted to search, his heart sank into his stomach as he watched whatever potential evidence was in there being destroyed by the flames.

He wanted to arrest them on the spot. But arrest them for what? There was no evidence of any crime whatsoever, and both Wren and Marc had cooperated with his request for a search. He could haul them in for tampering with potential evidence or obstruction, but he knew those charges would never stick. What he did know was that he'll be keeping a watchful eye on the odd pair from now on.

Something wasn't adding up. Carver could feel it in his bones. Something was wrong. Something was very, very wrong with these two.

"You know…" Carver called as he approached the bonfire. Marc and Wren both had their backs to him as if they were worshipping the fire. "When an officer is conducting a property search it's usually best not to light bonfires."

He noticed Wren eyeballed him from the corner of his eye, but Marc stood unwavering, his cane in the palm of his right hand. In his left hand he gripped the end of the green rope tied around his right wrist, rolling the rope between his thumb and forefinger. Carver noticed he was staring at the fire watching the flames lick the charred embers, mesmerized.

"It is cold, detective," said Wren without looking at Carver. "Do you wish to deprive us of basic heat, too?"

Carver let it pass. Obviously, no one likes police officers snooping around their home. Especially officers accusing them of murder. Carver looked from Wren to Marc.

"You two really enjoy staring into fires." Neither Wren nor Marc would cease staring into the flames.

"Reminds me of home." This was Marc. He wiped a bead of sweat off his scar before turning to Carver. "Have you completed your search, detective?"

Now Carver could get a better look at Marc's eyes, confirming his first suspicion. His irises were large and black, covering most of his sclera, but the pupil was tiny, almost nonexistent, as if the black irises squeezed the frosted blue pupils into the size of a pin. Carver couldn't be certain, but he believed he saw a thin red ring outlining the blue pupils. So strange, thought Carver. Aren't irises supposed to hold color and not the pupils? It was as if everything about Marc was inside out. And his face, just looking at it, pinched Carver's brow with a fit of confusion. It was as if he looked like a different person depending on the light or how a shadow fell across his face.

Carver had to force himself to answer. Felt hypnotized, staring into Marc's eyes. Thought that if he stared for too long, he'd fall right in and lose himself. "That I did."

"And did you find any evidence of foul play?" Marc's voice was rigid.

Carver shook his head. "None at all."

"Of course not, because there's nothing to find."

Carver paused, assessing the gaze in Marc's stare when the dark clouds completely blocked the sun, turning what had been a sunny day into the dark of night. Marc looked different in the darkness, as if his features morphed into something sinister. Wind ripped across the property, bending the flames towards Carver. He could feel the heat on his bones through his coat.

"Well, it's our duty to follow up on potential crimes. We wouldn't be much use to the public if we didn't. Most are a wild goose chase but every once in a while, the accusation holds weight."

Marc looked at Wren. "This is the state of the world, Wren. Where anyone can make an accusation that defiles the reputation and sends police officers to trifle through every aspect of your life." He looked at Carver and shook his head while gritting his teeth. His stare was hateful, as if he could eat Carver's heart right here and now. "Tell your accuser we don't take kindly to accusations."

Carver raised an eyebrow as he transferred his toothpick from one corner of his mouth to the other.

"Now if you'll excuse me, detective, I have work to return to."

And with that, Marc turned and left. Walking through the snow, laboring like an old man with his cane. There was something about him Carver couldn't put his finger on.

Reminds me of… a walking tragedy.

"I trust you'll find your way back, detective?" Wren was standing behind him.

Carver nodded his head. "I'll be fine, thank you."

"Good," said Wren and bowed. "Have at it, detective. I must return to accompany my host."

"Of course," said Carver, watching Wren scurry towards the home, leaving Carver alone. He turned to the flames, scanning through the bonfire but of course there was nothing. Nothing but heat and flames roaring and crackling, licking the air.

He came to put the overactive imagination of a traumatized child to rest but found what he considered was far off the beaten path. There was something sinister about those two. He could feel it in his bones. Carver looked up to the house and the second-story window.

He noticed Marc was already in the room, watching him like a hawk.

He watched the detective return to the woods, beginning the half-mile trek back to his car. The officer had been searching the bonfire, but Wren had removed all bones and remnants that hadn't been turned to ash earlier this morning. So, search all you want detective, you'll find nothing in return.

But why the police officer was at his front door he did not know, although he had his suspicions. He scanned the woods, searching as far as his eyes could see. In the distance, he could see the rooftops of houses.

Someone in one of those homes had seen the bonfire and was watching Wren dispose of the body. Was it the boy, he wondered. The one who Wren visited last night. The one whose blood carried the essence of his ancient rival. Or perhaps it is the council. Perhaps they have become aware of his presence. But why not call the police last night? Why wait until morning? No responsible person would wait until the next day to inform the police of their discovery. It didn't add up, but the why or who behind it wasn't his greatest concern. It was the police officer snooping around his business that mattered most. And Detective Carver was already suspicious. He had no doubt that the good detective would maintain a watchful eye on their activities from now on.

"And here we are... so close to the endgame." He looked down at the rope between his fingers, listening to Wren climbing the stairs.

"My master," said Wren, "I apologize for the unlawful intrusion."

He said nothing in return, standing by the window while watching Detective Carver disappear behind a thicket of trees as he rolled the rope between his fingers.

Heard Wren clear his throat. "What should be done about this intrusion?"

He turned around, twisting his cane as he did so, the bottom kneading into the drop cloth. Noticed Wren was nervous, his eyes downtrodden, avoiding the master's gaze when the dark cloud hovering over the house turned the room into a host of shadows that darkened Wren's visage.

"In time," said the master. "Everything in time. I don't have the strength today to take full form. Not under duress because of circumstance, and not without the absinthe." He stepped forward, hobbling across the floor, closer to Wren.

"Understood." Wren watched him closely as he walked to the door.

"Continue as instructed. Volunteers are required. Our plan remains as it was." He took the first two steps down then turned. "Tonight, we capture what we need to bring us to the alignment." He paused, thinking. "Are the shackles ready?"

134

"Yes, my master. I completed the task when the officer arrived."

The master stood tall, stretching his shoulders, breathing heavy. "Good," he said, as if to himself. His gaze turned to the ceiling. "Tonight, our work officially begins." He looked at Wren. "Give no concern to the good detective. I'll deal with him in time."

"As you wish, my master. As you wish." Wren couldn't help the grin that spread across his lips, knowing his master's mind and what he planned to do with the detective when the time came.

"Now, I must return to the ether to garner my strength." He looked up and over the house, thinking. "My cells become tapped so quickly. The third dimension depletes the strength from my bones. Until my union with the host has been completed, it will be as such." He looked at Wren. "Come," he instructed. "The host will return soon, possibly with questions. You'll need to placate him until tonight."

"Yes, my master. I only wish for our success. I will do all that you instruct."

And with that, the master turned and took the steps to the first floor. Wren followed. Followed him to the red leather chair and watched as he sat, his cane draped across his lap. Watched as he rested his head against the leather and closed his eyes.

And Wren waited for Marc to return.

Lori Francon kept reading. The more she read, the more she discovered that Marc's fictional story reflected the reality she was living. The only exception was the demon because demons don't truly exist, they're simply a metaphor for the darkness that exists within the human heart.

Is this why Marc wrote the letter? Maybe the injuries he suffered from the accident sent his mental health into a tailspin and now he was melting between reality and fiction, unable to decipher what was real and what was imagination. The nurse... *what the hell was her name?*... had said Marc suffered a serious head injury. Perhaps the injury scrambled his neurochemistry like a master chef mixes a vat of eggs. And now he was playing out the story, not in his mind, but in real time.

Which scared the bejesus out of Lori. In the book, the demon requires hearts to bring back to hell as an offering to the devil. Lori couldn't see Marc committing such acts, but what if he spiraled into madness after the accident? Marc had always been a bit unhinged. Brilliant but disturbed was how Lori first referred to him, but his heart was pure. Lori knew this was true. She'd witnessed it firsthand on multiple occasions.

No, there's no way possible Marc would do such things. It wasn't adding up, and Lori had to tell herself repeatedly that it was just a novel. Fiction. Imagination. The ravings of a fictional genius and nothing more. In the book, it's John Ashton who receives the letter that ends the relationship that spirals poor John into the darkness of murder and mayhem. But did Marc send the letter to produce the same effect? Too much to think about, and too much to weigh on the conscience. There were too many similarities that reflected Lori's current predicament as if Marc had written the novel years from now, recounting all that had taken place in the present. But that's just not the case. She was with him when he wrote it.

And then everything went to shit.

She looked through her window to the icy winter sky. *Where are you, Marc Saduj? Where have you gone?*

There was more than a third left to read. So many questions and yet so few answers were given. She couldn't wait to finish.

The wind kicked into overdrive as if a portal had been opened and the wind went rushing into it. All Marc could hear was the fierce pounding of wind in his ears. The wind that melted the black and white images of the mansion. His gut hurt something awful. He felt depleted and defeated as if every ounce of strength had been drained from his bones.

Felt sick, lethargic and nauseous. Hard to think. To put words together. To connect one thought to the other. Scattered were his thoughts. Heard the wind whistling, howling, in his ears, across his skin. His head was weary, heavy too, and all he wanted to do was rest. To put his head down and catch a few winks of sleep.

Exhausted. Where is here? Where is anywhere? His stomach churned with noxious toxicity. Thought he was going to puke. But he didn't. Instead, he opened his eyes, or maybe they were open the entire time.

So quiet now. So still and quiet. Staring through the window, he leaned his head against the red leather chair. His limbs felt like they weighed a thousand pounds. He could barely move, nor did he want to, gazing at the bonfire raging outside his window, mesmerized. Hypnotized by the fire.

Marc felt like he aged a hundred years since this morning. His eye, his left eye, burned in his skull. He could feel it watering and dripping across the rim of his eye. Burning and coated with discharge. And then the itch. His scar pestered his skull with a constant uncomfortable burn. Never satisfied. Always wanting more.

Noticed the cane in his lap, he stared at it mindlessly before tossing it off his lap where it skittered across the floorboards. He saw his drink on the side table.

Perfect. Wren brought scotch this time. The ice had yet to melt, as if Wren had placed the glass on the table the moment Marc awakened. He's quite efficient, thought Marc, as his hand drifted to his drink. The ice rattled against the glass when he lifted it to his lips. Felt the burn on his tongue, cascading down his throat and filling his stomach with a comforting warmth.

I think I'll stay here for a while. Sit in silence and watch the sun set behind the fire.

Marc took another sip and waited for the darkness to arrive.

Carver walked into the county courthouse hoping he'd find some records on the abandoned mansion. He knew that the house had been abandoned since he moved to Sleepy Hollow thirty years ago and if Marc and his cohort Wren were telling the truth, that would mean Marc purchased the house recently and there would be a record of the transaction.

He introduced himself to the county clerk-Bonnie was her name-identified himself as an officer of the law and inquired about the house. Bonnie was a middle-aged woman with thick blonde hair cut short just above the neck. She was efficient and helpful and located the most recent documentation.

The house did belong to Marc Saduj. Although Carver suspected Marc and Wren had been lying, he'd given a 50/50 split on the matter and he wasn't surprised when Bonnie provided the information. But what truly piqued his interest was the date Marc officially received the property. August 31, 1996, was the date. Also, the date of the full moon. Carver remembered it vividly. He couldn't get that day out of his head no matter what he did. August 31st was the day Zoe Hardwood was murdered. The same day that Jerry went off the rails.

Well, that opens one hell of a can of worms.

"Who sold the property to Mr. Saduj?" Carver asked.

Bonnie studied her computer screen. She cocked her head; her brow knitted in confusion. "Well, it appears the house had been kept in probate for…" Her head snapped back. "A very, very long time. Since the twenties when it dropped into probate court and remained there until six months ago."

Carver took the toothpick from between his lips. "Interesting. Who was the owner at that time?"

She looked back at the screen. "Fredek," she said. "Fredek Francon. But there's no information on how he received the property, which doesn't make sense considering appropriate records had been kept since the 1800s. But there's nothing. It's as if the house didn't exist until that time."

"So, it sat in probate court for close to eighty years?"

"Apparently."

Carver shook his head. That's a long time for a property to be in probate. As if someone purposely kept it there. But why? The property was enormous, and he was certain any would-be developer would be delighted to take it over. Build houses or townhouses or whatever else they could think of. That much property in this area of the country was worth a fortune. It made little sense.

And who the hell is Fredek Francon? Sounds Russian or German. More importantly, what is the link between Fredek and Marc Saduj? Seems his inquiry brought more questions than answers, but it was a good start. At least he had something to investigate. He was about to leave when another question popped into his head.

"Are there any blueprints for the property and who handled the transfer of ownership?"

"Definitely no blueprints. I already checked. Let me see about the other." Bonnie returned her gaze to the computer screen. Carver watched as she scrolled across the screen, her head moving slowly from left to right until the mouse ceased moving and he could see her eyes roaming across the words on the screen. Her stare narrowed; her lips pressed tight together. She was quiet, reading what was on her screen.

"Bonnie?"

Bonnie shook her head and turned to Carver, her eyes narrow, brow pinched in confusion. "Hardwood Realty."

And Carver's eyes went wide. "Well, I'll be damned."

Hardwood Realty was locked up and forgotten. Carver stood in the parking lot, staring at the building with the sun slowly descending beneath the horizon and with it, the temperature dropped a few degrees. It seemed like the building was staring at him with its dark bay windows on opposite sides of the front door providing the illusion of eyes staring at him with a sinister scowl.

The yellow tape had been removed long ago. After Jerry was carted off that night, the building had turned into a hot spot for forensics to comb through every inch of the office. Although that all ended abruptly when Captain Flannery ordered the investigation to be closed. Why spend tax dollars investigating when the killer was caught red-handed? Literally, red-handed.

The smartest thing to do is bulldoze the office and start new.

Carver knew the office would be deemed haunted for the rest of its days. Small-town people were superstitious and considering two murders took place in the building he was certain no local citizen would step foot inside no matter what type of business took occupancy. Especially in this town. Sleepy Hollow has always had its superstitions, myths, and lore. The Headless Horseman rode through town every Halloween like a national treasure and that lore alone provided enough star power to forever alter the psyche of every Sleepy Hollow resident as if the legend permitted the residents to stake a claim to all that was spooky and went bump in the night. Carver was certain the Hardwood Murders would join that lore in time.

Give it a few years and it'll all come back like some sick hellish nostalgia, turning Jerry Hardwood into the son of the horseman.

He popped a new toothpick between his lips.

Or some shit like that.

Carver had enough with staring. He approached the front door and gripped the handle. Locked. Not that he cared, Carver had gone to the precinct and rummaged through the evidence to find the key. It took a while, but he found it sitting at the bottom of a box filled with knickknacks retrieved from Jerry's desk. The same key that he now retrieved from his pocket and unlocked the door with.

Can't believe I'm going back in here.

Truth be told, the office gave him the creeps, and it wasn't because Jerry Hardwood had eaten a human heart within the building's walls. It was the energy consuming the building. A rather nefarious energy. The same energy that erected the hair on his arms and the same that cringed across the nape of his neck. The one telling him to run in the opposite direction and hide.

The door opened with relative ease, releasing the stale air in the office as if the building had finally exhaled. Carver noticed the faintest scent of decay and the metallic taste of blood on his tongue. He stood, holding the door open, staring into the office. Everything looked the same. Looked the same as it had before the murders. Carver expected footprints from firemen, paramedics, officers, and forensics to be stained across the floors, but there were none as if someone had mopped the floors. Maybe someone did.

But who?

The Hardwoods owned the building, and Jerry had no living relatives other than his son, John, and Carver knew that Claude refused to come here and would be damned before allowing his grandson entrance. So, who cleaned? Certainly not the police.

Maybe I'm wrong, thought Carver. Maybe there were no footprints.

But Carver remembered that day like it was this morning. The rainstorm had blanketed Sleepy Hollow in a downpour, kicking up dirt and muddy puddles that no doubt would have been trampled across the linoleum floor. He craned his head, looking in, assessing while rolling his toothpick across his lips. So still and quiet, the silence was accompanied by a thick anxious energy that brought tension to the detective's bones. He took a deep breath before stepping in, allowing the door to close behind him.

Stepped into the freezing cold. Frigid was the word on the tip of his tongue. Sure, it was cold outside, but the office temperature dropped ten degrees the moment he walked through. Dropped in temperature like Marc's property. He'd never been so cold. His breath released across his lips in vapor. He tried the light switch next to the door. Nothing happened. Obviously, the electric bill had never been paid so there wouldn't be electricity, and the state of New York certainly wasn't paying the bill. He flipped the switch a few times with the same result. Now, since the sun was setting, Carver had little time before he'd be plunged into total darkness.

Time to get moving.

He wasn't certain why he was here or what he was looking for. He had that nagging feeling that he should be here. For what reason he did not know, but he hoped he'd find out soon. His instincts brought him here, his wit and expertise. Carver moved to Jerry's office on his right, all the while keeping his eyes open and his instincts on high alert. Stepped past the door and his stare immediately went to the opposite wall with the pentagram and the words that, when he read them out loud for the first time in six months, stifled his heart and breath.

"Initium Novum."

Written in blood. The blood that had turned dark brown with a tinge of orange after sitting for so long.

Carver was aware of his heavy breathing as he stared at that wall. As if the cold froze his lungs, he couldn't get enough air. His breathing was labored, and he couldn't take his eyes off the pentagram and those words. Those damn fucking words that followed him everywhere he went.

Initium Novum. A new beginning.

Whatever the fuck that means.

He had to force himself to turn away from the wall. To snap out of it as he told himself. Carver transferred his toothpick from one corner of his mouth to the other while he scanned across the office. Blood stains were on the floor behind him-where Jerry had eaten the heart and took a few bullets to his torso. Other than the blood on the floor and the wall, everything was as it should have been, clean and pristine. No one would ever know a crime had taken place between these walls if the blood had been cleaned.

But if someone did clean, why didn't they take care of the blood too?

He stepped into the room's center, closer to the desk and looked around. Scanning. The nape of his neck cringed as if someone had drifted two fingers across his neck. Heard a growl in his ears. Or maybe it was the wind. Outside the window, the wind kicked into overdrive as the sun dipped further below the horizon, casting dark gray hues across the sky and darkening the office.

"Well, what are you doing here, officer? Either get on with it or get out."

Carver stood a moment longer, feeling like a fool when he turned to leave and his stare landed on a file on Jerry's desk. Placed perfectly, as if it was left for him to find.

Left by who?

He craned his head, staring at the file then took a good look around the office. For some odd reason he had the feeling he was being watched and whoever was watching was waiting with bated breath for him to look at the file. Nothing but cold and quiet greeted him. Carver pursed his lips and swallowed, then went around the desk and stared at the file. It was in a green and brown file folder. No name on the file, so he flipped it open and immediately recognized the name and address.

This was Marc's file. The file that provided Marc with the deed to the house.

Was this here the entire time?

Carver snapped his head to the reception area outside the office. He thought he saw something shuffle past the door.

"Hello," he called, but received nothing in return. His bones were tense, and he noticed his hand was shaking as the sun dipped further below the horizon, darkening the office even more. His breath caught in his chest, and he gripped the file folder while scanning the office. Waiting. Waiting for something to come running into the office with murder in their eyes.

Nothing.

This place gives me the creeps.

He tucked the file folder under his arm then beelined out of the office. When he passed the hall leading to the back of the building something flashed in the corner of his eye that stopped him cold in his tracks. His heart froze. His bones and limbs tensed as his arms rippled in gooseflesh, erecting the hairs on his arms as his spine shivered.

He stared straight ahead, not wanting to turn and look. But he did. Had to. Had to see with his own eyes what he couldn't believe.

Sheila was standing at the back of the building. Or, what looked like Sheila draped in darkness, a silhouette that seemed to be a part of the darkness, embedded into its shadowy embrace. Her head had a hole in it where the bullet had gone through. She stared at him through black eyeballs. Carver had to shake his head as if what he was seeing was simply a matter of a tired brain and shaking the cobwebs away would dissipate the apparition standing in front of him.

He had no such luck. And the stare across her face was dire and filled with pain. He felt frozen, his feet refusing to follow his thoughts to run and get the hell out of the office. His toothpick dropped from his lips and the file folder fell to the floor. She looked like fear was her only emotion. She stepped to her right and disappeared.

"Sheila?" Carver ran to the back of the building, into what was a breakroom for the office. A printer, a table and four chairs. A sink with cabinets above it. But no ghost. He looked around the room, then turned to where she had gone. Saw a wall and nothing more. Carver took a deep breath, looking around the room.

Nothing. Nothing at all. Heard the wind outside kick into overdrive. Carver stepped back. Back into the hall, staring into the breakroom, waiting. Waiting for a threat to come barreling out of the darkness. Stopped and looked. Assessed. His head craned, feeling the cold race across his skin. He shook his head and turned.

Carver grabbed the file folder off the floor, rushed out of the building, then locked the door, taking long backward steps away from the building. When he was certain nothing was going to come out of the darkness and snap his head off, he turned and hurried to his car.

He didn't feel safe until he was inside.

88

Marc watched the sun disappear behind the western woods. The bonfire now more prominent in the darkening sky. He sipped his scotch, the ice rattling against the glass. The burn on his lips and the sting across his tongue crinkled his nose and bared his teeth. His scar a forever itch and he pressed on it now; his skull bruised with pain.

His eyes were wet, as if he'd been crying. Not that he remembered crying, but it was possible. His drunken fits of isolation often brought some tears. Plus, he'd been thinking about Lori. The love he lost. The one who tossed him to the curb like yesterday's garbage and why that pain cut so deep was another tragedy he'll need to puzzle over.

He wondered what she was doing now, so many months after the accident. Did she find someone to fill the void? Did she take up a new hobby to pass the time as she sat in her Hamptons mansion placating the world with her gentle assassination? Like she did to him. Shattering the hearts of those who love her most.

Marc gripped his glass tight, grinding his jaw, his lips trembling. Holding back the tears.

Felt hollow.

Empty.

Cold.

Twisted and knotted from within.

Pretending he was all right. Knowing he was changing. Turning. Not a care in the world. Not a care for the world.

Let it all burn, he thought, staring at the bonfire. *Burn and turn to ash.*

Marc closed his eyes tight, his face pinched as his breath stuttered across his lips. Felt that whining cry erupt in his throat. He squeezed his glass in his left hand. His right hand balled into a tight fist, squeezing, his knuckles turning white.

"Lori," he howled, lovesick and heartbroken. The glass cracked in his fist, and he tossed the shattered glass to the floor. Felt the cut on his palm but he paid it no mind, leaning his head back against the chair. Curled his legs beneath him and closed his eyes.

Fought those tears and cries and whining, forcing them down his throat into his darkening heart while gritting his teeth. His scar burning, itching, he rubbed it feverishly against the chair. Whipping and ripping and tearing. Blood rushed into his eye, across his temple and cheek. He pressed his head into the chair, grunting into the cushion.

Heard screaming. Blood curdling wretched wails. Saw a pendulum slash across a stomach. Saw blood jump into the air when that holler reached into the heavens with maddening fury.

"Don't look," he said, more like whispered as if his child self were speaking to his adult life. Cover your eyes and don't look. Don't even peek. The man in black is doing evil deeds.

"My master?"

151

Marc shot his head off the cushion. Wren stood in the hall, holding a tray. On top of the tray was a bottle. Marc could see the liquid inside was pale green.

"Our time has come, my master. All has been prepared." He stepped forward, his feet clomping across the floorboards while Marc wiped the tears off his face with a gasp. He sat up and rubbed his palms together while shaking the cobwebs from his head. Wren placed the tray on the side table when his boot crushed some of the glass on the floor and he paused. "Whatever has happened here?" Wren looked from the floor to Marc. "You're bleeding."

Marc looked down at his hand. A thin stream of blood dripped from his palm, cascading across his wrist. The wound was small, nothing deep. "Yeah, broken glass can do that."

Wren craned his head. "I was referring to your face."

Marc furrowed his brow, then remembered the scar. "Damn thing breaks open every once in a while."

Wren grunted. "Let me fix your drink and then I'll tend to the wound. We can't have you running around the Hollow with blood all over you. Think about the reaction that will have with the locals."

Marc laughed, rubbing the sting on his left palm.

Wren returned his attention to the bottle and his tray. A shot glass, tall and thin, sat on the tray along with a second glass filled with sugar cubes. A feuille spoon-a stainless-steel spoon designed in the shape of a leaf with holes for liquid to pass through-sat next to the glass with sugar cubes. Wren placed the feuille spoon on top

152

of the shot glass, followed by a sugar cube that he positioned on top of the spoon. He gripped the bottle and stood tall, pulling the cork from the neck then breathed in the scent with closed eyes, relishing the pungent aroma.

He poured the absinthe over the sugar cube, filling the shot glass then re-corked the bottle and placed it on the tray. He took a match from the tray and struck it against his palm. Marc watched the flame dance in the darkness as Wren touched the match to the cube, then to the candle on the side table. The sugar cube bubbled and fizzled, dripping down into the glass. A moment later, Wren twisted the spoon and dropped the cube into the absinthe. He then picked up the shot glass.

Marc sat forward, gazing into the green liquid at what looked like little green fairies dancing in the glass, although he knew it was an illusion. The burnt sugar cube was disintegrating, shooting sugar particles to the top of the glass. But there was more to it. The candle's flame reflected the fizzling dancing sugar fairies buzzing in the liquid.

Now he could feel the sun fall away from the horizon, allowing the dark night to unleash its talon across the city. His heart jumped with a startle when the wall sconces erupted with fire down the hall.

"Initium Novum," said Wren, offering Marc the glass.

Marc's gaze darted to Wren and his sickly tightlipped grin. His pasty skin glowing within the dark and fire riddled home as if the wall sconces framed his nosferatu features in perfect clarity.

"It'll help with the pain," said Wren as he tapped the glass with the feuille spoon. "Both of the mind *and* the heart." He stretched the glass closer to Marc.

Now Marc saw the shot glass in front of him. Everything else seemed to drift away and vanish as if the glass floated in the darkness. He watched as tiny particles of sugar danced in the green liquid. Like they were dancing for him. Spinning. Arms stretched. Back and forth. Swaying. Floating in the liquid. Dancing and spinning with marvelous wonder. Those little fairies brought a smile to Marc's lips.

As if those fairies were little friends spawned with the purpose of returning joy to his heart and mind. To forget the past and bring center stage the dark subconscious. Saw his reflection in the glass, but he looked different. His eyes were red. Or is that the candle's flame? The red eyes drifted, wavering in the liquid as a fae dropped through the reflection to the bottom of the glass. Now all he saw was the green glow and the fairies jumping and spinning and dancing.

Marc took the glass and cleared his throat. Looked at Wren, standing over him. He seemed anticipatory, seething, grinding his jaw with bated breath.

"To all who have come and to all who have gone. To those who are here and those we've yet to see. We drink in honor of thee." Wren grinned, tightlipped, as he held his arm over his stomach, palm up.

Marc stared into the liquid. Saw that green rope around his wrist and everything went silent. Quiet. He could hear his own breathing. Could feel and hear his heart beating in his chest. Heard a massive gallop rushing towards him, as if something was coming, barreling towards him in a mad fever. He tipped the glass to his lips and drank the liquid down his gullet, warm and savory across his throat. His eyes closed, feeling the absinthe race to his stomach.

Felt the wind across his brow grow heavy and thick with a hurricane force. Heard fire and the crackling burning of trees as if the earth had been set on fire. Heard the howling from the dead, the hiss from owls and the screech off the lips of the unsavory.

Marc pursed his lips and swallowed with a gasp. He opened his eyes. Opened his eyes and found himself in that old familiar place.

Opened his eyes and found himself in the cemetery.

89

John was watching from the window when Detective Carver pulled his car into the driveway. John was grateful the detective made it out of the house alive. He'd been at the window for the better part of the last hour, waiting. Grandpa had asked him if he was okay, and John just nodded. He couldn't take his eyes off the outside.

He watched Carver stroll across the driveway to the front steps. John was opening the front door before he even knocked.

"Did you see him?" John blurted the moment the door opened. "I told you he looked like a vampire."

"Well, hello to you too, John. And you told me he *was* a vampire. Not that he looked like a vampire."

"What's the difference?"

To that comment Carver had no reply. All he could do was grin. "Grandpa home?"

Seemed like the energy dropped at that moment. John wasn't expecting Carver to talk with Claude, but he understood that was what the adults should do in such a situation. All John wanted to know was when Carver was bringing the SWAT team to the house in the western woods. What did he find when he was there? What did they say? Those two strangers he saw waiting outside. Questions he'll obviously need to wait a little longer to receive answers to.

"He is," said John, although reluctantly before he called over his shoulder, "*Grandpa!*"

"Damn, that was loud enough."

"Stephen." Claude called from down the hall. He was in the kitchen, preparing dinner. "Come on in. I just started dinner."

"Thank you." John moved to the side and Carver stepped in. The moment his foot hit the ground the lights went off. The television that had been on in the living room shut down. It seemed like all the electricity was funneled out of the house.

"Shit," said Claude. Carver heard him in the kitchen. The three of them drenched in darkness. "Power must've gone out. That's the fourth time in two days."

Carver looked at John when a sliver of moonlight graced the boy's face. Carver's eyes adjusted to the darkness, and he could have sworn he'd seen a shadow pass over John's face. He seemed older, with a narrow chin and thin cheeks. And his eyes...

Carver did a double take, staring at the boy and the eyes that seemed to reflect total darkness. He looked over his shoulder and noticed the lights were on in the other houses.

"I'll grab some candles," Claude said. Carver could hear him walking into the living room. "Who's in the mood for Chinese?"

90

Lori flipped through the rest of the notebook. Breathing heavy as if she'd just run a marathon, she passed feverishly over every blank page.

"Can't be it," she whispered. Her head darting left and right, looking over every single page all the way to the end. Biting her lower lip, she turned to the back cover.

The words Initium Novum seemed to call to her. She ran her fingers over the words, then said them out loud as if she needed to hear them. To hear them to make them real. Was this real? Did Marc pen a story that then came true, possibly through the will of imagination?

Initium Novum. Lori knew she'd heard those words even before the booming voice said them in her nightmare last night. But where? Maybe Marc had repeated the phrase when they were together. Someone wrote the words on the back cover, and it had to be Marc. This was his notebook and his story, but she would swear that she'd heard the phrase well before last night. As if the words existed in the dark recesses of her past. She sat on the bed, thinking it over, disappointed and needing answers. Answers that weren't in the book. The story just ended, and Marc never had the time to finish it. Obviously, the accident stopped his progress.

She wondered if Marc thought about the story at all. If he had searched for his notebook or asked about it, but of course he didn't. Considering the hospital dropped it off along with all their belongings from the car, it was quite apparent that Marc never sought the notebook out. Perhaps it was too painful? Perhaps he wanted to put the past to bed and that included anything that tied him down to Lori Francon.

The story ended with the return of John Ashton's wife, Alena, to Sleepy Hollow. And that was it, all blank pages after and no conclusion. No way to determine how the story was going to end.

She looked at the notepad where she'd written all the similarities between the story and real life. The list filled up an entire page. But what did it all mean? Did Marc conjure a demon to save Lori's life? Or did he slip into the dark recesses of lunacy because of a head injury and now he's lost in a battle between insanity and rational thought? But how far would his madness go? Was he playing out the story as we speak? Choosing his victims and spilling blood by the bucket in some deranged sideshow wrought with anguish?

The thought was enough to send a shiver through her bones. Plus, she found it disrespectful to the man she agreed to marry. Thinking of him like that-a sick and sadistic, murdering son of a bitch-brought a pang of guilt and shame to her soul. There was no conceivable way Marc would ever hurt another human being. The man was all heart. Heart and alcohol. Alcohol and derangement, but she'd always tossed his eccentricities off to his artistic ability. After all, history is littered with mad geniuses sitting in dark corners slaving over page after page with a pen in hand, or typewriter, or computer. But was there a breaking point to their derangement? An event that could push the genius over the edge where they fall into their own insanity, never able to recover what they once had because they'd gone too far blending the boundaries between reality and fiction. When fiction becomes reality, there can be no recourse back to fiction.

She hoped Marc hadn't blurred those lines. She hoped he was safe and sound and moving on with his life. She wished him the best as she took up the notebook and added it to the junk drawer in her desk, placing the list of similarities on top of it then closed the drawer.

Felt a certain sense of loss, as if she'd finally realized she'd never see Marc again. Over the last six months she had held onto the hope of a reconnection, but now the thought seemed distant as if the notion was funneled into the past and was soon to be forgotten.

A knock on her bedroom door. "Lori, darling. I'm going to the club for dinner. Would you like to join me?"

Lori's stomach gurgled with the mention of food. She hadn't eaten all day, but spending the evening with Elena and her stuck-up social circle was not worth the meal. Not at all. She opened the bedroom door and Elena just about jumped out of her skin.

160

Strange response, Lori thought. As if she caught Elena doing something she wasn't supposed to do. She found the response odd. Lori cleared her throat. "Thank you for the invite, but I'm staying in tonight." She looked back at her desk. Felt like the notebook was calling her.

"Are you sure? It's good to mingle with good people. Helps with…"

Lori cut her off. "I'm good, thank you. Gonna take a bath, open a bottle of wine, and do some reading."

"Not with that notebook, I hope?"

Lori shook her head. "No, mother. I'm done with that one."

Elena seemed to jump with glee. "Splendid," she said and wrapped a scarf around her neck. "Well, you know where I'll be."

"Enjoy your time."

"That I shall." And she smiled before retreating to the stairs. Lori noticed there was a bounce in her step.

She listened while Elena went through the front door. Lori could hear the car outside, the engine humming. Heard Elena's door close, followed by the car motoring down the driveway. Lori could see it from her window, exiting through the gate then driving down the road. The hum from the engine faded, replaced with a profound silence when the house turned quiet. And in the silence a thought surfaced.

She didn't know why, but she had a sudden need to go to the basement.

Felt it in her bones. There was something down there she needed to see.

91

Carver sat with Claude and John at the kitchen table. Two candles sat on the table, their flames dancing. Carver had wanted John to allow the adults to talk, but with the electricity having gone by the wayside, what was he going to do? Allow the boy to sit in the dark while he waited for Carver to finish his inquiry? It didn't seem right to Carver, so he kept his questions to a minimum. He could always come back and talk to Claude tomorrow when John was at school so he went right into it, asking about Jerry and hoping Claude could shed some light on the Hardwood heritage and, more specifically, about the house they kept in probate for close to eighty years.

"Honestly, I don't know too much," Claude said, and Carver noticed he was tightlipped on the subject. Perhaps John's presence was the deterrent. "I know they've been a mainstay in Sleepy Hollow for more than a few centuries, even before the Revolutionary War. They came here like many of the Dutch settlers at that time. Jerry's grandfather started the agency. How long ago I'm not too certain, but from what I could gather is that Jerry's father grew up in the agency, so I assume it was before he was born."

Carver nodded, and Claude took a sip from the glass of scotch he had gripped in his palm. "Did Jerry or Sheila ever discuss the family business? Have you ever heard them speak about a property in the western woods?"

Claude licked his lips and paused, thinking. Carver noticed John's eyes darted from Claude to Carver, then back to Claude. "Not really. Most of what I heard were simple statements in passing like, business is good type of conversation but nothing about the property. Nothing about the past or his family." Claude cleared his throat and sat back in his chair. "He was always very cryptic about his family."

"Cryptic?" Carver took the toothpick from his lips.

"Yeah, like just about every American family, tightlipped about the family secrets type of cryptic. Keep the skeletons in the closet so no one ever sees them, and we can go on in life as if they don't exist. Because the façade is everything and people's perceptions matter most."

"Seems like you think they had something to hide?"

Claude shrugged. "Doesn't everybody? If you go back far enough, eventually, everyone's got a skeleton in their closet."

Carver paused before he said, "Ever witness anything concerning about the family? Anything weird or off."

Claude was already shaking his head. "Nothing at all. As far as I was concerned, they were your typical American family. Until… well, you know."

Carver locked eyes with John, gave a smug smile and a nod. The conversation was going nowhere. Obviously, Claude wasn't up to date on all the Hardwood secrets.

"What is this about, detective? What did you find in the woods?"

Carver sat forward, closer to the table. "Well..." He gestured to John. "Our little man here reported this morning that he saw someone in the western woods last night... and he also reported having seen a dead body."

Claude's head whipped around so fast to look at John Carver wouldn't have been surprised if the man suffered whiplash. John's eyes went wide as Claude shook his head. "Why didn't you tell me this last night?"

John went to speak, but no words were spoken. Carver intervened, "Well, he said something today. Which is all that matters."

"Did you find the body?" Claude's eyes were narrow, staring in disbelief.

Carver shook his head. "I did not."

"What *did* you find?"

"Two people are living in the house. I checked into it, and they are the rightful owners. What's weird is that the house was held in probate for close to eighty years." He shook his head, then popped his toothpick back between his lips. "I've never seen that before. It's as if no one wanted the property to be sold. It just sat there unnoticed for eighty years. And then these two people come along... it's just... strange." Carver left out the part that the property was under the watchful eye of Hardwood Realty during that time. As if the agency was founded for that specific purpose. He also left out the part that the new owners took occupancy on the same day

Jerry Hardwood went off the rails and murdered three people, his daughter included.

Claude paused. Everyone paused. Claude wiped his hands across his face with a sigh. Took up his glass with trembling fingers and finished his drink. The pause was thick with tension. Quite obvious to Carver that Claude was experiencing an existential crisis knowing his grandson, the one who lost his family in the most tragic of circumstances, was now seeing people with dead bodies creating fires in the middle of the woods on an abandoned property. Yeah, that's a cause for concern for anyone, let alone a single grandfather.

"Strange indeed." Claude sat up from his chair, grabbed his bottle off the counter and poured another drink.

"There are evil things that go on in that house." Both Claude and Carver looked at each other, then at John, who cleared his throat. "My mother told me."

"When?" Claude said, his voice was abrupt and gruff. He sat back down.

John sat, startled by the question. Carver could see the cogs in his brain working, looking for an answer. Or making one up. "A long time ago. I remember because I was always afraid of the woods." Carver had a sneaking suspicion the boy was lying. "She said there were rituals that went on in the house a long time ago. A lot of bad stuff happened there. People went missing, she said, and later on they found their bones in the house and all over the property... she said it had been going on for a long time, and the Hardwoods were a big part in stopping it. She said they tried to burn the house down, but it wouldn't take because there was magic in the house. Evil magic that wouldn't allow the house to be burned."

The look on Claude's face was skeptical and aggravated. He was shaking his head. "Your mother said this? I can't believe it."

"It's true, grandpa."

"She never said anything like that to me."

John had no response. The boy just sat there, dumbfounded as if he was ashamed of what he'd said.

Claude looked at Carver. "Well, there you have it. Straight from a child's imagination. Maybe we should get some torches and pitchforks and have ourselves an old school witch hunt." He downed his scotch, then spun the glass across the table. "Maybe we should talk more tomorrow?"

Carver noticed John cringed, his eyes darting from one adult to the other. He seemed on edge.

Carver nodded his head. "Agreed." He sat up from the table and shook hands with Claude when the doorbell rang.

"Foods here. Are you sure you won't join us?"

"Thank you, but I've got more investigating to do." He looked at John and that innocent, frightened stare. "You stay out of the woods until the investigation is over. Understood?"

John nodded.

Again, the doorbell.

"I'll walk you out," said Claude.

Carver took one more look at John. It seemed that there was more he wanted to say. Carver gave a quick nod with a tightlipped smile then followed Claude to the door.

He'll have to wait to talk to the boy again. In the meantime, what Carver had on his mind was his next step. He had a sneaking suspicion he'll need to pay Jerry Hardwood a visit.

92

Lori was standing in the center of the basement, looking over the clutter of boxes and old furniture she never knew existed. It looked like the furniture was decades old. She placed the designs to the 1940s. Maybe the 30s. All of it stuffed in the corners and against the walls. She wondered who it all belonged to. Considering she'd never seen it before, the furniture had to belong to the previous owners, her father's cousin Fredek and his daughter Alena.

She had never been in the basement before. Lori and her family moved in when she was twelve and there was never a reason to come down to the basement. There were so many rooms in the house to explore, and the basement always seemed drab and old and filled with dust. No reason whatsoever. But now that she was standing in the middle of it, she felt a sudden sense of comfort, as if she'd been down here before. And not just before, but many times over the years. So surreal and familiar.

"Okay Francon, why are you down here?" Lori said out loud, scanning the basement. She hugged her arms. It was so cold in the basement. Goosebumps rippled up her arms as her breath drifted across her lips like vapor. She took a step forward, squeezing past the boxes, towards the back of the basement.

When she took the stairs down from the kitchen, Lori wasn't sure what to expect, nor did she expect how large the basement would be. It was huge, as big as the floor above. The size of a house but wide and open. At the bottom of the stairs, she pulled the string on the light fixture secured in the ceiling. The floor was basic concrete, although she noticed that in some places the flooring would angle upwards and then back down a few feet away, as if the concrete had been poured over mounds in the earth.

She had her eye on the tall structure beneath a thick blanket towards the back wall. In front of the structure was a waist high slab of marble with an old bronze lantern on top of it. She touched the marble, and a shiver ran down her spine. Covered in a thick layer of dust, she wondered why the slab was so long. Long enough to carry a human body if necessary.

Was it a table? It was certainly long enough to be a table but not wide enough, unless the people sitting around it were okay with very little room. She scanned across the marble, noticing a round ring of rope that disappeared into a hole in the marble to the bottom of the table.

"Wrist restraints?" Her face pinched in confusion as her stare drifted to the tall structure on the opposite side of the marble slab. So tall, it dwarfed Lori. She scanned the structure then squeezed between the boxes and the marble table, shuffling over to the structure, then pulled the thick blanket that was caught on a nail hanging from the ceiling. She tugged again and heard it rip as the blanket dropped to the floor.

Beneath the blanket was a pedestal made from marble-white marble. Lori realized she had been mistaken. There was no statue or structure beneath the blanket. The fact that the blanket had gotten caught on the nail made it appear like there would be a statue beneath it. Maybe there had been a statue at one point in time, but not now. Lori judged the pedestal to be close to four feet tall. There were cracked pieces of marble on the top as if whatever structure had been erected on it had been removed or smashed to smithereens. A thick line of dark brown was stained across the front of the pedestal. But there was more. Lori couldn't put her finger on it, but it seemed as if the energy shifted, more confined, suffocating and difficult to breathe. As if the gravity around the pedestal was thick, turning her bones heavy and dense.

Heard a creak on the stairs as if someone had taken a step onto the stairs. She looked over her shoulder at the steps bathed in darkness on the opposite side of the light. Felt a cool, subtle wind grace her skin.

Maybe Gerard is home?

"Hello," she called. Her voice cut off when the basement door slammed shut and the lightbulb exploded. Slam. Pop. Glass rained across the floor as darkness drenched the basement. Lori jumped with a startle, covering her mouth.

Total darkness, her breathing heavy. Heart racing. She darted to leave and slammed into the marble slab. Face pinched in pain. "Fuck."

A scurry in the corner, on the opposite side of the basement.

Rats, Lori thought. Maybe it's rats. She was certain Elena would not be happy if there were rats down here.

Lori hollered, "Gerard? Hello. I'm in the basement. Can you open the door?" Nothing. No response other than a thick silence as she waited with bated breath. "Hello," her voice caught in her throat. Saw something float in the corner of her eye and she snapped her attention to it.

Nothing but dark greeted her.

She felt across the marble slab, remembering the lantern, which she took and placed in front of her, feeling for the knob and hoping. Hoping it would light. She wasn't sure if she had the strength to make it to the stairs without a light on. Lori twisted the knob and, yes, there was light. It was weak and glowed a pale orange, but it did the job. Lori lifted the lantern.

"This was a big mistake," she whispered before clearing her throat, scanning the basement. Turning, shifting between the slab and the pedestal, when the light glowed across the wall and Lori saw faded paint on the wall above the pedestal. It looked like a circle, the paint worn and faded into the concrete. The circle was incomplete, but it was obvious there had been a circle on the wall at some point in time.

She heard a shift behind her, like feet shuffling across the concrete, when the hairs on the nape of her neck stood erect, and her neck bones cringed as if a hand had wrapped around her neck and was inching towards her throat.

"What the fuck is that?" Her voice a cringed whining whisper. Her breath stuttered as she turned her head to where the noise had come from, watching the orange glow sweep across the

172

room to the red eyes that stood prominent in the glow before they darted away. Her heart jumped in her chest, her blood curdled, and her bones contracted. Circling the lantern back to the wall where she was certain those eyes had gone.

Holding the lantern high as blood now cascaded down the wall, forming an inverted pentagram. Lori never noticed that the lantern shook in her hand, watching the blood stream down the wall from the pentagram, forming words.

Words that seemed to have always been there, as if they required blood to be revealed. Her jaw hung loose, her eyes wide as the words were revealed.

Initium Novum

The letters dripped with blood. A moan rose from the far side of the basement. Then more, as if all the dead in the world were suddenly awakened.

Lori didn't remember running out of the basement. Didn't remember slamming into boxes or that the boxes tumbled to the ground. She didn't remember stepping across the broken glass from the lightbulb either or how it took three tries to get through the door to the kitchen.

All she remembered were the words written in blood and the red eyes in the darkness. The same words from Marc's book.

How is that possible?

She knew then she would need to return to Sleepy Hollow. She needed to find Marc. Lori had a strange feeling they were connected by more than she realized.

Lori Francon packed her belongings. She didn't know when she would return or if she would return. Despite what Elena had to say, she was going back to Sleepy Hollow.

93

The Sleepy Hollow Tavern was packed elbow to elbow with patrons. Talk was thick among the patrons and staff. Laughter and the occasional angry holler. A mix of regulars and college students from the local university filled the small tavern. The bar was long and occupied most of the wall on the left from the entrance. Ten booths occupied the opposite side from the bar and were packed with college students drinking pitchers of beer and downing shot after shot as the locals sat on their designated bar stools. Some had been frequenting the tavern for decades.

Marc knew most of the regulars. His memory and knowledge of them were cast like shadows to the man in black now occupying the mortal coil that belonged to Marc Saduj. Marc was confined to the ether of Sleepy Hollow Cemetery but the man in black knew all that Marc knew and, as he sat in one of the booths, he used what he knew to his benefit. His red cane held close to his hip, he befriended a few college students who were standing between the bar stools and booths. He offered them a place to sit and bought them pitchers and shots. Of course he bought shots. The man in black watched with a keen eye and bated breath as each downed shot broke down the barriers of wit and inhibition. His charm. His intellect. His knowledge thrilled his patrons, who gathered around his booth as if he were a worldly movie star.

Hypnotizing.

Mesmerizing.

His pupils swirled like a funnel, a downward spiral that led into the depths of his mind, capturing their attention and refusing to relent. His patrons could do nothing more than sit and stare and drink and laugh. So comfortable they became in the presence of the man in black. Time seemed to stop when he talked. The actions and conversations from the barstool patrons were muted to their ears. His voice carried a calm and confident vibration. It was all they could hear. His words dripped off his tongue like honey. They were entranced. Even when he smiled that half-cocked grin that crept into the corner of his mouth, they were taken by his smile. Sitting with their jaws open and their eyes ablaze.

The chatter was loud, growing louder the longer the night continued. Minds buzzing with the freedom infused from alcohol. And the man in black laughed, counting his thirteen guests. Thirteen mesmerized students.

He stomped his cane against the floor twice, and it seemed as if the world suddenly paused to pay attention to the man in black. Promises were made. Promises of a mansion in the woods and ancient rituals no human has witnessed in centuries. All promised with a half-cocked grin and spiraling eyes.

And they followed like dutiful children into the galloping glow of eternal night. To the frigid cold of early morning where Wren waited. Waited in the limousine. He opened the door for them, and they all filed into the back. The man in black waited to join them, standing on the sidewalk counting heads and grasping the top of his cane. Wren passed a knowing stare to his master.

"Let us have some fun tonight, Wren." The man in black looked up to the night sky and the crisp, clear twinkling stars. Music spilled through the door of the tavern. Laughter from his guests in the back seat.

"It will be a most glorious night, my master." Wren stood, holding the door open. "Only you could have snatched such splendid game."

The man in black gave a quick nod before taking his seat. Wren closed the door and the man in black watched as Wren shuffled to the driver's seat, taking his seat behind the wheel. He studied each of his guests. Their drunken eyes and lost inhibitions. Seven men and six women. All with blazing eyes and laughter in their throats.

It was when Wren pulled away from the curb that the master presented them with the cane.

"Look at what marvelous tricks the cane can do."

They all sat, wide eyed and mesmerized as the man in black twisted the round golden handle. Twisted it to the right and then the left then back again. The limo picked up speed as a green fog spewed from the cane. The man in black watched through the windshield as Wren barreled towards the cemetery wall. The wall was an illusion. It wavered when Wren drove through it into the tunnels towards the house in the western woods.

And the man in black laughed. Sitting among his guests who were all sleeping.

Incapacitated by the power of the cane.

94

Carver shot up in bed with a gasp. His hand went to his chest; his heart was beating so fast. His forehead was slick with sweat, he could feel it cascade across his temples. Felt sick to his stomach too like he needed to puke. His dream faded from his memory. He tried to catch it, to remember what the dream was but it fell into the void of his memory. He rubbed his neck. Saw a flash of a knife cutting into his throat and he jumped out of bed in a rush and paused. His hands were clenched into fists.

The room was dark. His eyes adjusted as an icy wind nipped at his skin from the cracked open window. His breath stuttered across his lips. The thought of Sheila drifted to his conscious mind. Seeing her in the office. Or what he thought was her. Her ghost. He felt that same presence in the room with him now.

A creak from his desk. Scratching now like a fingernail tracing across wood. Carver inched his head around to his desk, holding his breath, his heartbeat on pause. He could feel it. The energy around the desk was thick. He stared into the darkness. Stared at the faded outline sitting at his desk.

He swallowed his breath. "Sh-Sheila?"

Wind rifled through the window with an icy sting. He could hear pages flipping, crinkling under the heavy gale.

Heard the whisper, incoherent as it was. Moving too fast for clarity, he couldn't make it out. Breath across the nape of his neck. His spine shivered and cringed. Felt incapacitated as he heard something drop on the desk. Thought he saw long bony fingers stretching across the desk when the lamplight went on in a hurried flash and Carver gawked, covering his mouth.

His eyes narrowed, staring at the desk and the Hardwood file that was now open on top of it. His coffee mug had fallen, and the last remnants of coffee cascaded to the desk's edge then dripped off the ledge. He stepped closer, eyeballing the folder and coffee that pooled on his desk. His eyes widened as he watched what he assumed was a finger move through the coffee. Writing letters. Letters that formed words.

He knew what those words were: Initium Novum. Written in script.

Ithasbegun.begunithas.hasbegun.ithasbegun.begunithas.

The whispers in his ear.

Has begun. It has begun.

He stood over the desk, staring down at the coffee written words and the file. The paper contained a list of rooms in the house in the western woods. He stared at it with his jaw hanging open. It was always in front of him. Right under his nose. He picked up the file and read the list of rooms.

What he hadn't seen before was now apparent. Included on the list was a basement.

Carver had no recollection of a basement. No entrance to a basement either. He rifled through his memory certain he had not seen a basement during his search. Clearly, the basement would have been a room he would have wanted to search.

But if there is a basement, that would mean the entrance had to be hidden. Hidden for nefarious reasons because why hide something if there was nothing to hide?

Thebasement.dungeon.gotothebasement.inthebasementiswhereital lbegins.inthebasement.

Carver slapped the file closed. It was early in the morning, but his drive would take close to six hours. His previous thought of visiting Jerry Hardwood was never as clear as it was now. He needed someone to verify there was a basement. Needed someone other than a child to shed some light on current circumstances. If he drives all night, he'll be there by morning. Without a second to waste he dressed and climbed into his car then paused to look over his neighborhood.

"Just hold on Sleepy Hollow," he whispered. "I'll only be gone a little while."

95

Wren carried the last victim up the stairs to the dungeon. The man in black stood by the stone slab, leaning on his cane. His victim was already restrained on the slab. Her name was Jennifer, and she was selected to be the first victim, a result of her kind nature. The master had planned her demise while in the car. She will serve as an example to the others. Her torment was required.

Wren bent down, sliding the man's body from Wren's shoulder to his feet then leaned him against the wall where he clamped the steel clasp secured to the wall around his throat. Andy. That was the man's name. Or student. Wren couldn't fathom calling this young boy a man. He was at best a grown child. Wren then clasped Andy's wrists to the steel restraints, followed by the ankle restraints. Andy was still sleeping. They were all sleeping. Now he strapped the gag around Andy's mouth, clasping the latch behind his head. The master was adamant about gagging them. The screams were required, but having a host of victims clucking their tongues was unnerving. Distracting too, when torture requires focus. Wren turned to investigate his work. Twelve victims were shackled to the wall. Awakening moans began to groan from their throats.

The master's gaze was fixed on Jennifer. Her skin so soft and pasty, and her blonde curls looked like a pillow beneath her head.

Her naked body seemed so fresh, without a blemish or wrinkle. Taut around the bones. Her wrists and ankles were secured to the slab. She looked strange lying down with the gag wedged between her lips.

"Shall we wake them?" Wren looked over at his victims. His heart was racing, thundering against his chest as his breath huffed from his lungs. He was excited for the games to begin.

The master lifted his gaze to Wren; a tightlipped grin plastered across his lips. He turned and regarded his victims. One by one, he regarded them. "Indeed." He turned to Jennifer, then to the hot coals burning in the firepit next to the slab. The one where Michael's heart had been reduced to the size of a bean, charred and burnt to a crisp. "Perhaps we are best suited with a scream from the lovely Jennifer." He leaned his cane against the stone slab, then dipped his hand into the coals. The master's hand burned from the heat, although he revealed no pain as if he welcomed the agony. The master plucked four coals from the fire then turned around to the slab.

"Time to wake up, my dear Jennifer. Let me hear you scream." He placed the first coal on Jennifer's throat. Her eyes shot open, and a squeal bellowed from her throat. Her body cringed, then started trembling, her jaw tight. Face pinched in pain. Huffing moans ripped across her gag, a scream in the back of her throat. Crying. Weeping from the pain as her skin welted. Eyes wet with tears. Moaning. Crying. The master placed the second coal between her breasts and Jennifer's body stiffened as her stomach jumped off the slab as if she could slip away from the burning coals. Wren heard her teeth crack; her jaw was so tight. More cries. Heavy whines gagged her throat.

Her head snapped from side to side and the painful stare that gripped her eyes was priceless. Pain was replaced by fear when she realized where she was. To understand her predicament. He placed the third coal beneath her chest bone and the whimper that escaped through her gag would have been an all-out scream if she could scream. Her skin was welting and melting from the heat. Her body was twisting and cringing when the pain and fear erupted in an even flow of tears cascading across her temples. Heavy whining bellowing cries raged from beneath her gag as the master, so cold and calculated, so silent and meticulous, placed a fourth coal over her navel and the burn, the singe from the coal tightened Jennifer's bones. Her legs contracted when an all-out cry and whine guffawed through her gag. Wren gazed at the other victims as their eyes fluttered open to the never-ending muffled wails from Jennifer.

The master turned to Wren. "I do believe we have *earned* her attention." The grin across the master's lips curled into the corners of his mouth as his eyes delighted in Jennifer's pain.

Wren enjoyed the confusion that tore across every victim as they realized their predicament. Locked up and chained to the wall, the neck, ankle and wrist restraints kept them upright. Their legs will be like jelly within a day or two.

"Burns, doesn't it?" said the man in black, staring down at Jennifer. Her eyes staring wide at the ceiling as her chest heaved up

184

and down with thick huffing breaths. Confusion and pain pinched her face as muffled whimpers erupted from the surrounding victims. One male turned mad, his face a darker shade of beet red as he attempted to free himself. His anger surging into his arms.

Jennifer was watching him through the corner of her eyes as she cried, and cried, and cried. The man in black turned his gaze to the boy and grinned. "Oh, that's right. He's your lover, isn't he?" The master watched as the boy fought with all his strength to free himself, grunting madly and determined. Wren loved it when they fought, when their anger boiled to the forefront of consciousness and all they saw was rage and hate. And the man in black laughed. Wren joined him a moment later.

The master took up his cane then pulled the hidden blade from the top when all the noise and grunts and anger and cries and whines spiraled into silence. As if everyone stopped to stare at the blade. He offered it to Wren. "Please, Wren... pluck out his eye. His right eye." The master looked at the boy. "I believe his name is Ian, if memory serves me right." Ian immediately ceased fighting, looking from Wren to the master then back to Wren, whose hand trembled when he took the blade.

Wren was honored to be given access to the coveted cane, even if it was only the blade.

"And then I'll inform you all of your purpose." He locked eyes with Ian. "I'd rather not have to speak over your petty complaints Ian. But your eye will serve as a warning to keep your wits in check." Jennifer was shaking her head, talking through her gag. Her voice mumbled and muffled, but Wren was certain she was pleading for Ian through a veil of tears and cries.

Wren stepped in front of Ian whose muffled words Wren was certain were *Fuck you*. The anger in Ian's eyes burned deep into his pupils. Wren gripped Ian's forehead, holding the blade close to his eye, assessing. Ian attempted to turn his head away, his jaw tight, grinding his teeth, but the neck restraint offered limited mobility, and he struggled to force himself free. Fighting with all his strength and rage to break through his chains when Wren slammed the back of his head against the wall. Once, twice, three times and then more, smacking the back of his head into the stone until he stopped flailing. Ceased his rage and Wren held his palm over Ian's forehead, his thumb raising the eyelid. Ian's eyes were stiff and staring at the blade. So close to his eye. Ian swallowed his breath, thick and heavy down his throat. Now he was trembling. Every inch of his skin, every bone and muscle were shaking. The blade inched closer, and Ian snapped his head back, snapped his whole body back as if he could jump through the wall. But there was no place to go, and Ian was slowly learning this fact.

Another guffaw from beneath the gag, and Wren was certain Ian had pleaded for his eye. *Please. Don't. Please.* His stare carried that same plea for mercy. Wren grinned when he dipped the blade into the eye socket and Ian screamed, his head stiff but his body was wriggling. Screams thundered from his throat as Wren carved his eye out with the precision of a surgeon, circling the blade around the eye as blood gushed from the wound across Wren's hand and wrist, dripping to the floor. A river of blood flooded across Ian's face, across the gag, saturating his neck and shirt. His wails were never ending, screaming from the top of his lungs. Wren plucked the gelatinous ball from its socket, pulling the eye out and holding it as blood rushed from the open wound and Ian's wails reached a fevered pitch.

"Place it on the coals, Wren." The man in black turned to the three doors. "Another offering to the ether."

Wren did as he was instructed. The eyeball simmered on the coals until it popped and fizzled, boiling, bubbling. Jennifer's cries and Ian's wails were prominent through their gags. The other victims were quiet as they gazed at their wounded friends. The master removed the coals from Jennifer's skin. One by one, calm and cold and calculated. He then placed them back in the fire pit. Jennifer's skin was welted where the coals had burned. Her cries and screams settled into a consistent whimper as tears cascaded across her temples, saturating those blonde locks.

Other than Ian's constant painful wails and cries, all else was quiet in the torture chamber. The master seemed lost, staring at the coals-or maybe he was savoring the moment-when he lifted his gaze to the wooden doors. His head dipped to the right, staring before he turned and took up his cane then stretched his hand to Wren, who handed him the blade that the master returned to the cane. The master then regarded Ian, whose relentless cries soothed the master. He stomped his cane against the stone floor twice as if to signal to his victims to pay attention.

"Shall we begin?" The master looked over at his victims. All staring, frantic, panicked, and fearful. Staring at Wren. At the master. Staring at Ian's eye and his blood-soaked face. The empty hovel where his eye had been so dark and foreboding. A warning to the others not to suffer the same fate. Tears in their eyes or fear or rage plastered across their faces. Wren bowed to his master, a gesture signaling he was ready.

"Very well, then. It is time." The master breathed deeply, pinched the bridge of his nose then opened his eyes and regarded his audience. "You have all been selected to serve a higher purpose. The end of humanity begins tonight with the offering of blood." He pointed at the three doors with his cane. "Beyond those doors is a doorway to Xibalba." His cane drifted to his side as he looked, one by one, at his victims. "You have all heard of Xibalba. In the past and throughout your lives, although by other names that have come down through your history. Hades. Sheol. Inferno. The underworld. Tartarus. Gehinnom." His voice seemed to vanish, to drift into silence, but echo in all their ears. And the master grinned when he said, "Hell is the word most commonly used. And it is hell that is here in this room. We are the harbingers of death and fear. Your sacrifices are necessary. Required to open the portal to my home. The portal feeds on a fear vibration and that is what your purpose is now. To feed the portal what it needs to breathe. Most humans spend their lives searching for purpose. But for all of you, that purpose is now clear." And he stood as if at attention, holding his cane tight against his side. "Your sacrifice will open the portal

188

and will usher in hell on earth. Humanity's end as a new beginning starts tonight."

He stomped his cane twice as if to signal the end of his speech. He stepped closer to Jennifer, leaning close to her eyes, her wet, tear-filled eyes. Ian's wails had faded. Wren noticed he passed out. Passed out from the pain and blood loss, Wren was certain.

"My dear," said the master. "I'm going to remove your gag now." He stood tall, leaning his cane against the stone. "You may scream all you want. There is no shame." He regarded his victims. "And to all of you, let it be known there is no hope coming. No possibility of escape. And every night, a new torture will begin." And he grinned, staring at his victims. "Very well then. Let us begin." He reached behind Jennifer's head, unlatching the gag, then pulled it from her mouth. He handed it to Wren, who took it and placed it on the floor by his feet.

"You don't have to do this," said Jennifer. "You can let me go. I won't say anything to anyone, I promise." Her voice was a whining plea.

The master gazed into her eyes. "Is it better to know your fate, Jennifer, or do you desire for your torture to come without knowledge? Which suits you better? To know or to remain in the dark?"

Jennifer recoiled into herself. She turned her head away from the master and closed her eyes. "This can't be happening," she whined, attempting to free herself, tugging on her restraints. Pulling. Slithering across the stone slab and yanking her wrist and ankle restraints. "I'm dreaming. I know it. This can't be real." Her eyes shot open. "It can't be. It just can't be real. Can't. I'm home. In my bed. This is a nightmare, and I'll wake up soon. I'll wake up real soon." She pulled her restraints again, then flopped on the slab. Paused, then pulled some more, her lips quivering, crying, helpless to free herself. Deep, bellowing cries erupted from her throat. Tears spilled from her eyes as she shook her head violently, her body shuddering. Huffing breaths then turned calm. Her cries quieted, staring blank and lost.

"Seems we've broken the weary Jennifer," said the master. He regarded Jennifer and her shallow breathing. "I believe she has disassociated." The master waved his hand over Jennifer's eyes. She never blinked. Her stare was locked in place. "Indeed, she has." He looked at Wren. "I do not enjoy such states of mind." He retracted the blade from his cane. "Let us awaken Jennifer to a new state of consciousness." He leaned his cane against the slab.

Incoherent whispers arrived off Jennifer's lips. Wren wasn't certain, but he believed she was whispering prayers. Or maybe a plea. Difficult to tell in her disassociated state.

The master dipped his head close to Jennifer's eyes. "Prayer only leads so far, my lady. God gives free will." He raised his head, regarding his victims, who all stared wide-eyed and fearful at the knife in his hand. "And with my free will..." His lips stretched into that conniving grin. "I'll take her skin."

The master gripped Jennifer's hair, dipping the blade into her forehead then dragged the blade to her temple and down beneath the jawline when Jennifer wailed something awful, her eyes bulging from their sockets, her mouth open wide, her tongue erect as the master circled the knife beneath her jaw to the other side of her face, then dragged that blade up and back around to the forehead. Blood raced from the open wound like a dam had been opened, raining across the stone. Jennifer's teeth were gnashed, her face pinched in anguish. She whimpered in her throat as her cries arrived in stutters.

"See, Wren. I knew she'd come back to us." And the master laughed as he dug his fingernails beneath the flesh on her forehead then pulled. The flesh ripped and tore off her face, splintering nerve endings and unleashing a river of blood. It looked like the master was peeling off a mask, revealing Jennifer's bloodied fleshless skeleton features. The skin came off with a wet pop and tear that tugged the meat on Jennifer's cheeks, ripping off tiny chunks that remained attached to the skin. She looked priceless to Wren. A mass of bloodied meat, veins, bone and cartilage. Teeth and bulging eyeballs, screaming to God Almighty for the torture to stop as her blood rained across the stone and the Xibalba doors creaked and groaned, buckling under pressure. The master tossed Jennifer's skin onto the hot coals, then stopped to admire his work. Staring at the screaming, hollering, faceless Jennifer.

"We'll save the scalp for last, Wren. Such a prized torture deserves the final bow." He pinched Jennifer's hair, rolling the strands between his fingers. "Such beautiful hair will burn so quickly." The master then craned his head, assessing his work while ignoring the consistent screams bellowing from Jennifer's throat. They were like music to his ears. "Her neck, shoulders and arms come next. Then the torso and legs. Let us carve all the flesh from her bones."

He fileted the skin from her neck to her shoulders, depositing chunks of flesh into the firepit with a murderer's delight.

Jennifer's screams were eternal. With every prick from the master's blade, her agony tore from her throat in restless abandon. The master had been right; Jennifer was the perfect choice to begin their tirade. Her torture bathed every atom in the dungeon with agony. Wren regarded the other victims, terrified and silenced because of the gags although their muffled whimpers could still be heard. He enjoyed watching them gaze upon the scene-the nightmarish foreboding of what was to come for all of them. Some were crying, silent tears in their eyes. Some were praying, and a few had their eyes closed, as if not seeing the torture made it less real.

The master continued to carve. To carve and admire his work, drinking Jennifer's anguish like a fine wine. Her screams were relentless, echoing across the dungeon as the doors groaned, buckling, splintering, the wood popping, grinding.

And Wren couldn't wait for Xibalba to return.

96

The screams were everywhere in the cemetery. High in the night sky, the screams echoed across the stars. They were relentless, as if the entire world was screaming all at once.

Marc sat huddled against the crypt he'd come to know like an old friend. The same crypt where the blonde woman had gone and disappeared. He hadn't seen her since, but he'd come to realize he felt safe when he was near it.

His arms were wrapped around his knees, rocking back and forth. His scar burned something awful, turning his stomach into a noxious boil. Felt blood across his face from the scar but he was too frightened to wipe it away. Too afraid of the screams. Let it drip, he thought. Let it burn my head off. He wanted to cut the scar off. Wanted it gone. The itch was a constant player that refused to relent. He grinded his teeth, listening to the blood-curdling screams raging across the cemetery.

Whoever those screams belonged to, Marc was certain they would be joining him soon. He'd never heard such screams before, never in his life had he heard such pain and terror. He stopped rocking when his stomach wrenched with a thick pain that boiled acid into the back of his throat. He tightened his grip around his knees and dipped his head to them, rubbing his forehead against his jeans, rubbing that scar feverishly, with a whining cry in the back of his throat. Marc felt depleted, as if all his energy had been drained from his limbs, restless yet exhausted all at the same time.

"Marc," said the voice, subtle yet profound. "Marrrrc." Again the voice, calling to him. "It's in the drink, Marc."

Marc lifted his head off his knees. His eyes were wet with tears. Tears and blood that he could feel across his skin. His head drifting, rising, when his eyes absorbed the sight of his father standing beside a mausoleum ten feet away from him.

"Dad?" Marc's voice was like a child's, soft and vulnerable. His lips quivered, staring at the ghost of his father. His skin was decomposed, pale gray with blotches of green where there was skin. Marc could see his skeleton where the skin had completely deteriorated.

"It's in the drink," his father said. "That's how they get you here."

The screams continued. Blood-curdling screams, and Marc stared at his father through a narrowed, confused stare. He watched as his father turned his head up, listening to the screams with a painful wince.

"This pain is too much, Marc." His father kept his gaze on the sky. "He can't win. Someone has to stop him."

His father turned to him. "*You* have to stop him," he said as his ghost form faded. Marc jumped up and took a few steps in the direction where his father was, watching as his form thinned. "Beware of the gong, Marc. When it tolls… the end is near."

His father's voice faded into nothing along with his ghost form when another scream echoed across the firmament. Marc looked around. Looked around as the moans and groans began. Starting in low and guttural, they rose to meet the screams in the sky. Rising from the ground, the cemetery ghosts revealed themselves. They, too, were staring at the sky. Their stares lost and filled with pain as if they agreed the terror must stop. So many of them. Marc looked over the cemetery and there had to be hundreds, if not more.

He stood among them. Stood with the ghosts, listening to the never-ending screams that stabbed the heart.

It was the first time Marc felt as if he was a part of something. A part of something larger than himself.

97

She awakened with a jolt. Lori was in a daze, her eyes wet with tears. Her feet were moving, moving towards the bathroom where she dropped to her knees and retched into the toilet. Her head was spinning. Seemed with every slight movement, the world tore across her vision at lightning speed, her eyeballs floating in their sockets.

Hard to focus, to put her thoughts into a coherent sentence. As if her thoughts hit a wall and shattered and all she could do was pick up the pieces, one word at a time.

Visions. Flashes from recent memories were stained behind her eyes. The blood on the wall in the basement. The words Initium Novum dripping with blood. The pentagram. Her mother screaming. So angry, her rage caught in her throat, turning her complexion into a dark blotchy red.

"You're not going anywhere!" Her mother's voice, thick and piercing.

Lori's face was hot and slick with sweat as she retched again, feeling small chunks pass across her lips and plop into the water splashing across her mouth and chin. Weak and weary, she collapsed on the cold tile floor, her head beating like a drum. Her heart in her throat. Gasping. Trying to breathe. Now she was trembling. Shivering.

"What's gotten into you?" Lori's words from the conversation with her mother earlier this evening. "You can't force me to stay."

She saw herself in the memory standing on the second floor, arguing with her mother. Then Elena's face, her scowl filled with hatred.

Gritting her teeth when she said, "We'll just have to see about that."

The memory faded then with Elena stomping into her bedroom and slamming the door. Lori had stood for a few more minutes. Her arms were shivering, shivering like they are now, on the bathroom floor. Her brain felt like it was hit with a sledgehammer. Her stomach yelped and twisted, and she gripped the toilet bowl tight then lifted her head again, retching with her mouth open wide. She saw blood in the water, but the room was spinning.

"My god! Lori!" Elena's garbled voice floated to Lori's ears.

Lori dropped back down to the floor with a thud. Her head felt like it weighed a thousand pounds. She saw Elena standing at the bathroom door.

"What did you do?" Elena scolded Lori; her face pinched in disgust. She was holding a pill bottle. "Took all of them, didn't you?"

Lori couldn't be certain, but right before her eyes closed, she would have sworn she saw Elena's face contort. It looked like a monster snarling with large, pointed teeth and big bold black eyes.

It was the vision that followed her into darkness. The dark where she found comfort and calm. Where all the pain subsided. Where quiet was as profound as laughter and content as natural as sleep.

Another jolt and she was on a stretcher. Strobing red lights waxed across her eyes. Paramedics rushed her to the ambulance. The air was so cold it felt like ice in her bones.

And then the pain arrived with vengeance.

The pain of living as natural as death.

98

Wren pulled forcefully on the rope. The weight was heavy, the screams relentless.

He and the master had crucified the young Jennifer. Hammered nine-inch nails through her wrists to the cross Wren had crafted that afternoon. They hammered nails into her feet too, after the master had removed her skin. Now Wren was lifting the cross above the dungeon's entrance, across from the three doors to Xibalba. The rope was tied to a metal hoop attached to the top of the cross then weaved through a second hoop above the doors. Wren pulled down on the rope, lifting Jennifer.

And with every pull of the rope, Jennifer hollered even more. The master had done well; her skin was completely removed. The slab absorbed the blood, and the fire ate the flesh. The entrances to Xibalba creaked and groaned the entire time. Wren could feel evil waiting with bated breath beyond the entrances. The sensation brought elation to his heart. And the master watched it all, watched Jennifer lift above the entrance. That tightlipped grin plastered across his lips as he leaned on his cane. When Wren had the cross set above the entrance, he tied the rope to the steel circle secured to the ground.

"Perfect, Wren." Wren regarded his master. "She makes for the appropriate ornament." And he laughed. Wren did too. Laughed, as their victims looked on, horrified.

Wren ran his tongue across his lips. "She'll probably be dead by morning. I'm surprised she survived the procedure."

"Indeed. The blood loss alone should have killed her." Jennifer's screams faded into thick groaning and whining huffs. The master stared at her. All veins and blood and cartilage and bone. A bloody disfigured skeleton. Her blue eyes seemed oddly peculiar, bulging from their sockets. Blood dripped off her feet to the floor. Dripped from her arms too, off the elbows and armpits. Her teeth were pearly white and prominent behind a lipless mouth. Wren turned to the floor, watching Jennifer's blood being absorbed into the stone.

The master stepped closer to her; a certain stare filled with satisfaction plastered across his face. It was clear to Wren she was on the verge of entering the darkness. Whether that was sleep or death, he wasn't certain.

"You're beautiful, my lovely." The master's voice was soft, almost caring. Jennifer's breath was ragged now, spilling from her throat in thick huffs that raised her chest. "The minions of Xibalba will enjoy feasting on your bones." Her screams fell into a void. Her heavy breathing vanished into shallow instinct. The master stepped closer, craning his head to study her.

"Dead?" asked Wren. He looked from Jennifer to the master then back again, running his tongue across his lips.

"No, just sleeping." The master clucked his tongue, gazing at the blood absorbing floor. Little pitter patters of blood fell from Jennifer's toes in front of the master. "In the morning, Wren..." The master raised his head again. "Take her heart. Cut it out and offer it to the ether. We need hearts Wren."

Now Wren felt a surge of warmth at his back. He turned to the Xibalba entrances when a gargantuan boom rattled into the doors as if some hellish monster was pounding on it to gain entrance. The doors buckled, straining, creaking, the wood crunching, the portal strengthening with the offering of fresh blood. "Master, the portal. It strengthens from our deeds."

The master turned on his heels, twisting his cane as he did so. His stare intent, eyeballing the doors when a thunderous rattle shook the foundation beneath them with a growl born from the depths of hell. The middle door looked like it was going to implode, buckling then swelling. The sound coming from the door was ear piercing. Sounded like a loud buzz, a sonic boom thundering in their ears.

And then the door cracked, opening a fissure in the wood no longer than a foot and no wider than three inches. The crack looked like a single tear from the claw of a wolf.

Then silence. The buckling ceased as did the growls. Wren craned his head to look inside the fissure when he noticed the scent of sulfur slithered through the crack, but all he could see was blackness. All he could hear was the gentle wind funneling through the fissure.

The master closed his eyes when the heated wind waved across his skin. "My home," he whispered, opening his eyes as that grin spread across his lips. "So long have I waited. Soon, Wren. Soon we will be with our brethren. Soon we will have all the power of Xibalba in our hands." He strolled towards the door when Wren regarded their victims. Petrified and quiet as if being quiet turned them invisible. Every one of them, their faces pinched in pain and discomfort. Fear and terror. He wondered if they'd thought about their own demise, and what form of torture would deliver death to their doorstep.

He noticed more than a few had lost control of their bodily functions. A pool of urine sat beneath them. The master stepped in front of the Xibalba door, staring through the fissure. He reached his hand to it when electrical sparks tore from the slit to greet his hand.

A subtle rickety growl erupted from behind the doors.

"It's beautiful Wren." The master laughed. He stared into the darkness existing beyond the fissure, mesmerized. "My cave speaks to me." He turned his stare to the top of the door then turned to Wren. "Our gateway waits for us. Once Baphomet has been appeased, he will grant me dominion over humanity and the armies of Xibalba will walk the earth like gods."

Wren snickered. "And then we can unleash hell upon the earth."

"Indeed," said the master. "Soon, Wren." He curled his fingers into a tight fist.

"So very soon."

Part IV

99

Carver arrived at the state hospital just after nine am. His eyes were dry and tired, although his brain was functioning at an optimal level. His arrival in the parking lot brought with it a renewed vigor. Plus, the amount of coffee he'd ingested during the drive had him wired to the eyeballs.

He introduced himself to the two people-a young man who seemed like he just started his job looking like a deer in headlights, and an older woman Carver placed at about his age who clearly knew every in and out of the hospital-sitting behind the front desk as a friend of Jerry Hardwood. He thought it was best to keep his official duties away from the public eye. Considering he was a friend to Jerry and his family he wasn't lying, and he decided it would be a lot easier to speak with Jerry if the staff didn't know he was here on official police business.

The older lady-Esther, Carver read on her employee badge hanging from a lanyard around her neck-studied him, assessing every part of him with a skeptical stare as she gnawed on her bottom lip. She requested he add his name and signature to the visitor log as she took a badge from a basket in front of her. He had to wear the badge at all times. The word Visitor written in thick black ink on the pink-colored paper wedged inside the plastic. Carver clipped it to his collar.

"Follow me," said Esther.

And Carver did just that, looking around, assessing the hospital and the tall ceilings he walked under. The hospital was clean and pristine and looked recently renovated. Windows lined the walls, allowing the morning sun to drape the hospital in natural light. Esther pushed the button for the elevator while providing information on what, and even more so, what Carver could not give Jerry. It was a long list.

The elevator opened to the third floor where they entered a small sitting room no bigger than a broom closet with three chairs. Directly across from the elevator was a thick white door with no window. On his right was a window and behind that window sat an older gentleman who opened the window when he saw Esther. They exchanged pleasantries before Esther introduced Carver.

After one look at Carver, he said, "You'll have to get rid of your toothpick. Wouldn't want one of our patients to drive it into your eyeball." And he laughed, Esther did too. A slight chuckle, a joke among coworkers.

Carver took the toothpick from his lips. "Does that actually happen?" He dropped the pick in the garbage can in the corner.

"More than you know. You'd be surprised what can be used for contraband."

Carver shook his head.

"You ready?" He cocked his eyebrows as if there was some secret joke that Carver wasn't in on.

Carver looked at Esther. "You'll be fine," she said.

"I'm not worried about it."

"Well good. Jerry never had a visitor before. This may be good for him. Then again, it may be the worst thing that can happen. I guess we'll just have to find out." The man smiled and cocked his eyebrows as his hands disappeared beneath the desk when Carver heard the buzz on the door. "Come on in," he said, delighted. "The orderly will seat you."

Carver stared at the door. It seemed like it was now or never.

He couldn't wait to see Jerry but as he opened the door, for the first time, he wondered if Jerry would reciprocate Carver's sentiment.

The thought never occurred to him that Jerry might not be happy with Carver's little visit.

100

Lori drifted awake. Her eyes floated across a blurred room; the walls smeared across her vision. Her brain wasn't working. Her head was pounding with a headache so strong she believed her skull was on the verge of cracking open. She paused the roaming eyes and kept them still. She found the movement ramped up the pain from the headache. Staring straight ahead. Staring at nothing. Everything was dull and it seemed as if the world had gone quiet, as if on pause.

She rested her head on the pillow, closing her eyes then twisting her body to roll over but her wrist refused to follow. She pulled her wrist, but it caught again. Tugged a couple more times, but her arm wouldn't move.

What is going on?

Lori forced her eyes open. Forced them open to study her wrist. Her head was weary and felt like it weighed a thousand pounds. Her headache pulsed in her skull, ballooning her head to an abnormal size. She felt depleted. Raw. As if every organ in her body had been tapped and did nothing more than sit like stones in her body. She turned her head to see her wrist. She looked at it, numb and absent. Studying her wrist and the thick strap around it that was secured to the bedrail.

Strange. Is that my *wrist?*

Her eyes wandered. Looking around the room. No windows. No paintings. All white concrete walls. A wooden chair in the corner. A door with a small window, the door was thick and stood like a guard. The single lightbulb on the ceiling hurt like a son of a bitch when the light washed into her eyeballs. Lori's head was so weary she dropped back down on the pillow and closed her eyes again. She pulled on her right arm, but it too was secured to the bedrail. An itch on her leg. She tried to scratch it with her foot, but her ankle caught.

Her legs were strapped, too.

Tried to think, but no thoughts arrived. Her brain was tapped, struggling to connect thoughts and synapses. Felt drool drip from the corner of her mouth. Her jaw and neck were wet with spit. A shadow in the room. Lori looked around, the room buzzing and vibrating.

Or is that just her brain?

With a weary head, she looked at the door and saw a face in the window. Someone was watching her. The doorknob turned, the door opened and then there was this person walking over to the bed. Their footsteps tapped across the linoleum floor sending waves of punishment to Lori's head.

"Ms. Francon?"

Lori dropped her head on the pillow and closed her eyes.

I'm having a night terror.

Heard the scrape of the chair across the floor and her stomach boiled with acid when her head ballooned even larger than it had before. Whoever it was put the chair beside the bed and sat down.

"Ms. Francon? Are you awake?"

Lori felt the person's hand on her forehead. Then her eyelid was lifted and now she's staring directly at the person. A woman. Older, Lori placed her in her sixties considering the mop of gray hair. She wore glasses over dark brown eyes. She shined a light into Lori's drifting eyeball then clicked the light off and replaced it in her shirt pocket. Now she was taking Lori's pulse and when she noticed Lori staring at her she smiled.

"Do you remember me?" she said. "Dr. Reese. I was your doctor the last time you were admitted." A pause. Lori said nothing, her brain was depleted of thought. She still didn't know where here was.

Lori's head drifted, looking around the room as if that would prompt the good doctor to answer the burning question her lips refused to ask: *Where am I?*

"You're in the mental health unit at Holy Cross Hospital," Dr. Reese reported as if she'd heard Lori's question. "You downed a bottle of painkillers last night."

Lori turned to the doctor. Dr. Reese had her elbows on her knees and was hunched over. Lori rested her head on the pillow.

"Do you remember what happened? Your mother called 9-1-1. You owe her a debt of gratitude. She saved your life."

Lori went to speak, but no words followed.

"I see you're having trouble speaking. It could be from the pills or the charcoal suspension the ER used to bring you back to life. Your system took a jolt, and a side effect is confusion and a suppressed neural connection." She cocked her eyebrows. "Taps the strength too. We've been seeing a lot of overdoses lately with those new oxycodone pills. You're lucky we had a stocked supply for that purpose, or you'd be dead right now." The doctor paused. "It seems that fate has superseded your desire to be dead."

What is she talking about? What pills?

Now Lori's memory passed in front of her eyes. Elena stood in the bathroom, scolding Lori while holding a pill bottle. The memory shifted then to the moment Lori told Elena she was going back to Sleepy Hollow to find Marc.

You're not going anywhere.

We'll just have to see about that.

The words had jumped off Elena's lips. And that scowl, that hateful, angry scowl, beamed from Elena's eyes like daggers filled with vengeance.

Lori drifted back to the here and now when the doctor slipped a blood pressure cuff off her arm. Lori wasn't aware she had put the cuff on.

"What you need now is sleep. You'll be here for at least a day, and I suggest you get your rest. We'll talk more when you're ready but this time I want a plan, Lori. A plan for how you're going to get your life together and that plan needs to include therapy, both individual and group. And let's not forget medication, too. Your mother told me you stopped taking your medication." She shook her head. "Not good, Lori. You don't have to be ashamed of taking medication. Just look at it like a vitamin for your brain." And she smiled. Smiled and gathered her blood pressure cuff before she stood. "Get some rest. I'll be back to check on you in a few hours."

She turned and went to the door but stopped in the doorway, returning her attention to Lori. "Your mother's waiting for you to wake up. I suggested she return home but she refused. She's waiting until you're up and ready to talk. You gave her a good scare, so I allowed her to stay but if you don't feel like talking to her, I'll tell her to go."

Lori said nothing. She couldn't put two words together. Not now, at least.

She wanted to tell Dr. Reese that she didn't try to kill herself. Wanted to tell her that Elena was the cause of her current circumstance. That her mother tried to kill her. Lori knew she didn't take those pills.

But what Lori knew all too well was how the system worked, and she wasn't about to raise bloody hell over it. They'll have her committed for a very long time if she tosses out accusations. It's better to placate the doctor and get the hell out of the hospital. She'll deal with Elena on her own time.

Instead, she shook her head, closed her eyes and rested against the pillow.

"Ok. I'll tell her," the doctor whispered.

Lori heard the door close with a click. She opened her weary eyes. The doctor looked through the window but left a second later, leaving Lori alone. Alone with her thoughts and nightmares.

101

Carver was sitting at a small square table while waiting for Jerry and nursing a cup of coffee courtesy of the orderly who escorted him in. The coffee tasted like burnt oil, but he couldn't care less. His long drive was weighing him down. He needed caffeine, so he swallowed the coffee one bitter sip at a time.

He reached for the phantom toothpick between his lips, realized it wasn't there, and laughed at himself. A slight chuckle escaped his throat before taking a sip from his cup.

They might think I'm the crazy one. Laughing at myself.

Which brought out more laughter as he stretched his arms and back.

How long is this going to take?

The room he was in was large and open. The cafeteria, as the orderly had said, was recently renovated, bright, clean, and pristine. The walls were painted mauve and Carver remarked to himself that the color was calming. Soothing was the word he used. The windows had bars on them, but they did little to stop the sun from bathing the hospital in natural light. Ten tables sat empty around him. Carver was in the center of all those tables, alone, except for the staff who occasionally walked through the hall outside the cafeteria.

Carver wondered why there weren't more visitors.

Probably too early. Either that or not many people like visiting the psych ward.

He was staring through the windows that were lined across the wall behind him when he heard feet shuffling in the hall and when he turned the orderly was escorting Jerry by the wrist to the cafeteria. Carver stood up to greet his old friend. The old friend whose stare was blank, his expression flat, his eyes like tiny pins revealing the hell he was going through. Jerry wore sweatpants, thick yellow socks with what looked like sandals provided by the hospital, and a gray sweatshirt over what Carver could see was a white T-shirt. His hair was a mop of disheveled grease and wiry curls. His skin was so pale Carver was convinced Jerry hadn't seen the sun since he arrived. Jerry's beard was thick, unkempt, and filled with gray and the skin beneath his eyes was pale red and sunken.

Other than the fact that Jerry had lost a substantial amount of weight- substantial doesn't give it justice, he was as thin as the toothpick Carver wanted to pop between his lips-he looked like what roadkill would look like after being trolled over by a line of cars exiting a frustrated Yankee game.

Carver went to walk around the table to greet Jerry when the orderly waved him off.

"Need you to sit on the other side of the table. Remember the rules, sir."

Carver remembered the rules the orderly had rattled off when he brought Carver to the table. No hugs or handshakes of any kind. No sitting next to each other. Hands where I can see them. Keep your voice down, even if you're frustrated, keep the volume to a minimum. No passing anything without inspection. And the last one, no sex. The fact that the orderly had to say that last rule spun Carver's imagination in a million directions.

"Of course, my apologies." Carver was staring at Jerry, who had yet to acknowledge his existence. Jerry barely moved; his stare fixed on the window.

"Here, Jerry. Take a seat." The orderly guided Jerry by the wrist and plopped the old man on the bench. Jerry's expression never changed, nor did his focus. Carver wondered if this trip was all for nothing. If he'll be here the entire time and all Jerry will do is stare through the window. "Enjoy your visit, Jerry." The orderly gave him a pat on the shoulder that Jerry never acknowledged. "I'll be right over there." The orderly pointed to another table not far from where he stood. Carver looked at the orderly, realizing he was talking to him and not Jerry as if Carver required protection.

Carver rubbed his chin. "Thank you." The orderly nodded, then turned and posted up on a table a few feet from where they sat, allowing enough room for them to talk in private but close enough to move into position if he had to. Carver's attention returned to Jerry. Jerry, who looked like a shell of the man Carver knew over the last few decades, sat unmoving, stiff as a board.

Hopefully, I can get something out of him.

Carver stepped over the bench and took a seat, staring eye to eye with Jerry and his lost stare. Jerry turned away.

Tragic. Where do I start?

Carver cleared his throat. He didn't know what to say, so he said what he came here for. He figured if this was all for nothing, at least he'd know sooner rather than later.

"The house, Jerry. The house in the western woods, the one you brokered on the same day that brought you to this hospital…" He paused to assess Jerry, hoping for a response; even a small acknowledgment would help. Again, there was nothing. "Were you in the basement? Did you see what they have down there?"

Nothing.

Damnit.

They sat in silence. Carver looked over the room, scanning across the tables to the orderly posted up by the table.

This is all for…

When he looked back, Jerry was staring at him. It looked like he was going to speak. His mouth opened, but no words arrived off his lips.

"Yes, Jerry. What is it? Tell me, please."

A sudden terror-filled stare tore across Jerry's face. It looked like his innards were wrenched from his stomach.

"Are you, okay?"

Jerry stared directly into Carver's eyes and whispered,

"There's a portal to hell in the basement."

102

Wren forced Ian's head back against the wall with a gentle hand. The blood had dried across Ian's face and was now dark brown. Wren had done well with the incision. Ian's eye socket was a dark cavern reaching towards hell. His breathing was shallow. Indeed, Ian was sleeping. Exhausted from fear and pain and terror.

Subtle moans over Wren's shoulder. He didn't have to look to know that Jennifer was still alive. How she was alive, he wasn't certain. Perhaps her will to live superseded the pain of death. He paid her no mind.

Let her rot on the vine. A slow, painful death is required for the Xibalba fires to rage into this world.

When he first entered the dungeon this morning, he immediately assessed the Xibalba doors. Last night he'd seen the astral plane strengthen resulting in the crack in the middle door. He had heard the growl from the ghost demons, but now, the astral plane had vanished and all that remained were three thick doors. The middle one with the crack, but all Wren could see was darkness beyond the fissure. He was disappointed.

We need more blood. More sacrifice. More torture.

He chose Ian to dole out that torture. And why not? Wren took pleasure in knowing he could carve Ian up one piece at a time. He could carve something off every single one of them if he chooses and he may do just that in time, but he'd taken a liking to Ian after cutting out his eyeball. A torturer's bond, as he called it.

We all have our favorites now, don't we?

The master had given explicit instructions to keep it to a minimum. The blood and carnage, that is. The master enjoyed torturing them and wanted to be in attendance when the astral plane finally broke through. So, he allowed Wren to have his fun while he slept, gathering his strength until Wren provides the absinthe to Marc, although not too much fun.

Marc? What a tool.

Marc was sleeping when Wren had checked on him. No doubt he'll be up soon. Ready to paint once again.

Wren still wondered how much Marc knew about their little venture. After all, where did he go when the master took over the body? The master referred to it as the ether. The in-between. A dimension that exits between life and death. A limbo of sorts.

He'll be up soon, thought Wren.

His grin curled across his lips. Wren looked around, over his shoulder, wanting to see who was awake and who was sleeping. Soon, so, very, very soon they will all be up. They will have no choice in the matter. Screams and wretched cries of anguish, even with the gag in place, typically awakens weary eyes. He noticed seven of them were awake, watching Wren and the devilish grin across his lips.

Now he applied pressure to Ian's forehead to keep his head still, then used a scalpel to cut into Ian's ear. Once that blade carved into the cartilage Ian's eye snapped open, bellowing a thick holler in his throat. His head twitched, his face pinched in torment. Wren gripped his forehead tighter as he carved into the ear. Blood rained across his hand and wrist and down across Ian's neck. A full out whining cry emanated from Ian's muffled throat in thick gasps and wails.

"Just hold still, little pet." Wren gripped Ian's hair tight, holding his skull with an iron grip as he carved and sawed and fileted the ear. "It's so much easier if you don't fight."

Ian's screams, cries, and whining whimpers echoed across the dungeon as Wren removed the ear. There were tears in Ian's eye, cascading like a waterfall across his cheek. Wren gripped the ear and stared at Ian, returning the scalpel to his pocket while Ian howled like a child with one less eye and one less ear. Wren felt the heat from Xibalba rise in the dungeon; his stare fixed on Ian as he took a cloth from his pocket and pressed it to Ian's ear to cease the blood flow.

"I'll take you piece by piece my little pet." Wren glowered at Ian, grinding his teeth beneath the gag. "I want to keep you alive for as long as I can. Carve you up and make art with your skin." Ian's left eye stared at Wren as his wails subsided. "I think I'll end it by taking your heart. Rip it from your chest while you're still alive. You'll be awake during the procedure. A witness to the destruction of your own heart." And he smiled. Smiled when Ian froze. Wren craned his head, wondering what thoughts just raced through Ian's brain.

Satisfied he'd stopped the blood flow, he stuffed the bloodied rag into his pocket then dropped Ian's ear onto the coals, listening to the muffled grunts and whimpers from his victims when he heard a creak from upstairs. Wren looked at the ceiling. Heard more creaks. Someone was walking across the floorboards upstairs. He turned to his victims.

"The master is awake." Wren had one arm behind his back, the other in front of his stomach, palm up. He looked around. "I'll leave you for now. But in my absence, please think about me. Think about which one of you I'll cut into next." And he paused. Paused as those steps creaked across the ceiling. "Well, enjoy your day."

He walked towards the basement, eyeballing Jennifer on the way when he paused, staring at her and how beautiful she looked without her skin.

"If I do say so myself, Jennifer, you look absolutely stunning."

Jennifer groaned something awful. Her eyes rolled to the back of her skull as a single drop of blood dripped off her toe. He was supposed to cut out her heart, but she looked so precious in her current position he decided to put it off for a few hours. He hoped the master would not mind.

"Absolutely stunning," he repeated then continued to walk. Walked and laughed, pinching the bridge of his nose. Repeating, "Absolutely stunning," as he took the stairs up, laughing and cackling.

"Absolutely stunning."

103

Now Carver believed he was getting somewhere. Jerry may be acting erratic, but he was talking, albeit in whispers, but it is what it is.

Carver couldn't help but think about the tragedy Jerry endured, although he found it odd that Jerry never asked about his son, nor did he mention anything about his wife or daughter. He'd expected Jerry to inquire about John from the outset, but Jerry was obviously a man beating to a different drum.

There's a portal to hell in the basement.

A portal to hell. A portal.

What the fuck does that mean? At least he acknowledged there was a basement.

Whatever this portal is, Carver deduced that Jerry might be filling the gaps in his reality with his current psychosis. What happened to this man to make him go off the rails like this? Carver had seen Jerry not a week before all hell broke loose and he seemed fine, natural, like he always did. Normal. Well, at least as normal as any human can be. And definitely not the shell of a man sitting in front of Carver. The Jerry sitting across from him was a man possessed, as if he'd always been that way. As if he'd spent his entire life under the watchful eye of the orderly sitting in the corner.

The transformation nagged at Carver. How can a perfectly sane and prominent member of society lose his mind and go on a murdering rampage? Someone who has never so much as had a run in with law enforcement. Never had more than a parking ticket and then he suddenly wakes up one day and rips his daughter's heart out.

The only logical conclusion to Carver was either trauma or possession, even if that possession was simply a matter of a cracked psyche brought on by the severe pressure applied by a nefarious mind.

The master.

Marc Saduj.

The memory of Jerry's statement surfaced in Carver's mind: *I need hearts for the master.* Followed by the memory of that damn tree Marc had painted with a heart carved into the trunk.

Carver hunched over with his elbows on the table, reaching for his nonexistent toothpick. Jerry sat motionless, staring at the floor, sitting sideways on the seat. Carver mulled over what to ask next. Clearly, he would need to be careful with his questions and chosen articulation. No one wants Jerry to go off on a tirade, nor does Carver want to contribute to his already demented distortion of reality.

"How do we access the basement, Jerry? Where is the entrance?"

To this, Jerry glanced at Carver, his eyes steady and suspect. He traced his finger over the table when he said, "Through the hall," with his head bent, watching his finger glide across the table to the end where his fingers dipped off the edge, then he shot up, staring at Carver with his hands on his lap. His stare was stoic, as if he'd turned to stone.

Carver searched through his memory of the house. *Through the hall.* He remembered the hall on the first floor, but there was no entrance to a basement he could recall. Carver saw it in his mind's eye, the stairs to the second floor and two doors at the end of the hall but no stairs or door leading to a basement.

A hidden door. The revelation popped into Carver's mind like the toothpicks he pops between his lips. It made sense to Carver. If they're committing evil deeds in the basement of course they would do all they could to cover up those deeds.

"Past the wall and down the steps. The stone steps that lead to hell." As if Jerry read Carver's mind. Jerry's voice sounded like he was singing a nursery rhyme.

Carver studied Jerry when he noticed a few more people had entered the cafeteria. More visitors, taking their seats and waiting. Carver looked at them before returning his gaze to Jerry whose stare was locked in on Carver.

Jerry said, "Sheila comes to visit too."

Carver's head snapped back. *Does he not know his wife is dead?*

"She comes and sings me to sleep. When the voices and whispers are too much. She comes and sings." He looked down at the floor, his eyes brimming with tears. "Such a beautiful voice." Jerry blinked his tears away, returning his gaze to Carver.

Let it go, Carver told himself. What does it matter anyway? Look where the man is. Where he'll spend the rest of his life. Carver's throat gagged. He wanted to cry himself. Instead, he cleared his throat and cupped his hand over his mouth, grinding his teeth to squelch those tears. Carver had more questions. Questions he didn't want to ask any longer but after a six-hour drive and with all that's going on in Sleepy Hollow he felt he had too. He just wasn't sure how Jerry would respond to the inquiry.

"Who is the master, Jerry? The one who needs hearts? And what does he need the hearts for?"

Jerry said nothing, staring at Carver as if he never heard him.

"Is Marc Saduj the master?"

A slight shake of Jerry's head.

"Is it his servant, Wren?"

Jerry slapped his hand on the table. The sudden movement jolted Carver. Jolted everyone in the cafeteria and Carver noticed the orderly shot up from his seat, assessing the situation. When no other sudden move was made, he stood and stared. Carver returned his attention to Jerry as he lifted his hand from the table, pinching a petrified cockroach between his fingers. The roach squirmed and scurried, attempting to free itself from Jerry's grip.

Carver watched as Jerry swallowed the roach down his gullet. Carver's eyes narrowed, and his stomach churned.

"Mr. Field is a good man," said Jerry, now bobbing his shoulders and glaring at Carver with his nose curled in a snarl as if that roach was not sitting right in Jerry's stomach. Or it was crawling back up the way it came. "He serves the master well."

Serves the master, Carver thought. So, it is Marc Saduj. Maybe Jerry refers to Marc as the master?

"All will be done soon. All under the moon will rise again at the master's behest. A new beginning is coming."

Initium Novum.

Carver sat quietly as Jerry turned his gaze to the floor. He appeared so lost and fragile Carver's heart bled for his friend. What made the most sense was that Jerry was the victim of brainwashing. Marc and his vampire-looking servant really did a number on him. It was wrong, setting the man up for the big fall while they took over the house to perform their evil rituals in a basement they kept under lock and key.

Now Carver was well aware he'd received all the information he could from Jerry, and it was time to go. What was he going to do anyway, stick around to play chess? He's got more investigating to do. More pieces to the puzzle to fit together. He knew he couldn't use anything Jerry said in a court of law, but he could begin with a stake-out, hoping he would witness a deed or act that'll allow him another search of the house and, more specifically, the basement. Now that he's confirmed a basement exists. Although there was one more thing he wanted to tell his friend.

"Just so you know, Jerry, I'm doing all I can to look after John. He's been good. Starting to get on with his life and Claude has been great with him." He paused, waiting for a response, but Jerry just sat there as if he hadn't heard a word Carver said. "Anyway, I just wanted you to know that your son's being looked after."

Carver paused when he realized this was more than likely the last time he'll ever see Jerry. Considering the two men had no one else in their lives, this ending was weighing heavy on Carver.

Funny how life turns out sometimes. Life either changes on a dime or over time and Carver laughed at this adage, thinking of himself and Jerry, two prime examples of the statement.

"The boy must be sacrificed. He is the last in a long line." Jerry's head was turned, his eyes were downcast, slowly lifting to meet Carver's stare. Something nefarious existed in that stare. "The missing piece to the puzzle."

"Jerry, that's your son we're talking about." Carver had to check himself, remembering that the person in front of him was a lifetime resident in the hospital for murdering his own daughter. Although, Carver never expected Jerry's contempt included his son too.

"And what a dastardly boy he is. Meddling in things he doesn't understand." Jerry's voice changed. He didn't even sound like Jerry. He sounded like Marc Saduj.

Carver watched as a shadow passed through Jerry's eyes. Like a switch, a click that transferred personalities in Jerry's mind.

"Jerry, what're you talking about? He's a good kid."

Jerry tilted his head. "If he's such a good boy, why is he roaming around the woods in the middle of the night? Spying on good people and making up stories about their deeds? Is that what good boys do, detective? Perhaps we should have taken his heart instead. What do you think about that?"

Carver's eyes narrowed. Jerry's stare was burrowing a hole in Carver's soul. His stomach twisted, grinding, churning.

"Look at you, detective. Going the long mile in your pursuit of evil." Jerry's elbows were on the table now and Carver didn't like how he just inched closer to him. He grinned then, a tightlipped, half-cocked grin. His eyes beaming with nefarious intent.

Is this some multiple personality shit I'm witnessing?

"Yes, detective, that's exactly what this is. A switch in personality if you wish. Call it what you want. I truly don't care."

Did he just read my thoughts?

Jerry's smile grew even wider across his lips.

"The boy will burn, detective. His heart will be offered to the ether. Sooner or later, the sins of the ancestry must be brought forward for retribution." Jerry's head tilted to the left, glaring at Carver. "I am everywhere, detective. Don't think for one second I'm not privy to your dealings."

"And what would they be?"

"You wish to dismantle my progress. You wish to destroy all I've sacrificed for. But I can't wait. I can't wait, detective… to take your head." He stretched his hand out then curled his fingers into a tight fist. "Then tear out your heart though your decapitated neck."

Now that one hurt. He wanted to reach out and choke the life from Jerry. Instead, he nodded. "I think that's about it for today,

Jerry. It was good talking to you." Carver sat up from the table. In fact, he wanted to get as far away from Jerry as possible. This change in personality was not expected. It put all Carver knew into a different light and as a detective, he had to consider all possibilities. Namely, that Jerry was out of his fucking mind. If there are two personalities inside Jerry's mind there is a large possibility he committed all those murders on his own. Everything else could be deemed suspect but not nefarious, born from a troubled mind.

Carver looked at the orderly and gave a quick nod as if to say, we are done here. The orderly immediately shuffled over to the table. Now Jerry was also standing, glaring at Carver.

"Leaving so soon, detective? But I just got here. Why not stay a while longer? Maybe the two of us can come up with some sort of deal."

"Are you a police officer?" asked the orderly, now standing directly behind Jerry.

"That he is. Did the good detective not inform staff that he was an officer of the law here to question a potential witness?" Jerry shook his head and clucked his tongue with a demonic tsk.

The orderly stared at Carver, waiting for an answer.

"I am an officer, yes. But my business here was personal." Carver looked at Jerry and his obnoxious stare. He looked like Marc Saduj.

"Well, I believe it is time for you to go." The orderly wrapped his hand around Jerry's elbow. "Come on Jerry. Let's get you to bingo."

The sudden shift in Jerry was apparent. His shoulders slumped forward, and his head bent down. His eyes too. It seemed as if whatever personality had taken over suddenly vanished. Now he seemed weak and pathetic. Carver watched the orderly escort Jerry into the hall before taking his coat off the table and draping it across his shoulders, squeezing his arms into the sleeves.

"DETECTIVE!"

Jerry's voice boomed through the ward. Carver snapped his head towards Jerry. Jerry suddenly spun around, breaking the orderly's grip from his elbow.

It happened so fast as if Jerry developed the speed of a cat because he had the orderly spun around and was squeezing the nape of the man's neck. Jerry snatched the plastic identification cover clipped to the lanyard around the orderly's neck and in one quick snap of his wrist he swiped it across the man's throat.

Carver stood unmoving, unsure of what he'd seen. It seemed like the world had suddenly hit the pause button. His eyes narrowed as he cocked his head back. Staring as blood bubbled from the throat. Just a little. Just a little and then the floodgates opened. The orderly's eyes were wide open. Shocked as his hand went to his throat, the blood gushing from his windpipe before he dropped to the ground with a thud, his leg twitching. Blood everywhere, pooling beneath the body around Jerry's feet. So much blood, it looked like a river of red right there in the hall.

And then someone screamed. A bloodcurdling scream that echoed across the hospital. Carver stood in awe with his jaw hanging open watching as nurses and staff huddled around the orderly, working feverishly to save the man's life. And standing there within the chaos was Jerry.

Jerry, who glowered at Carver.

His stare burrowed into his soul, but all Carver could see was the grin. That tightlipped tell-all grin that squeezed Carver's heart.

104

Marc awakened out of a nightmare. Shot up out of bed like he was in a trance with scenes from the cemetery stained on the back of his eyes. His feet thumping across the floorboards, he almost tumbled down the steps he was thumping and thudding so fast.

In the nightmare, he was locked in a cemetery crypt where the darkness wrapped around him like a blanket.

His mother was in the darkness, spewing insults that stabbed his heart like a dagger. Cut into his brain and mangled his neurochemistry. His head trembled as he took the stairs down. Cold. So cold, he was shivering. Felt spit on his lips and across his chin. His hands were shaking. His insides were on fire, burning into his veins. Hot. Cold. Hot. Cold. Nothing was consistent other than the shaking. And the pain. Unimaginable pain tore through his liver and he felt sick. Started vomiting in the kitchen sink.

His eyes were wet with tears. Vomiting and trembling. Shaking like a leaf in a storm. He dropped to the floor, the pain in his solar plexus was so strong it pinned him to the ground. So, he crawled, arm over arm to the cabinet where he knew Wren kept his alcohol. Huffing and groaning, he reached for the door and opened the cabinet then reached for the bottle, his arms refusing to obey his thoughts, shaking so badly that he could hardly grip the glass bottle. After his second try he knew he had to readjust his position and he did just that, forcing himself to sit with his back against the kitchen cabinet.

He swallowed his breath to stifle his heavy breathing and with trembling hands he reached for the bottle, then stomped it onto the wooden floor where he proceeded to twist the cap, needing both hands to do so. One to steady the bottle and the other to twist.

You ain't no good. You're a sad sack of shit. How the hell did you come out of me?

His arms shaking, the bottle clinked against his teeth. The moment the vodka touched his lips felt like ecstasy. He guzzled it down and the moment it hit his stomach he puked it all up. Couldn't even get the bottle away fast enough. The puke came so quickly, projecting across the kitchen. He tried again, stuffing that vodka down his gullet. Coughing and gagging now.

I wish you were never born. I should have aborted you when I had the chance. Now look at you. Pathetic you are.

He managed to hold that last gulp down. He could feel it, softening his organs, giving them what they wanted and restoring his strength. Just a bit. Just a little bit. The shaking seemed to calm then. But still, his mother's voice followed him.

Nasty little vermin. You're nothing. A feeble existence if there ever was one.

And then she laughed. That cackling, heckling laugh. He could see her, with her strawberry blonde hair all nappy and disheveled. Her skin was moist with sweat. Her skin was like parchment paper, pale and soft and delicate. Yellow teeth and blotches across her skin from where she'd picked and picked and picked until the flesh bled.

Marc drank again, numb to his core. The vision shifted behind his burning, itching, watering eyes. He saw the man in black, slicing into flesh with a devilish grin. Then another shift and all the ghosts in the cemetery were standing at attention, listening to the eternal shriek that raged across the night sky. He saw the crypt then, that dark and gray crypt with the inky-black, glass-looking rock across the door where a name should be. Where darkness exists like a black hole into hell. Where his mother was. Where she doled out her punishment, clucking her tongue so vehemently. Marc's mother was one issue, but what existed beyond his mother's insults was another. The woman in black waited for him with bated breath.

Why do you go in there? he asked himself; the question came from a part of Marc's mind, some part that was still the rational mind of Marc Saduj.

He sees his hand opening the crypt door as if his dream was alive in waking consciousness. Felt the pull towards the crypt. Like a drug he couldn't resist. Like the bottle he was guzzling between pauses in his labored breath. Felt a hand on the bottle, forcing it from his lips. He didn't realize his eyes were closed. Either blood or pus leaked across his eyeball. His scar was burning across his skull.

Saw the body hanging from the rafters. Devoid of skin. Blood dripped off the toes in heavy sheets to the stone floor.

Fucking useless piece of garbage. A rat, if there ever was one. Let her rot. Rot like little rats should.

236

Not his mother's voice. Those thoughts carried his own voice.

"Mr. Saduj…" The voice was soft and calm. "My master. Let me get you back to bed."

Marc forced his eyes open to the light that sent waves of anguish to his brain. Gritting his teeth, his jaw tight as if it could ward off the pain swelling in his abdomen. In front of him was his servant, Wren.

"Come, let me help you."

With gentle ease, Wren lifted Marc to his feet then wrapped Marc's arm around his shoulders, steadying Marc with his free arm around his waist. So easy it was, this short man so inhumanly strong.

"You need rest, and you must sleep. Sleep is required."

Wren brought him to the second floor where Marc dropped with a thud to the mattress. Wren kneeled beside him, wiping the sweat from Marc's brow with a bloodied rag. Marc gasped, tired and wavering between sleep and awake.

"I don't want to go," Marc pleaded. "There're devils in my sleep."

"All is well, my master. When you wake up, I'll have your drink ready. We have much to do. Much to be ready for. You will need your strength."

"So… much… pain." Marc's liver squeezed his insides with a pain that rolled his eyes to the back of his brain. He brought his knees to his chest, suffering eternally. Shaking, his breath stuttering across his lips.

"Soon the pain will be gone. Soon you will rise again."

Felt Wren's hand on his forehead, drifting across and closing his eyes. Darkness everywhere. That dark black hole. His breathing calmed. He opened his eyes to the light through the open window when the chilled air crawled across his flesh. Closed his eyes again and drifted off to sleep.

105

"What was the reason for your visit?"

Carver was being questioned by the hospital supervisor, Cheryl Raven, in her office. After Jerry slashed the orderly's throat, Carver couldn't just leave. Such an action would have been suspicious, and Carver had nothing to hide. He'd come as a friend, and that was that. Keep it simple. Besides, how could he know Jerry would go off like that?

Maybe the three murders he's accused of?

That voice in his head, that nagging voice filled with reality. His conclusion was that Jerry was possessed. By what or whom he wasn't certain, but the sudden change was confirmation that there was someone else living in Jerry's head who wasn't Jerry. He kept replaying the flicker that crossed through Jerry's eyes that brought out the change in Jerry's voice. As if he was talking to a completely different person.

Jerry, who was now lying on a bed in four-point restraints and pumped with so much Thorazine he'll be sleeping until his next trial date. Not that the court system could do too much more to Jerry. He was already serving three life sentences for the first three murders, albeit in the confines of the hospital for the mentally insane. So, add another life sentence and be done with it. The man's never getting out, anyway.

Carver gritted his teeth, gnawing on his toothpick while staring at Cheryl with her shaking hands and startled expression. Her white doctor's coat stained with blood. He was certain that Cheryl had seen some shit go down over the course of her career, but he was also certain she had never seen a murder before. Perhaps none of her patients had executed a bloody murder in the swift manner that Jerry pulled that one off. She was visibly shaken by the ordeal.

"Just came to visit with an old friend. I wanted to check up on him and provide an update on his son."

Cheryl paused while staring at Carver. "You drove all the way from Sleepy Hollow to give an update to a patient about his son when that very same patient is responsible for the murder of his daughter?" She paused again, assessing Carver's response. "You didn't think that might be inappropriate?"

"I did not." Carver shifted in his chair. "I guess I didn't realize the extent of Jerry's... condition."

Now Cheryl looked at him with suspicion. "How is that possible? You were the lead investigator on the case. I've read the reports written in your own hand. It seems to me you knew exactly what the extent of Jerry's *condition* was."

Carver took the toothpick from between his lips. "I've known Jerry for decades. He... before all of this, he never so much as had a parking ticket. Sure, he may have been anxious, but for the most part, he was a good man with a good family. I never truly believed that Jerry operated on his own. There had to..." He cut

240

himself off and had to check himself. He closed his eyes and breathed calmly to ease the lump growing in his throat.

Cheryl was chewing on her bottom lip, assessing Carver when he noticed her demeanor changed, less on guard than it was before. Perhaps witnessing Carver's startled reaction and shocked expression put the woman at ease. Her voice inflection changed too, more empathetic than probing. "Well, in a way, you are correct."

Now Carver perked up. "What'd you mean?"

Cheryl paused before she said, "Jerry suffers from dissociative identity disorder. Otherwise known as multiple personalities."

I hit the nail on the head with that one.

But it still made little sense to Carver. He noticed the doctor was looking at him as if she couldn't read his reaction, waiting for him to respond. All he did was gnaw on his toothpick, thinking.

Not guilty by reason of insanity. Jerry's case was settled quickly after a doctor diagnosed him as clinically insane prior to the trial. Two doctors, actually. One for the defense, and the other for the prosecuting attorney. *And they're the professionals. This is their line of expertise. Who am I to question their judgment, especially since I thought the same myself not more than an hour ago?* Even so, there was a part of him that didn't believe it. And he had questions.

"Let me ask you something, doctor. If you don't mind."

"Of course not. Except if it concerns private information, because I'm not…"

Carver waved her off. "No private information required, just questions about the diagnosis."

Cheryl put her hands up. "In that case, please ask."

Carver took the toothpick from his lips. "When someone has such a diagnosis, wouldn't there be signs or noticeable changes in behavior? And wouldn't that type of diagnosis show up years earlier?"

Cheryl leaned into her desk. "Detective Carver, did you not just witness the change in behavior yourself?"

Carver shook his head. "I'm referring to before today, and before all the murders." He paused to collect his thoughts, then continued. "Understand, I've known Jerry and his family for decades and I've never seen anything like what I just witnessed. It seemed like he was possessed. Like a demon just jumped into his body and took over. Complete change in everything. Even his voice was different."

"Because you were talking to a completely different personality. It's like speaking to two people. You may have even witnessed changes in posture or little ticks that show up out of nowhere. It may look like the same person, but the personality is unique and has all the attributes that come with the new personality."

Carver remembered the flicker that ran through Jerry's eyes. Remembered how he thought he was staring at a different person. He even looked like Marc Saduj.

After receiving no response, Cheryl continued. "Changes in the personality are usually caused by stress. So, may I ask you a question, detective?"

Carver shrugged, dropping the toothpick back between his lips. "Of course."

"Did you discuss anything with Jerry that may have caused him undue stress?"

Carver looked at her all crooked-eyed. "Are you saying I caused this?"

Cheryl shook her head. "No one is to blame for what happened. There are risks associated with working with the criminally insane." Carver noticed how she paused when she looked at her hands. They were still stained with blood, albeit faded across her palms. "But as his doctor, I'd like to know what the cause was."

"Understood. We were discussing his son, John, when the change occurred."

"His son," Cheryl repeated. Her eyes downtrodden, staring at the floor. Staring into space.

Lost, Carver thought.

"I do have a few more questions. If it's, okay?"

Cheryl lifted her head. "Go ahead."

"What are the causes for the diagnosis? And is it really possible for such a diagnosis to go undetected? I mean, if Jerry was living with this for a long time, how did we all not notice?"

She was shaking her head when she answered. "Maybe you didn't notice because it was kept a secret. You'd be surprised how many people live with mental illness and you'd never know it. Most people today... most families keep their secrets behind closed doors. So, it could have gone on for some time and if you weren't living with him on a day-to-day basis and only saw him when his mental state was stable, you wouldn't see the other personalities. But to answer your other question, multiple personalities are typically created under duress."

"Meaning?"

"Meaning, detective, the other personalities are created to protect the host personality from suffering through traumatic experiences. Grief can also trigger such a change."

Carver nodded, silent, thinking.

"You're trying to find the reason behind it all? Don't think too hard, detective. According to the reports, Jerry suffered with multiple personalities since he was a child and considering the amount of medication that was found in his home, it was apparent he stopped taking his medications after his father's passing."

"What?"

The doctor nodded. "I've read through all his medical records. Jerry was first diagnosed when he was ten years old. At that time, he was the victim of satanic worship and pedophilia."

Carver was shaking his head. "I'm... flabbergasted."

"Secrets detective. Every family's got them. That's why Jerry's case was sped through the court system. There was a clear

244

history of his condition, and two forensic psychiatrists confirmed it."

Carver stared wide-eyed, holding his toothpick. His jaw hung loose, thinking.

How the hell could I have missed it? It makes no sense. Since he was ten? Satanic worship and pedophilia? What?

"I see you're having trouble processing." Cheryl stood up from her chair, fingertips pressed against the desk. "Just let it sink in and accept it. For most of Jerry's life he was taking medication for his condition. From what I understand, he was stable until the murders. No one could have predicted he'd go off like that."

Carver said nothing. He had no response, still reeling from the doctor's revelations.

"If that is all, detective, I've got more than a few fires to put out and a mountain of reports to file, not to mention a staff who are all bent out of shape." She paused, shaking her head, eyes downtrodden. "Every agency in New York will be up my ass for the next six months over this incident, and I'm not looking forward to it. I've got to get all my ducks in a row so, if you have no more questions, I'll leave you to it."

Carver looked at her. "I am sorry for what happened."

"We all are detective. It wasn't your fault. I know that may not help at the moment, but it truly wasn't your fault. How could it be? You're not the one who slit his throat." She paused, then said, "The investigating officer wants to speak to you too. Please do so before you leave. He'll need to take your statement."

Carver nodded. "Of course."

"Very well then." She went to leave, opening the door. Carver noticed her hands were still shaking.

"I do have one more question," said Carver when Cheryl stopped cold in her tracks. "If you don't mind?"

"Always the police officer," she said. "Go ahead, detective."

Carver stood, removing the toothpick from his lips. "You said Jerry's condition was caused because he was the victim of satanic worship. Do you happen to know if his family was involved?"

Cheryl's eyes narrowed. "Going on a search, are you?" She shook her head. "Be careful detective, you might not like what you find."

"Even so, the question still stands."

Cheryl smiled smugly, staring at Carver. "Reports revealed that Jerry was kidnapped. No family member was ever implicated in his kidnapping. He was found a month later on the street, naked and clearly abused." She swallowed hard. "That's when the first personality was discovered."

"The first?"

Again, that smug smile. "Correct. From what I've been able to discover, there's an army of personalities in Jerry's mind."

"Army?"

"Yes, an army. He calls them ghost demons and says their purpose is to bring an end to humanity."

Carver paused before whispering, "Initium Novum."

246

"Correct, detective. Jerry's calling card."

106

"Heart Eater. Heart Eater, come and take your soul. Heart Eater. Heart Eater, eating hearts... *all night long.*"

Michael, Chad, and Logan were at it again. John couldn't shake those little fuckers. And that stupid dance Michael did when chanting *all night long* like he was dancing the twist made him want to pound on their faces until he heard the snap of their bones under the weight of his fist.

John walked with urgency, hoping to put as much distance between them as possible. Hoping they'd give up their tirade and leave him alone, but he could hear footsteps behind him.

"Where are you going?" It was Michael. Always Michael, the biggest ass Sleepy Hollow had ever produced. So close, John could feel his breath on the nape of his neck.

John kept walking, squelching his tears. He could see his house, just a few houses away. He needed to get in front of his house, hoping Claude was watching from the window.

"I said, where are you going?" Michael's voice rose when John felt the push at his back, and he tumbled to the ground.

His palms and wrists hit the asphalt before he dropped onto the street. A painful sting ripped through his arms.

"Fucking heart eating family."

John forced himself to his knees when he felt the kick in his ass and his body leapt forward. His face and skull wracked against the street. Felt a cut across his brow. Pain raced up his spine and his ass hurt something awful. A sting above his eye.

"Piece of shit."

Felt a kick in his ribs that ripped the air from his lungs, and he flopped over, his face pinched in pain. The sun washed into his eyes and all he could see was Michael's silhouette hovering over him, about to unleash holy hell when...

Logan pushed Michael away.

"Cut the bullshit," said Logan, glaring at Michael's angry expression.

"Well, aren't you the savior of the day? You gonna let this murdering fucker off easy?"

Logan shook his head and helped John to his feet.

"He didn't do anything to you or anyone else. Leave him alone."

John didn't know what to do. He never expected one of the terrible three to come to his rescue. Something wet cascaded down the side of his face. He touched his brow and saw blood on his fingers.

"Whatever. Looks like you'll be the one with your heart ripped out, Logan. If his father is a murdering pig, what'd you think he'll turn out to be?" Michael stepped forward, glaring at John. "He's probably already planning his first murder."

"If anyone should be worried about turning into their father, it should be you." Logan's voice was sharp and cut like a knife. Michael looked like Logan just twisted a blade in his gut. "Your father ain't no prize either."

It was Chad who intervened. If he hadn't, John was certain Michael and Logan were about to throw hands. Considering the hateful stare in both of their eyes, the tension could only be released through violence or diverted completely.

"Fuck this," said Chad, stepping between his friends. "If he wants to hang out with a heart eater, let him." Now Chad eyeballed Logan. "It's only a matter of time until this little fucker starts cutting up hearts." Chad's attention turned to John. "He'll probably start fucking his mom's corpse, too." He was shaking his head as a smile graced his lips. "Isn't that right, heart eater? You gonna fuck your mom's corpse?"

John didn't know what to say. It seemed like every thought just flew out of his brain and his heart froze. His entire body too. Standing there with his jaw open, dumbfounded or just dumb. He felt dumb.

"Look at his face." Michael stepped forward. "I think you hit the sweet spot, Chad. Fuckers foaming at the mouth." He paused, the moment thick with tension and John was worried that his heart wouldn't start beating again. "You jerking the monkey to mom already?" And he smiled. "You are, aren't you? You sick fuck."

"You're both twisted." Logan gripped John by the elbow. "Come on. Let's just get out of here."

250

John followed, eyeballing Michael and his sinister scowl as he passed. When they were a few feet away from the dynamic duo that stupid fucking song started again.

"Heart Eater. Heart Eater, come and take your soul. Heart Eater. Heart Eater, eating hearts… *all night long.*"

The two of them repeated the song, doing that stupid dance John was sure of it, and one quick glance over his shoulder confirmed it.

"You, okay?" asked Logan. John looked at him and shook his head. "Don't worry about them. Their brains aren't screwed on right."

They stopped in front of John's house and no, Claude was not waiting by the window. The dynamic duo finally gave up their efforts and were walking in the opposite direction.

"You're still bleeding. You should get that cleaned up."

John didn't know what to say. He felt like crying and had to force the lump down his throat. He looked down the street, watching the duo walk away.

"Go ahead," said Logan. "Get inside and clean up. They're not coming back, so don't worry." He looked down the street too and laughed. "Michael will get an ass kicking from his dad if he doesn't go straight home." He turned back at John. "You're fine for now."

John nodded before walking up his driveway. He stopped when he came to the steps to the front door and turned to Logan, still standing in the street.

"Thank you. That took a lot of balls to stand up to Michael."

Logan shrugged. "He's not as tough as he looks. His bark is bigger than his bite."

John paused, thinking now that his brain was operating again. "Would you like to come in? I've got the new *Street Fighter* game, and my grandpa can make sandwiches."

Logan looked up at the house when John wondered if he was afraid he'd get his heart cut out if he agreed to the invitation.

After a moment, Logan shrugged. "Sure, I can go for some food."

107

Wren stood in the dungeon, staring through the crack in the door. Staring into the darkness existing beyond the Xibalba doors. He could hear wind howling quietly in the darkness as if the wind were caught in a funnel and he wondered what would happen should he force his hand through the fissure. Would one of Holer's ghost demons grip his hand and pull him through?

He hoped so.

Now he could hear a low, guttural growl and he felt like he was being watched. Felt eyes on him and he knew, he knew they were there, somewhere deep inside the darkness waiting to be released.

Not too much longer, thought Wren. With every sacrifice, we come closer to opening the portal. In time, my friends. All in time.

He reached his hand to the fissure and could feel the energy pumping from beyond the doors. It felt like electricity rippled through his fingers and he closed his eyes. Closed his eyes and basked in the portal's glory. It felt like pure evil, like venom in his blood, and he couldn't help the smile that graced his lips. He could feel the power that comes from hatred and in his mind's eye he saw mountains of dead bodies in city streets, and fires raging across the planet. The living humans like zombies with their black eyeballs, standing in line and at the whim of the master, all living under the darkness of a forever night.

The living humans are like playthings for the ghost demons, like puppets, living in a forever nightmare, their minds twisted and programmed for torture and hate, eating animals and each other raw.

A literal hell on earth.

And he, Wren the Merciless as he enjoyed referring to himself, standing at the right hand of the master.

An electric shock shot through his chest. Wren jumped back from the door as his vision faded. He saw eyes glaring at him from the darkness. Red beaming eyes filled with hate that quickly disappeared into the thick blackness that consumed the portal.

He closed his eyes, sensing the power in his fingers, in his bones and heart. Wren the Merciless with the power of mind control and manipulation, seen as a God to humanity as he cut into their flesh and feasted on their hearts. Wren knew all too well. Eat the heart and the person is doomed to be your slave in hell.

And he wanted all of humanity to be his slave.

Gritting his teeth, he breathed deeply, then opened his eyes. "In time," he whispered. "So soon in time."

He turned and studied his patrons. Studied the dungeon with its vast expanse, so large and beautiful, beaming with a red-orange glow from the sconces scattered across the walls. Wren was proud of his dungeon. For what murdering wretched fiend in today's society can say they have a dungeon?

The master makes all things new.

He eyeballed the cane leaning against the stone slab. He wanted to touch it. To take it as his own. There was otherworldly power inside the cane that was born from the fires and the power of Xibalba. He reached his hand to it. Let it hover just above the cane. His fingers curled like talons. The energy beaming from the cane felt like sweet ecstasy, drenching his cells with a thundering vibration that rippled through his heart. Wren's eyes rolled behind his eyelids, his mouth opened, his jaw hanging loose as a smile curled in the corner of his mouth.

"So sweet," he whispered, closing his mouth, his teeth chattering as his jaw fluttered. He rolled his neck, feeling waves of pleasure buzzing and fluttering with vibrating pleasure ripple across his flesh like goosebumps filled with ecstasy. "Like a drug."

The master said the cane was powerful, although Wren never knew how powerful and that power intensified with the coming of the alignment as if it knew and was aware of the coming glory. The cane was aligning with the astral plane and the energy of the house, strengthening its power and the magic within it. Wren knew he was on sacred ground. Knew why the house was built in this exact location. According to the master's teaching, there were several like it across the planet. Places where the energy converged, punching a hole in the universe's ether. A portal that allows easy travel to other worlds.

His master had been brought through the astral plane so long ago. Brought by the witches of the time as a God to aid them

255

in their endeavors. For protection of their ways and manners and lives. But they didn't know, couldn't know how wretched the master is. They didn't know their portal led to hell and the protector they conjured was nothing more than pure evil.

The master had attempted to strengthen the astral plane and bring his ghost demons to Sleepy Hollow, but his plan was thwarted, and the master was cursed to live in the cemetery ether. Cursed by witches.

Until now. Evil is always meticulous by nature. As time passes, every curse fades in strength and the master learned to influence the weak from the cemetery ether, biding his time until he could unleash his tirade across humanity. Waiting for his negative to be reborn.

Mr. Saduj.

Wren grinned while thinking of his host. The battered drunken host was nursing his alcohol infused weary mind while he slept. Wren understood how the astral plane was occupied by dense gravity pulling down on the organs and weakening them, hence Marc's already alcohol saturated liver was deteriorating at a faster pace. But the master paid this no mind. All he required was a host body until the astral plane reached its apex and the final ritual concluded. Then the curse will lift, and the master will molt Marc's body like a snake leaves the old all crippled and opaque and left to rot and then the master will rise as flesh and bone. And even more than flesh and bone, his full power will burn through his veins.

Now Wren felt a surge of strength, sensing how twilight beamed across the firmament welcoming dusk into its embrace. Not long now, just an hour and the master will return.

And what beautiful deeds they had in store for their patrons. Wren eyeballed them again, one by one. Their weary eyes filled with fear. Their limbs were weak, and their strength depleted. The astral plane did that too, drained their energy while feasting on their lifeforce, drinking it down like a fine wine.

Their muffled grunts coughed back into their throats from the gags.

He took inventory, recounting their names. Other than the sweet Jennifer and the nefarious Ian, there was Carl, with his dark hair and blue eyes. Then, Hal, Andrew, Victor, Philip, and Liam. Funny how all the men looked on with fearful stares while the women's gaze revealed fury and wrath. Perhaps the memory of sweet Jennifer's skin removal burned their guts with vengeance.

Witches, Wren thought. All human women are either witches or gypsies.

He regarded the women now. Other than Jennifer, he was certain the others were witches. Savannah, Nikita, Sarah, Cheryl, and Heather. They looked weak, but Wren knew differently. Knew they were like tigers getting ready to pounce once their shackles were removed.

Wren grinned at the thought, looking over them, assessing intentions.

"The master will arrive soon." He noticed some of them cringed within their shackles. Some had wide eyes, and some narrowed. "Who among you will run with the hunt? Who shall be chosen for tonight's sacrifice?"

He closed his eyes when a few of his patrons muffled grunts in his direction that he was certain were filled with expletives.

"Ahh," he grunted, holding his right arm behind his back, his left arm draped across his stomach, palm up. "Looks like I already have a volunteer."

The grunting and muffled expletives immediately stopped.

"But which of you it is, I'll keep to myself. I wouldn't want to spoil the surprise."

He then looked at Jennifer, the sweet Jennifer hanging from the rafters crucified and skinned alive. He craned his head to the right, assessing her state of life and living. Her eyes bulged from their sockets, wide and staring. Unmoving. Even the blood had stopped dripping off her toes. Her veins, muscles, tendons, and bones were on full display. He could see her organs beneath the bones.

Wren examined the ground beneath her where all the blood had spilled. Not a drop remained. The stone had consumed all of it. Every drop. Drunk by the astral plane. "My lady, I believe it is time to take your heart." He clucked then ran his tongue across his teeth. "But worry not. I'll be certain to return you to your humble abode when I am finished."

108

Carver had a long drive ahead of him. He thought about a hotel but decided that being locked in some shitty room for the rest of the night would drive him insane. Instead, he opted for the long drive and the time he could use to get his head together.

His endeavor had turned into a big mistake. Mistake wasn't the right word. He fucked up big time, and a man lost his life because of it. If he hadn't paid a visit to Jerry Hardwood the orderly would still be alive, breathing oxygen and making decisions and not on a slab waiting for embalming fluid to be pumped into his veins.

He wanted to put it out of his head. Wanted to forget what happened, but he knew that was impossible. He was a police officer, and he was questioned by several members of law enforcement and the medical director like he was a child in way over his head. Not that the murder could be pinned on him. Jerry was clearly insane, and it wasn't like Carver had caused his insanity. He hoped there were cameras in the hospital because if there were cameras, they'd confirm his story. Jerry may have been acting weird, but who the hell could have predicted what had happened? Using a plastic covering to cut the man's throat.

Carver could see the blood as he steered the car onto the highway's ramp.

DETECTIVE!

Heard Jerry's voice, although it wasn't his voice. Carver shook his head, attempting to toss off the blood image that appeared like a stain on the back of his eyes.

"It was Marc's voice," Carver whispered, accelerating onto the highway.

Multiple personalities. Dissociative Identity Disorder. First diagnosed at the age of ten. The victim of satanic worship and pedophilia.

What the fuck?

He knew Jerry for decades and would never have suspected that Jerry suffered from multiple personalities. All indications were that Jerry was a stable member of society and not harboring multiple people inside his brain.

Stopped taking his medications after his father's passing.

Which made sense to Carver, but still that gut instinct nagged and nipped at his brain. He reached into his shirt pocket and pulled out a toothpick that he popped between his lips. He thought better with the toothpick, pushing down on the accelerator and punching his vehicle into overdrive with the sun just out of reach, gliding down the side of the horizon and draping a blanket of night across the earth.

He had six hours ahead of him. Six hours to think about what had happened. Captain Flannery's going to be pissed when he hears about his visit. He might even force him to take another leave of absence. Once again, he's getting too personal, sticking his nose where it doesn't belong.

At least he received the answer he was looking for.

260

There is a basement in the house.

Marc Saduj flashed in his mind's eye, and Carver nipped at his toothpick. He thought about the basement, remembering Jerry's stare when he mentioned it and how the flicker ran through his pupils when the other personality took over. As if the personality had heard enough and wanted to change direction.

Or needed *to change direction.*

Perhaps Jerry was divulging too much information and the other personality needed to act fast. Maybe he didn't want Carver to know more than he already did. Although one thing was certain, according to Jerry at least.

There's a portal to hell in the basement.

Whatever that means.

109

The green fairies basked in the green glow of the glass. Fire gently fluttered across the surface of the sugar cube, spinning the fae into a dance beneath the yellow glow. The flame quickly extinguished with a gentle blow from Wren's lips.

Marc was lying on his mattress in the fetal position, shivering and burning with cold sweat, watching mesmerized as the fairies twirled and danced within the glass that Wren offered him. Night had fallen over Sleepy Hollow, drenching his room in darkness. The only light came from the glow of the crescent moon that hung outside Marc's window.

"Your sunset mixer," said Wren. "It will aid in the pain."

Marc turned his attention from the glass to Wren, his scar itching and burning into his watery eye. His skin was slick with sweat as he shuddered from the cold wintry breeze that rushed through the window, lying on the mattress against the wall in his art studio. He went to speak-tried to at least-but no words floated off his lips, his mind devoid of thought except for the pain. The pain in his solar plexus that twisted his liver into a mangled, wretched organ. Felt like it was being boiled in a vat of poison, twisting his gut with a drowning noxious boil. He could feel the poison in his veins, and it brought pain to every inch of his body. His lips quivered, dry from dehydration and cracked from the cold lick of winter wind. He could feel the cracked slits across his lips. They stung and burned.

He tried to move, but his liver pinned him to the mattress.

"Let me help you," said Wren. His words were spoken with empathy, but his voice inflection revealed nervousness or frustration over helping Marc sit up.

Marc shuddered in response, closing his weary, wet eyes. Heard Wren place the glass on a table. Marc's eyes opened, staring at the glass sitting on the easel beside his last painting. Saw the heart in the tree trunk. The fae seemed to want entrance to his dark cemetery painting. Wanting to be with the ghosts. Wren slipped his hand beneath Marc and lifted him with gentle ease when Marc groaned from the pain of moving. His legs, shoulders and arms ached from the movement as Wren propped him up against the wall and Marc had to gasp to earn his breath.

Marc watched as Wren's dark silhouette reached for the glass. All Marc could see was the glass. Didn't even see Wren's fingers pinched around it. Just the green glow and the fairies with sinister smiles waiting for entrance into Marc's veins so they could live and breathe and dance and set his blood on fire to twist his mind into rage.

He licked those dry, cracked lips and tasted dried blood on his tongue. He reached for the glass, but his hand shook like a leaf in a hurricane.

"Here, allow me." Wren crouched in front of him, slipping his left hand behind Marc's head, gripping his hair tight to keep his head steady. Marc's lips shuddered when Wren tipped the glass to his lips and that first touch of absinthe awakened his senses and set them on fire. The drink flowed across his tongue with a sting and burn. The burn raced down his throat as if those fairies dragged daggers down his windpipe all the way to his stomach.

Heard the boom and saw the room tremble around Wren. He felt like he was falling, plummeting in fact, and listening. Listening to the high-pitched cackle from his mother's lips, ready to bring torture to his already tortured soul.

110

John was playing a video game when he felt the shift in his bones as if the earth had spiraled out of its orbit and was plummeting into space.

He dropped his controller. His lips quivered. Staring at the video game but not seeing the video game.

"You, okay?"

What he saw was a dungeon. Wall sconces flickering with fire, casting light and shadow across a stone wall.

Descending. Stone steps led down into a dark cauldron. It seemed like those steps went on forever, leading down into hell. The air was musty, damp, and with a hint of iron beneath the fold. The ground was cool like the earth in autumn. He's on the bottom floor now, staring at three doors. Three openings with pointed tops standing tall like guards to the underworld. All he could see was a thick blackness as if the darkness were a shield for the underworld, choosing who was allowed entrance into the dark dominion. The wall sconces with their fire's delight could not penetrate the thick blackness that existed like its own entity beyond the doors.

The entrances called to him with a buzz he could feel in his bones. They came to him then; the entrances stretched towards him like mouths wanting to swallow him whole. To devour every inch of him.

"John?"

He saw people in chains, secured to a wall surrounding a stone slab like some demonic worship. Something dripped across his shoulder with a subtle tap, tap, tap, and he looked up to the rotting corpse crucified and hanging from the rafters as his heart leapt in his chest and he stumbled backward, landing on his ass.

A groan came from over his shoulder. Not from a victim chained to the wall, but from the three doors on the other side of the room. The ones that mirrored the entrances he'd come through.

He could hear burning like the subtle roar of a distant bonfire coming from beyond the doors and could feel the fire's heat on his sweat drenched skin. The victims were all staring at him with wide, fearful and black eyeballs. Their groans and pleas erupted in the center of his brain.

"John, wake up."

Electric sparks raged across the wooden doors. John's breath stuttered in his throat. Felt like he was running a marathon, and his lungs were running on empty. His stare drifted to the middle door that had a crack through the center. There were red eyes beyond the fissure that looked like blood in a river of black. Paralyzed with fear. Frozen, struggling to breathe as gray smoke slithered out of the fissure like a snake had discovered its next meal, moving cold and calculated towards him.

He saw eyes in that smoke as it approached. Red beaming eyes. Thousands of them. The smoke, like a blanket, so large and forever, stretched across him, his body shuddering as the blanket enveloped him in darkness. Silence then, like the quiet from outer space, but he could feel it. Feel the dark blanket as if it held all the power in the universe. Felt it in his bones, his muscles and organs, drenching every cell in his body in darkness, trembling through his heart that raced in his chest.

Heart eater. Heart eater.

My son. Boom!

He's floating now, above Sleepy Hollow. Above the house in the western woods.

He ate her heart.

Ripped it from her chest.

Spiraling down now, into the house with its crooked foundation and rickety walls. The dilapidated floors were covered in dust and dirt. Down into the dungeon.

"John. It's me. Grandpa Claude."

His vampire was standing by a stone slab and the demon, the master, the man in black, stood with his back to John when he looked over his shoulder.

His lips moved, his voice in John's ear. *I'm waiting for you.*

John didn't notice he was screaming. Screaming at the top of his lungs. Didn't realize Grandpa Claude was kneeling in front of him or that Logan had his hands on his knees and was hunched over, attempting to rouse him from his waking nightmare.

"John," said Grandpa Claude. "You're having a night terror."

111

You're a useless sack of pathetic.

Marc stood in the cemetery, nipping at his fingernail. He tore the cuticle from his finger and tasted blood on his lips.

His mother laughed, her voice crackling across the sky like lightning. *Pitiful vermin. Can't do anything right.*

His scar was itching, burning. His eye was on fire. Felt like his eyeball was being squeezed, burning inside his skull. His vision blurred when he pushed on the scar. An effort to satisfy the unrelenting itch.

The cemetery was quiet tonight, as if all the ghosts retreated into their caverns of eternal death. A breeze howled across the gravestones like an icy breath across his skin, turning over frozen leaves that scuttled across sporadic blades of grass brave enough to continue to grow. He raised his head, staring at the tall trees hovering over the cemetery with their crooked bare limbs reaching like spiderwebs across the night sky. The crescent moon hung like an Arabian night in the distance.

He was staring into the western woods. Just staring. Lost, with no thoughts at all. No thoughts but his mother's raging lunacy nipping in his ear.

You were always the sentimental fool. Always useless and pathetic. I knew you'd never amount to anything.

Her voice a rickety cackle, leaping across the cemetery. Marc deposited his finger between his teeth, nipping at his skin, gnawing on it. Tasting the blood on his tongue, he bit deeper.

And where is that nasty whore? She's got you wrapped around her pinkie. What kind of man are you? Just like your father, pathetic and weak. So weak you deserve cruelty. You deserve to be a slave.

Marc's heart stuttered in his chest. He could see Lori now, laughing. Smiling and happy. Her bright, beautiful eyes gleamed in the sunlight.

Typical, isn't it? Another Saduj playing the pawn to a whore.

He wanted to be with her. Wanted to see Lori's smile and those bright beautiful eyes as she looked at him. Wanted to share another moment filled with laughter and smiles and connection.

Look at you. Look all around you. You chose to be here. Chose to relinquish your heart so that she can live. And what did you receive in return?

The cackle again. The rickety cackle off his mother's lips echoed across the cemetery, but Marc kept his focus on Lori. On her smile and her eyes.

A letter tossing you out like yesterday's garbage. His mother's laugh surged across the sky like a crack of thunder. *Such a fool. Such a fool.*

He gnawed on his finger. Nipped at the nail and tore it off, his lips bathed in blood. He drank it down with a thick gulp down his gullet.

And then, silence. Quiet. The cemetery stood like a still-image frozen in time. As if the world had suddenly stopped. His mother's cackle was gone. No wind howling through the trees. No wind in his ear. Just the lonely quiet of the night and the quiver in his chest. Lori's image was gone too, now all he could see was the cemetery.

Marc was well aware of what was happening. The man in black was taking his stance, ready to unleash torture to satisfy his desire by inflicting pain and suffering. The revelation came to Marc after he sought refuge in the blonde woman's crypt. The crypt helped to clear his mind, but that clear head came with a conundrum. He'd become aware that he unleashed the devil into the Hollow. He didn't know how, but the man in black walked the Hollow as flesh and bone. All because of Marc and his need to save his beloved.

He could hear the footsteps now. The master's footsteps as he walked down the stone steps to his dungeon. Marc wondered where his dungeon was. In some far-off version of hell, he was certain.

Marc turned and started walking to the barrier outside the cemetery with a certain hurried anxiety in his step. His heart fluttered in his chest as he grinded his teeth. The cemetery fence was in his line of sight, his scar itching and burning, his eye on fire.

He wanted to dip his head into the barrier. Wanted to feel Lori. Her essence. Her heart. He could feel her calling him and he had a gut instinct that she was coming to the Hollow. Coming to find him, and that was something he could not allow. What if she comes under the thumb of the man in black and his torturous ways? Marc knew the man in black and knew he would relish the moment he had Lori in his grasp. He would do anything to destroy Marc's heart and devour the reason Marc chose the union. It would be his final insult, leaving Marc in a perpetual limbo with the knowledge that his sacrifice was for nothing. She must stay away from the Hollow, every bone in his body knew this was true. The man in black will not be kind to Lori if she returns.

Torture will begin soon, he told himself as he gripped the bars on the fence.

Marc wanted to be far away from the cemetery by then. He dipped his head into the barrier, hoping Lori was there.

112

Lori was dreaming. Dreaming within a state of medication induced delusion. Her dream was a mangled diorama of crunching steel from the accident she and Marc had been in. She saw the demon's eyes in the storm-drenched sky race through the car with a laugh that bellowed across the sky, followed by the screech from the tires across the wet asphalt. Spinning. Crushing steel then tumbling. Tumbling over and over. Exploding glass followed by eternal pain. She saw the street from when the car stopped upside down.

The scene is moving now as if she's floating across it like a phantom hovering within and above. She could see fine details, the notebook with the word Holer written across the cover. Her belongings were littered across the back seat. And then she was outside the car, standing in the street with the rain thundering around her, staring at her own body lying in the street. She'd been jettisoned from the car through the windshield. Lori stared at herself. Her bloodied self. The rain washed that blood towards her now. Crimson water funneled to her feet as the wind howled.

Now the demon was standing over her body. Tall and lanky and dressed in all black. The man in black, as Marc had called him. The demon from his past. The one who made him do bad things.

No Marc, that's just an excuse to find a reprieve from the evil deeds you've done.

He crouched over her bleeding body. He had a red cane cradled in his arms. He reached out to touch her forehead when Lori took a step closer.

"Get your hand off of me," she screamed in a voice filled with rage.

He snapped his head towards her, looking, staring, both hands now wrapped around his cane, but it seemed as if he saw nothing as if she wasn't there. His smile crept across his lips as he craned his head back, closing his eyes to the rain. She could hear sirens in the distance, and she turned to where those sirens were coming from.

"Hurry," she said. "Hurry, please."

She felt something bump against her foot and when she looked down, she saw Marc's notebook on the ground surrounded by a stream of rainwater dyed red with blood. The rain thundered against the street as she bent down and gripped the notebook, cradling it like a baby as she stood up. Stood up and saw the man in black was staring at her, although he no longer looked like the demon. He looked like Marc, but Marc with the same black clothes and the same red cane cradled in his arms.

"Stay away from Sleepy Hollow, Lori."

"Marc?" She shook her head. "What is this? What's happening?"

"Whatever you do, please Lori... please... stay away from Sleepy Hollow." He returned his gaze to the Lori lying in the street.

273

She could see his eyes were wide when he pulled the hidden blade from the cane.

"What're you doing?" She took a step closer.

"I'm no longer in control, Lori." Marc was shaking his head, his eyes closed. Lori took another step towards him. The sirens were getting louder. Her heart hammered in her chest.

She shook her head. "Don't do it. Please don't do it."

He raised the blade over Lori's body; the tip aimed at her heart. "I can't stop him, Lori." His hand was trembling, as if he were fighting the urge to sink the blade into her chest. "He needs your heart, Lori." Marc was gnashing his teeth and now his arm was trembling. His entire body was shaking like a leaf as if that blade weighed a thousand pounds.

Sirens now, over her shoulder. Tires screeched across the pavement.

He's fighting with all his strength.

"Don't," she screamed, sprinting towards him.

"Stay out of Sleepy Hollow, Lori." She dropped the notebook and reached for his arm. "Because this is what he wants me to do."

He dropped the blade down at the moment Lori grabbed his arm. She yanked his arm back and when she locked eyes with him it wasn't Marc any longer. It was the man in black. He grinned as his red demon eyes glinted with satisfaction.

"Thank you," he hollered and with the speed of a cat he was on his feet. On his feet and plunging his fist into her chest.

Lori felt her chest bone crack and splinter. Pain twinged across her spine when he ripped her heart from her chest. He raised the heart to her eyes. It was still beating in his hand when a hollow sensation rippled through her bones. Like torture eternal. A zombie. No emotion. No sensation. Mindless and numb. A feeble existence, wandering the world in limbo for all eternity.

She looked into his eyes and saw it was Marc again. Marc with her heart in his hand and anger mixed with pain plastered across his face.

"See," he said. "I told you..." His voice roared across the heavens. "Stay away from SLEEPY HOLLOW!"

She awakened with a jolt in the hospital bed. Her wrists and ankles were free. Her hand immediately went to her chest as she sat up in bed. Hard to breathe. She had to coach herself to calm down. To take deep breaths to calm her heart. It was thundering in her chest. Sweat dripped across her forehead in a cold cascade.

She saw the demon's eyes in her mind's eye. Lori pursed her lips, then swallowed her breath with a gasp.

"It's okay, Marc... I'm coming."

113

Grandpa Claude wrapped a blanket around John's shoulders. He was shivering, sitting on a chair beside the desk in his room.

"There you go, buddy," said Claude, crouched down in front of John. Staring into John's eyes, he gave a reassuring nod with a quick, tightlipped smile for encouragement. Logan sat on the bed with his hands between his knees.

"Happens sometimes. Your mother used to have them too." Claude stood up. "I'll get you some water. Just try to relax. It's over now."

John glanced at Claude, receiving another nod and reassuring smile. He knew Grandpa was attempting to smooth the situation over as best as he could. Obviously, having a full-blown freak out in front of the only friend John has ever brought home was humiliating and Claude was hoping to save face in front of his new friend.

Not that John gave two shits about what anyone at school thought about him, but he was hoping-praying actually-that Logan wouldn't run down the block and give John's bullies another reason to inflict pain with punishment when he gets off the school bus tomorrow. Although, judging by Logan's facial expression he seemed more concerned than immoral, which settled John's nerves about the situation.

He waited for Grandpa Claude to leave, listening to his footsteps shuffling down the stairs before addressing the elephant in the room.

"Sorry," John said, shifting his arms within the blanket. "You must think I'm some sort of freak."

Logan shook his head. "Not at all. Everyone's got problems, why would you be any different?" He paused to swallow his breath. "My mother died a few years ago so… I get it."

John nodded his head. He didn't know Logan's mother had died. The only thing he knew about him was that his father was a suspected mafia stooge. He'd never heard anything about Logan's mother. John's gaze drifted to the window and a shiver rattled down his spine.

"So," said Logan, snapping John's stare from the window. "What did you see?"

"Huh?"

"In the nightmare… what was it?"

John cocked his head, his brow furrowed. The question was unexpected. He was surprised someone cared.

"You seemed like you were… somewhere else. Like not here."

John waited before he answered. Was it okay to tell? John was certain what he'd seen wasn't a nightmare or even a waking nightmare like Grandpa Claude had said. He saw the man in black. The demon and his vampire minion were watching him as if they knew he was there. As if they commanded him to join them and like gravity he had to go. The pull was too strong to resist.

He pursed his lips before he answered, swallowing his nervous breath down his throat. "The man in black."

Logan did a double take. "The man in black?" He paused. "Who's the man in black? Sounds like something out of a Stephen King novel."

John gestured to the window. "He lives in the house in the western woods. The abandoned house… well, it's not abandoned anymore. There are people living there."

"What? You mean that shitty old house in the woods?"

John nodded.

"And you saw people there? Like… when? How?"

"The other night during the Super Bowl. There was a bonfire on the property, and I used the telescope to see them."

Logan eyeballed the telescope standing in the corner.

"The police went there, and people are living in the house."

Now Logan turned to the window. He stood up and walked over to it where he remained for a long while examining the western woods.

"Do you believe me?" John's voice was soft, defeated, shameful.

"Well, there's only one way to find out." He turned to John and said with a shrug, "Let's go to the house."

114

The master waited by the stone slab, leaning on his cane while gazing at Jennifer's heart simmering in the firepit. Wren eyeballed the cane as he ascended into the dungeon from the steps that led beneath Sleepy Hollow. He was holding the knives the master required for tonight's first torture.

The torture was called lingchi, or, more properly referred to as death by a thousand cuts. The master required blood, pain, and flesh to produce the necessary fear to strengthen the portal. Jennifer had served this purpose well; her torture was necessary to force a plethora of fear and damnation. Energy that aided in the strengthening of the astral plane. But now her fear had given way to death and Jennifer's fear vibration had subsided. Time is ticking and the celestial constellation will not be aligned for very long. There were many tortures to conclude before the full alignment.

Tonight's torture will catapult the master's vengeance and crack open the plane, allowing the ghost demons access to this world. Wren had difficulty containing his excitement.

"My master…the blades are ready." Wren offered the knives to his master who turned on a dime, eyeballing the gold-plated serrated knives in Wren's hands. His stare then drifted to Wren.

A small smile curled across his lips. He took one of the blades and held it as if it were a lost friend finally found. His eyes radiated with delight. "My beautiful Wren, were they where I said?"

Wren bowed. "Yes, master. Exactly where you said they would be. Your ancient minions did well. They should be honored for their loyalty." He paused while gazing at his master. "Are you satisfied?"

The master leaned his cane against the firepit. He held the knife in both hands, devouring it with his eyes. "Indeed." He looked at Wren. "The other I offer to you, Wren. Delight with me tonight as we indulge in the flesh."

Wren couldn't contain his excitement. His face turned stoic as he closed his eyes. "I am honored, my master." When he opened his eyes, the master was eyeballing their victims. "Who will it be tonight, Wren? Which of our lovelies will sit center stage and offer themselves to the ether?"

Wren stretched his arm, pointing to the one named Victor whose eyes widened, staring petrified at Wren's finger pointing in his direction. His eyes darted to his friends as if pleading with them for help. "Our beloved Victor will fulfill our needs."

Victor immediately attempted to free himself, panicked and struggling within his restraints when a guttural grunt erupted from Heather's throat. Her eyes were wide with fear and rage. Wren regarded his master.

"Seems we have more lovers in our presence, Wren." The master's grin was ear to ear. "What to do?"

Wren held his fist by his side, staring at Heather who was shackled next to Ian. Ian's eye was closed, his head leaning against the concrete exposing his severed ear. The sight sent a flutter filled with pleasure down Wren's spine. His stare then drifted to Heather with her dark hair and dark eyes. Now he turned to the master as he gripped his cane. Wren didn't know what to do, although he knew the master had a plan.

"No worries, Wren. I know exactly what to do. Such a nuisance should be quieted so we can complete our tasks in relative harmony." He stepped towards Victor, shackled on the opposite side from Heather. The blade in one hand, the cane in the other, gliding across the floor to Victor. Victor stared at the master while petrified and flailing, pulling on his restraints as if he hadn't attempted to free himself before. More muffled grunts from Heather, but Wren paid her no mind. The master was in charge, and Wren knew Heather's grunts were of no consequence. The master lifted his cane to Victor's eyes. The golden top gleamed in the firelight. Victor ceased moving when Wren noticed the astral plane glowing beyond the fissure. The thick dark purple shade looked like smoke under a purple light.

The master's head craned to the left. "Look here," he told Victor, gesturing to the cane. Victor's lips quivered beneath the gag when he reluctantly obeyed. The master tapped the cane with the blade and not a moment later a thin, forest-green smoke slithered from the golden handle to Victor's nose. The smoke recoiled like a snake, and Victor cringed before the smoke sprang forward, snaking up his nostrils. His eyes rolled to the top of his skull. His head whipped back and forth as if he couldn't breathe, struggling to draw air into his lungs. More grunts from Heather as the others looked on, petrified.

"There you go, my good Victor," said the master. "Take your medicine."

Victor started flailing as if the smoke were eating his brain as he struggled and stretched within his shackles. His eyes were stretched wide open as if he were witnessing some horrific vision in front of him. Victor started screaming and even with the gag his scream reached a fever pitch. Wailing now. Tears falling as if a flood gate had opened. The master turned to Wren. "You may release him now." His eyes delighted when he said, "You will have no concern with Victor. He will come willingly." He turned to Heather. "As will you when the time is right."

Heather was muffling expletives through her gag. As were the others. A few at least, Wren noticed a handful of his victims looked on in a state of perpetual fear surfacing into a numbed stare. As if they accepted their fate, knowing their death was imminent.

Victor's wails and hollers subsided. He ceased flailing, his eyes were wide and lost as if caught inside a waking nightmare. Not here. Somewhere. Somewhere far away from the dungeon, locked in a prison of his own mind.

"As you wish," said Wren with a bow. The master returned to the eternal fire while Wren approached Victor. He glanced at the fissure where the purple glow beamed into the dungeon. He could feel the energy, thick like gravity, pulling down on his bones and turning his cells into a frenzy of packed atoms. It felt like ecstasy, fluttering his flesh into an orgasmic overdrive. Wren gritted his teeth with a clenched, quivering jaw. His eyes rolled to the back of his skull.

Wren opened his eyes to Victor who seemed more like a feeble child than a budding adult. His eyes were lost and filled with tears. Wren wrapped his hands around the back of Victor's head, unlatching the gag then dropped it by his feet. Victor gasped, his jaw hanging open. Now Wren used his key to unlock the ankle restraints.

"Mommm."

The word whined off Victor's lips as Wren came eye to eye with him, twisting the key in Victor's neck clasp, watching his tears fall in a constant stream across his cheeks. His jaw quivered. His face pinched in sadness and pain. Now the wrist restraints were removed and Victor's knees buckled. He slid across the wall to the ground where he hugged his knees, staring off into some dark distance only existing within his own mind.

"The cane's power strengthens along with the portal," said the master. "The power of Xibalba exists inside the cane."

Wren lifted Victor to his feet. No resistance. No running or attempting to escape. Like a child, he came willingly.

"The same goes for me," the master continued as Wren escorted Victor to the slab and Heather's muffled expletives raged through her gag. "Can you feel it, Wren? How the portal grows stronger with every sacrifice?"

"Yes, my master. It feels like ecstasy."

Victor was trembling. Subtle whines and whimpers grumbled in his throat.

"Here," said Wren. "Lay down." And he did just that, sitting on the slab then laying down, taking the necessary position as if he were a participant in his own torture. Tears cascaded across his temples, his skin flushed and beaded with sweat as Wren tied his wrists to the slab with no resistance from Victor. It was like strapping in a patient lost to the echoes of catatonia. Wren then tied Victor's ankles in place.

The power from the cane is immense. What a beautiful dream that cane is!

Now the master stepped towards Victor, holding the cane above his eyes. "Time to wake up, my dear Victor. We wouldn't want you to miss all our fun." He tapped the cane with the blade. Two taps, then a pause followed by three more taps when purple smoke drifted from the cane to Victor's nostrils slithering into his nose as the green had done before. Victor's eyes snapped open. His eyes darted around the room, frantic and urgent. "Do you have your blade?" asked the master.

Wren reached into his pocket then revealed the blade to his master.

"Very well, then. Let us begin." He turned to Victor, leaning his cane against the stone then gazed into Wren's eyes. "Blood,

Wren. Every slice reveals it to the stone. Let us indulge until Victor's blood is no more. With every appendage severed, drop it into the fire. Let it eat. As the fire rages and the stone drinks, the portal strengthens." Wren turned to the doors. He could hear a hum beyond the doors as if the portal was calling him, groaning for blood and flesh and fear. A smile crept across Wren's lips.

"As you wish."

"Just let me go." Wren looked at Victor, whose steady stare was locked in on the master. "Please, just let me go."

The master snatched Victor's mouth, squeezing his jaw and squelching Victor's voice. "Start with the legs," the master instructed. He looked at Wren. "Cut the flesh and muscle. Let the blood escape this mortal coil." Wren noticed the fire intensified as if ready to be fed, the flames licking the air with a roar.

Wren bowed then stepped to the feet. He gripped Victor's pinkie toe, then regarded his master. The master was staring into Victor's eyes, holding his jaw in a vise grip with his lips pursed in a kiss. "One last kiss, Victor. I'm sure Heather wishes it was for her." He cut into Victor's lips as a scream erupted in his throat, sawing his lips off as blood spouted from his mouth. The master dropped the lips into the waiting fire. Victor's screams raged across the dungeon as blood flowed from his mouth as if a dam had been opened. The master then dragged the blade across Victor's forehead, carving a cavern across his skin. Victor could do nothing more than scream. The master sliced across his cheek then carved off his ear.

Wren grinned, staring at his master as he slashed the other side of Victor's face. Blood raced to the stone slab then dripped off the edge onto the floor where it was swallowed by the ground. Victor's screams were eternal. He thrashed and stretched across the stone, his mouth opened wide with his tongue wriggling across his teeth.

Wren returned his attention to Victor's feet. He gripped his shaking leg, pushing the pants to his knee before carving a chunk of meat from his calf as blood surged across Wren's hand, dripping to the stone. He tossed the flesh into the fire then turned to Ian, his beloved, noticing he was awake. His one eye fixed on the carnage. Wren dug in again, eyeballing Ian while slicing across the tendons on Victor's ankle when his foot flopped sideways at an unnatural angle and the master dragged his blade from Victor's temple across his skull.

The master's hand came away with a lock of Victor's hair with a piece of his bloodied skull attached to it. He tossed it into the fire. The blood loss was substantial, raining across the slab then dripping in sheets to the floor where it hissed and burned like hot smoldering oil only to be absorbed directly after. The portal glowed beyond the fissure. Gnashing his teeth, Wren cut again. Cut off Victor's toes as the master severed a few fingers. All deposited into the raging fire and with every cut Victor's agony increased in severity.

The master licked his fingers before he tore away Victor's shirt, revealing his torso. He then dragged the blade across Victor's nipples as Wren sliced across the flesh above his knee. Wren cut through Victor's pants, removing the garment then followed with his shorts. He tossed the clothes to the floor then proceeded to carve into the pale flesh. Quick strokes created lacerations in the skin dripping with blood. Wren regarded how the gashes reflected the fissure in the door.

All the while, Wren kept his eyes on Ian. There was something special about that boy. He couldn't wait to discover what the master had in store for him.

115

The torture was ongoing and relentless. Marc returned to the ether from the barrier, back to the cemetery with its cold and groaning wind rippling across tombstones between foreboding trees and across sparse grass and frozen mud. His eyes rolled beneath lazy eyelids. He dropped onto his ass with a thud, weak. Marc wrapped his trembling arms around his torso, his breath stuttering across his lips as he looked at the stars and the crescent moon. Wispy clouds moved across them like a ghostly veil necessary to hide humanity's evil deeds. Screams and huffing fearful breaths raged across the firmament.

If he closed his eyes now, he would see. He would bear witness to the torture the man in black was inflicting at this very moment like a waking nightmare he couldn't control or wake up from.

"It's the union," Marc whispered. "He wants me to see what he does. To know how wretched he can be... To know that it's because of me." But there was one place he knew he could go that would drive away the sounds of torture. Silence the screams and wails. The crypt where the blonde woman had gone. It was the only place where he found any type of refuge. The only place he felt safe. He hadn't seen her since their first meeting, but he could feel her essence inside the crypt. The essence carried a youthful innocence.

A peaceful nostalgia that existed even when the ghosts called his name, goading him and delivering ridicule.

A shriek exploded across the stars and Marc's heart sank, knowing the pain was his. It was his agreement that brought the man in black to the Hollow and now he indulged his torturous ways and locked Marc in the cemetery to keep him blind to his ravings. Marc understood that if he hadn't acted in Lori's favor none of this would be happening and Lori would be the one in the cemetery, gone to the ether. Gone from him.

Like she is now.

Marc shook his head slowly back and forth, tightening his fist as another screech echoed across the cemetery. He looked up and noticed all the ghosts were gone. Another scream screeched across the cemetery. Marc could feel the victim's pain in his gut. In his bones, infecting his cells with venom. He felt tainted and noxious, his blood boiling, depleting his already depleted strength. The blonde woman had that right, too. The barrier tapped his strength. His limbs felt like anvils that weighed a thousand pounds. He needed to get into her crypt. To regenerate his strength and lock away the screams and torture. Marc ran his palms across his face then pushed himself to his feet where he stumbled, his hand on the fence to steady himself. His head was spinning, dizzy and lightheaded when over his shoulder he heard a choked back squeal and his heart leapt in his chest as he turned towards the sound.

It wasn't from the torture raging across the firmament. The squeal had come from the cemetery. Marc craned his weary head, staring in the direction of the squeal. Now he could hear a whining groan and crying. He'd heard so many screams and cries and wails during his time in the cemetery, but this was different. Marc couldn't put a finger on why, but it seemed more personal than the other screams and horrors.

Now the talking turned into rapid fire with a whine behind the voice that kept repeating, "It won't stop bleeding. Won't stop. Won't stop bleeding. It won't stop bleeding. Won't stop. Won't stop. Won't stop. Please stop bleeding."

He took a step forward towards the voice.

"Please help me... God, please help me. *It won't stop bleeding.*"

Marc came to a crypt. The voice was on the opposite side. He put his hand on the crypt to steady his feet.

"Stop, please. Just stop. Please stop bleeding."

He rounded the crypt then peeked around the corner to the ghost standing between an oak tree and the crypt. His eyes immediately widened. She had no skin or hair. Her body was slick with blood and veins and organs, and her eyes bulged from her skull, blue and petrified.

"It won't stop bleeding," she whined. Her hands wiped across every inch of her bleeding body.

Marc's eyes narrowed. She seemed different from the other ghosts, more confused and petrified, and he knew he'd seen her before. So familiar, although he couldn't place her. Couldn't put a finger on who she was but he knew, knew he'd seen her before. Her

290

breath rose and then fell in thick heavy huffs between whines and pleas for the bleeding to stop.

She was pacing now, her arms wrapped around her torso as if to provide comfort for her confusion. As if she could keep all her organs in place if she kept moving. "It won't stop bleeding." Blood kept dripping off her bones. Even as she wiped the blood away a second later there was more as if an endless stream of blood existed in her veins. He could see it flowing across her bones and organs as if the blood was trapped beneath some invisible veneer. The blood dripped off her elbows, knees, and hands as she wiped relentlessly across her arms, slicking the blood off her bones. "It hurts so much. So much pain. So much." She halted, as if seized by fear, then slowly crept her head around to Marc.

They locked eyes and stood, staring at each other. Her stare filled with confusion. Pain pinched across her bloodied face. Marc noticed she was staring at him as if attempting to recollect who Marc was.

"*You did this to me!*" Her voice trembled with a whine across her lips as she pointed her bloody bony finger in his direction. "It was you!" she screamed as Marc shook his head.

"Not me. I would never hurt you. I wouldn't do anything like that."

She gripped her skull as a shriek raged from her throat. "You did this to me…"

In the blink of an eye she had his throat in her hand. She seemed to move with the wind, like a flicker where one second she was standing away from him and the next, she was squeezing his throat with such immense strength he was convinced his windpipe was about to be crushed into oblivion. His eyes rolled to the back of his skull, his mouth gaped open, attempting to bring air into his lungs. His legs shook as she lifted him off his feet.

Her voice arrived like a child's whine. "You did this to me!"

Marc strained for air, believing the bones in his face were about to pop, his eyes bulging from their sockets. Her head was slick with blood that dripped across her nonexistent lips to her chin. He could see the veins pulsing, swelling across her face as what looked like smoke slithered across her eyes. Her fingers nipped into his throat before she tossed him across the cemetery. He crashed through a crypt door tumbling with a thud across the ground.

Marc grasped his throat, gasping for air. He saw her then, through the door as she gripped her skull in both hands and shrieked, "You did this to me." Her body flickered like a projection with every shriek born from her throat. She snapped her head in his direction, her eyes now black to the core. "It won't stop bleeding." Her feet pounded across the cemetery towards him and Marc backed up, anticipating she would throw herself on top of him when the door slammed shut.

She body-slammed into the door with such brute force Marc thought the door was going to rip open. The entire crypt shook around him as violet-colored energy rippled through it, reverberating back to him as though he were in an echo chamber. He could see the energetic ripples wash across the inside of the dark crypt. Her voice boomed through the crypt with the same reverberation. "It won't stop bleeding. It won't. It won't stop." She slammed into the crypt and again that same reverberation rippled through it. Marc climbed to his feet, listening as she slid across the door to the ground. "Please make it stop. Please."

Marc closed his eyes while shaking his head. "What have I done?" he groaned. His next thought was interrupted by a shriek that cut through the crypt like a knife followed by the all too familiar rickety cackle.

116

It was as if Victor's screams were stained into the stone, forever entombed in the dungeon. Wren looked at the bloodied mess they made of him. So many cuts across his flesh, so many severed extremities. Removed bones, cut cartilage, lumps of muscle, and chunks of meat were simmering in the eternal fire. Victor's entire body had slices and gashes across the flesh. So many, there was hardly any skin left. Wren could sense the fear in the dungeon. Like lingering smoke that imprinted on the molecules circulating in the air.

The metallic scent of blood burrowed into his nostrils. He loved it more than he could fathom. It turned his skin into flutters filled with ecstasy as he gnashed his teeth and watched his master approach the strengthening portal. His hands were red and slick with blood. He stretched his hand to the middle door; his palm pressed against the wood.

Painful groans and the rickety clucking of tongues erupted from beyond the doors. The master's head tilted to the right, staring, fixed on the fissure.

"It drenches my cells with hate." The master's voice was guttural. Wren was certain he was gnashing his teeth, his jaw tight. "The portal fills my heart with strength. My bones with density."

He turned abruptly, and Wren noticed that their victims all jumped. All except Ian and Heather. The master stepped towards Victor, raised his knife then cut into Victor's chest, sawing through the bone to his solar plexus. How easy it was for the master to cut through the bone. The blades were eternally hot; the steel forged from the fires of Xibalba. He dropped the blade on the slab then separated the chest bone before dipping his hands into the open cavity and pulling out Victor's heart. The master then locked eyes with Wren.

"So precious is the human heart. Where all emotion is kept. The essence of the owner is trapped within. Let us see just how pure dear Victor's heart has been." He dropped the heart into the fire with an immediate burst of flames. The flames turned a bold red as it devoured the heart when something glimpsed in the corner of Wren's eye. There were red eyes staring into the dungeon from beyond the fissure. Wren could see them over the master's shoulder.

Wren's heart stopped. His bones contracted. He could feel no breath in his lungs and no beat of his heart, staring at those eyes that were surrounded by a pale blue fog. Now he heard a guttural groan erupt from beyond the fissure when the fog slithered through the crack to his master's shoulders and the dungeon rumbled as if hit by an earthquake. As if some giant stomped across the earth in a rush to victory. Wren's stare then fell on the master.

"Oh," he said. "That would be Baphomet." His stare carried a certain vile glint before they closed as three fog plumes slithered around him, coiling like a snake. "My ghost demons... Baphomet has provided a reprieve. We have done well. Soon, all of you will have a place in the Hollow."

Now more quakes and rattling and rumbling. Wren's stare darted to the fissure where the blue fog beyond it strengthened with an intensity he could feel in his bones. The red eyes drifted up above the door and the house shook as if whatever creature those eyes belonged to trampled across the roof. Another quake and Wren had to steady himself against the stone slab to keep from falling over.

"They bring strength to my bones. Youth to my cells. Invigorating and awakening my senses."

Now Wren noticed the fire weakened. The red color dissipated within the flames. He snapped his attention to his master when he heard a vile screech that sounded like a call from a bat that curdled the blood in his veins. It was the fog that screeched. The fog that morphed into the shape of a jaw that gaped open, revealing jagged and long teeth with small rounded red eyes glinting with hellfire before dissipating into nothingness.

And then, quiet. Silence, except for the crackling flames. The master, with gritted teeth, looked over the dungeon then turned to the fire.

"It seems Victor's heart wasn't as pure as we expected." And he grinned. Grinned when he turned to Wren. Then to Heather. The defeated and depleted Heather. He then turned back to Wren. "Bring me the iron maiden." He gripped his cane and pointed it at Wren. "Let's give the portal some real torture."

117

Carver sat in his parked car with the windows down. The drive had been long, but he made it in under five and a half hours. His first thought was to go home and get some much-needed rest, but he couldn't do that. Not with all the thoughts spinning through his brain at high speed. So, he beelined to the house in the western woods the moment he got off the highway. Parked in the woods where he was now, gnawing on his toothpick with his binoculars on his lap.

The woods were dark and quiet. He thought about taking the trek to the house but knew that wouldn't be a good idea. He already had a lot of questions to answer for, and he was certain Captain Flannery was going to call him into his office in the morning.

Guess I'll stay away from the precinct.

And he laughed. Laughed because there was nothing else to do other than cry. Nonetheless, getting caught trespassing on private property was not the smartest move he could make.

He gripped his binoculars and brought them to his eyes.

Surveillance, on the other hand, is a cop's best friend.

The house was dark, not a light was on. It looked like a stain on the night with its blue hue cast from the crescent moon. A thin fog lifted off the ground as if ghosts had invaded the clearing around the home. No movement. No sounds erupting from within the home. No one trolling the ground and no bonfire raging on the property. Just an icy breeze that nipped the nape of his neck. Then again, he was a bit too far to hear anything other than an all-out blood-curdling scream.

He wanted to enter the house. He needed to see this basement for himself.

The portal to hell.

He laughed at himself, removing the binoculars. Laughed at the notion. Laughed, because somewhere deep in his bones and married to his instincts he knew this statement was true. Although, the relativity of it was in question. As in, not an actual portal, but a hidden room where evil deeds took place.

Yeah, that could be described as a portal to hell.

Carver knew that such portals did not exist and could never exist. It went against the laws of physics. And if it were true, then why is the portal not open? Why are there no devils or demons walking around the planet in what he would refer to as a literal hell on earth?

Because there's no portal to hell!

He gnashed on his toothpick and squeezed the binoculars. Turned to the woods outside his window, shaking his head and thinking. Thinking about his time as a police officer and all the criminals with their evil deeds.

Maybe they're already here. Maybe they've always been here. In the shadows, manipulating our minds and forcing our hands into evil deeds.

The house irritated him. It nagged at his instincts. Owned by Marc Saduj after the house sat in probate court for close to eighty years.

Someone wanted the house to remain unoccupied. Someone from long ago when Sleepy Hollow was in its infancy as a budding riverside town. The house boarded up and left unattended to keep everyone out. Or to keep someone in. He shook his head and took the toothpick from his lips.

"Now you're just being paranoid."

One thing was certain, he'll be spending his day in the library tomorrow looking through old books, scanning newspaper articles on microfiche and reading up on Sleepy Hollow's history. The house is a part of Sleepy Hollow's past, and he was damn certain he'll find it in the archives.

But for now, it was time to sleep. His bones seemed like they weighed a thousand pounds. His eyes were salty, dry, burning and tired. Carver dropped the binoculars on the passenger seat then popped his toothpick between his lips before turning the key in the ignition. His headlights beamed into the woods, illuminating trees with bare branches, brush and…

The ghost of Sheila Hardwood.

She pointed to the house then disappeared the moment Carver stepped out of his car.

118

"Come, Heather. Let us show you your worth."

The master unstrapped Heather's gag. His cane leaned against the slab. Wren watched him while wheeling the iron maiden into the room. Wren was certain the master was mesmerizing the fair Heather. He thought she would be screaming or thrashing or tossing expletives across the room. Instead, there was nothing. At first, Wren wondered if she had given up, accepting her fate and welcoming death, but after closer observation he was certain the master had mesmerized the young lady. She studied the master with a blank, unknowing stare as he used the key to unlock her restraints.

If she knew what she was about to endure, Wren was certain she'd be putting up a fight.

There was silence in the dungeon as the master unlocked the rest of Heather's shackles. The moment was thick with tension as the other patrons looked on. He noticed two were shaking their heads as if to warn Heather, attempting to snap her out of the trance that enthralled her. The fire's flames licked the air with a dull crackling, feasting on the skin and hearts while emitting a foul stench of cooking human flesh that mixed with the rotting corpse crucified above him and the stank rifling off the cut open body of dear good Victor. The fragrance was sweet, salivating Wren's tongue.

"Come, Heather," said the master. He offered his hand, and Heather took it as she stepped away from the restraints. "Let us be your escort into oblivion."

Heather's stare snapped to the stone slab; a sad look filled with confusion rifled across her face. Wren could see the internal struggle. Saw it in Heather's eyes. As if a part of her knew she was in trouble, attempting to run but with no means to do so. The master was in control of her movements. Her eyes flitted from one friend to the other. Petrified. Confused. Unable to take control. To take commands from her own mind.

The master held her hand. They looked like a macabre couple walking into prom with hell on their heels.

"Open the iron maiden, Wren." The master turned to Wren. "Our good Heather wishes to take refuge within its embrace."

And he laughed. That guttural laugh rippled up his windpipe as Heather's throat bobbed up and down as if she had taken a breath she had to force down her throat. There was a sense of urgency in her stare. Her expression was priceless.

Wren turned to the iron maiden-an upright iron casket with iron spikes on the inside, both on the door and within the casket. He felt over the latch on the side and flipped it open when his hand brushed across the wheel that either he or the master would all too willingly indulge with a twist and turn. The wheel brought the inside of the door and the back of the casket together, sending the iron spikes into the flesh of the person locked inside. Wren pulled the heavy door open, the bottom scraping across the floor.

"We shall cleanse your sins with blood," said the master with a conniving laugh as they walked around the slab. Wren noticed Heather's eyes darted to the mutilated Victor, then back to the iron maiden where Wren waited.

He enjoyed Heather's petrified stare, basking in the glory of the fear rippling across her skin. He could see that every thought she had was to run, confused and terrified that her body refused to follow her commands as the master had her step into the maiden, turning her around. Her jaw and lips were quivering. Her tears flowed endlessly.

"Any last words, Heather?" The master waited, craning his head, knowing Heather could not speak. "I guess not." And Wren laughed along with his master, who forced Heather to step back into the iron maiden. Her entire body was trembling as he closed the casket, locking her inside. The master could see her eyes through the small opening in the door. "Take the reins, Wren, and turn the wheel." The master stepped back from the maiden to gaze into Heather's terrified eyes. "I release you," said the master and without a moment's pause Heather's huffing cries could be heard. She'll find her voice again soon, but for now he could hear the whines vibrating in her throat.

Wren gripped the thick wooden handle on the wheel and turned. Heard the creaking wheels turning on the inside, the rusted cogs biting into each other with an iron crunch. He turned feverishly, the wheel becoming thick with tension. He gripped the handle even tighter then squeezed the wheel around another turn. He was certain the rusty cogs were giving him trouble but then Heather squealed and that squeal provided incentive to keep turning.

Slowly. That's how he wanted Heather to die. The blades inching into her a little at a time. The master was over his shoulder standing in front of the maiden, staring through the small opening to delight in Heather's tear-filled and fearful eyes.

Heather's voice was whiny and filled with sobs. Her screams came in fits in-between pleas for the Almighty to come and save her.

"Such sweet death," said the master when Heather belted a high-pitched squeal. Wren grinned just thinking about it. One of those spikes just inched into her skin. "What light will your heart bring, dear Heather? Will you be the one? The one to break open the cosmic highway between hell and earth?"

Wren used both hands now, turning the wheel when he felt resistance immediately followed by Heather's droning scream. He could feel the vibration in his hands when he turned the wheel over. The spikes inching into her skin and bones as he gnashed his teeth, reveling in the moment of death and blood and torture while turning that wheel over and over and over again.

Now blood started dripping through the crevice in the maiden's bottom. Another turn of the wheel and Heather's scream reached a crescendo between crying tears and guffaws filled with a

303

plea for mercy. Wren pictured her tongue jutting and wriggling inside that scream. He wished he could see her eyes, but that right belonged to the master.

He could feel the iron spikes penetrating her flesh as the blood flooded from the crevice on the bottom of the maiden spilling onto the stone where it was absorbed as if swallowed by hell. Gurgling from the back of Heather's throat. A blood-filled garble with a stiff scream raging beneath it.

And the wheel then stopped, catching resistance, but Wren knew there was more to turn. He pushed on the handle, forcing it over with all his power and might. Wren howled and turned that wheel to the sound of a final wet crunch that silenced Heather's screams and garbles. Blood flowed across the floor like a dark river. He turned to the master when the dark purple hue intensified. The chamber doors buckled then stretched, the wood twisting, grinding. The light radiated through the fissure, coating the dungeon in purple. Wren's heart twitched when the door on the right buckled and a crack split through the wood, releasing noxious fumes of sulfur along with three blue fog-funnels that raced into the dungeon. Now there were two doors with the same fissure split down the center.

"Oh, my Baphomet." Wren snapped his head to his master as the blue fog slithered around him. The three plumes spiraled around the master, his arms outstretched as if welcoming them to his embrace. It looked like a whirlwind circling him, his hair whipping in the wind. "Feel it, Wren." He closed his eyes, his head craned back, basking in the glory of the ghost demons. "The power of Xibalba is in my hands. It's been so long. So, so long."

The room glowed with that dark purple hue. Wren looked up, looked all around. His patrons looked on with wide, fearful eyes and when he looked down, he saw that Heather's blood had been absorbed. Not a spot remained.

"Come, my ghost demons," said the master, holding the cane in both hands. "Let us begin our next phase." He twisted the golden round handle, and the ghost demons spiraled into the cane with the force of a hurricane wind. The master held the cane tight as the ghost demons funneled inside it, the whipping wind dying at the same moment they entered. And then all was quiet. All except the huffing breath from the master as the purple hue dissipated with a wavering glow.

The master pursed his lips then swallowed with a gasp. The room was quiet, calm and quiet when Wren heard a rickety growl erupt from beyond the doors. The master turned on a dime. Turned to the blood-red eyes beaming through the fissures. He approached slowly as the eyes narrowed. The ragged breathing from beyond the doors was guttural, vibrating the walls.

"My Baphomet," said the master. "Thank you for your mercy. Soon, so very soon we shall be together again. Time quickens our union." The eyes bobbed up and down as if in unison with a huffing breath filled with anticipation. "The girl will be here in time. It is... inevitable. For now... enjoy feeding on the souls I sacrifice in your honor."

119

Marc stepped further into the crypt. He could see a subtle blue hue in the distance standing like a beacon in the darkness.

The skinless, bloodied ghost continued her tirade. She must be sitting against the door outside the crypt because he kept hearing her rock the back of her skull against it, the sound echoing with a reverberation inside the crypt. The same that happened to her desperate pleas. *It won't stop bleeding. Won't stop. Please stop bleeding.* Although her voice faded the further he traveled.

After he heard the cackling shriek erupt inside the crypt, the blue hue appeared. It started small, like a spark from a lighter that glinted in the corner of his eye but instead of vanishing the blue strengthened. It seemed to call him to it. The blue fluttered in the subtle wind drifting inside the crypt when he noticed edges around him. Understanding he was inside a crypt that was no larger than five feet wide and high and eight feet deep, Marc calculated he'd come to the edge of the crypt. He wished to not venture any further.

He stood at the precipice, staring into the dark recesses surrounding the hue. He knew he'd been here before. This is where the dark-haired witch lived. Her and her horde of devils.

"You did this to me!" The skinless one's voice rattled inside the crypt followed by a loud bang reverberating across the darkness in violet waves around him. Marc looked back, listening.

She was crying now, thick heavy sobs filled with confusion. Marc swallowed his breath, turning back to the blue hue flickering like candlelight in the wind when he looked down and realized he had stepped across the crypt's threshold. He froze when the cold wintry air raced across his skin and something gleamed in the distance, beyond the blue hue. Marc squinted to see what had caught his attention, staring past the hue and there, so far away, he could see a forest. Tall trees the size of redwoods stood like soldiers guarding the path. A path that cut straight through the trees. Marc scanned across it, following the path to the end where it dropped off the face of the earth. Staring at it saturated his cells in hurt. He noticed the pain in his chest, in his heart, as if someone had ripped it from his chest leaving a hollow sensation that funneled suffering to his brain.

He could feel his heartbeat and every thick beat reverberated with anguish, as if someone were squeezing the suffering from his heart into his bones.

Now he could hear murmurs, like incoherent chanting. It was difficult to remove his stare from the woods, but despite the pain it caused Marc's gaze drifted back to the blue hue. Pale figures blurred around the hue. They looked like specters inside fog funnels racing around the light. It seemed as if they were dancing around it. Dancing and praising the blue. There were so many of them. At first there were just a few but with every passing second the numbers grew substantially. Marc swallowed the lump in his throat before turning to walk back to the crypt door.

"Are you afraid of the light?"

The voice came from behind him and Marc snapped around to it, startled. His heart hammered in his chest. In the darkness at the edge of the crypt, he could see a silhouette immersed in the thick black pitch. Whoever it was, moved into the light of the hue where only the eyes were revealed. Blue-green eyes and as she stepped further into the light, Marc recognized her from before. The dark-haired woman who tried to murder him when he first arrived in the cemetery walked into the light. Her eyes, staring, unmoving, carried depths that Marc was certain were born a millennium ago.

Marc had no response. Fear tore his voice from his throat. She offered her hand.

"Come," she said, turning and looking over her shoulder before returning her stare to Marc. "I'll show you."

Marc looked at her offered hand, his eyes rising to meet her devilish stare that burrowed into his soul. He shook his head and took a step back. "No, thank you." He took another step back and noticed how she smiled. "I-I don't want to."

She craned her head, staring inquisitively. "Why so afraid? They are all your people. They mean you no harm." Marc looked over her shoulder at the pale figures that seemed to float across the woods as if they belonged to the fog. "We welcome you with open arms, Mr. Saduj."

Marc cocked his head back. "How do you know my name?"

To which the woman grinned. "I've always known your name, Marc."

Marc's stare narrowed, attempting to recollect who she was. For the life of him, he couldn't remember ever having known this woman.

"We've waited a long time for you. We've always known you." She took a step closer. "We've always known you because *you* have always been with us."

Another shriek from the skinless one outside the crypt and Marc snapped around to it when the witch's hands crept over his eyes and everything turned black.

Her voice followed him into darkness.

"Let me show you."

120

Carver had gone home. He sat in the dark at his kitchen table with a stiff scotch in front of him, listening to the wind howling outside.

After he got out of the car, Sheila's ghost vanished. He had thought about walking to the house but knew better. He required proof, a reason for him to be on the property.

Conflicted, confused and spiraling into oblivion, he sat and thought, staring at his drink but not drinking, lost and defeated.

DETECTIVE!

A river of blood poured from the orderly's throat. Jerry's stare burned into his memory. His conniving stare filled with venom.

Initium Novum.

Humanity's end as a new beginning.

Jerry's calling card written in blood on the wall outside The Sleepy Hollow Tavern. The heart missing from his daughter's body. *What did he do with the heart?*

I need hearts for the master.

What fucking master?

So many thoughts rolled across his brain, but he couldn't latch onto a single one. He needed to get into the house, and it was becoming apparent that despite police protocol and proper procedure he'll need to go no matter what his consequence was.

People are being murdered in that house. Not that he could prove it, but in his gut, he knew it was true.

He needed something. Something more than two strange characters living in an abandoned house. But what can he do?

Find it, he thought. Find something to give you access to the house again. *Find the fucking basement.*

There's a portal to hell in the basement.

He gripped his drink. "Yeah... I heard you." He took a sip, just a touch to burn his lips then gulped the rest down before spinning that glass across the table where it jettisoned to the floor, shattering into pieces.

What should I do?

121

Wren unlatched the lock on the maiden then gripped the handle on the door and pulled with all his might, feeling how those spikes tore out of Heather's body as the door opened with a creak. He stood and stared at Heather. The spikes in her back held her upright. He could see the tips of those spikes poking through her body. Two additional gaping holes from the spikes on the door were prominent across her torso. More holes in her stomach, thighs and legs and one that inched through her neck and jaw. Blood saturated her clothes, stained her lips and chin. Her neck was wet with blood. Her eyes were closed, her mouth hung open in a forever scream with her tongue draped across her bottom lip. He'll need to haul her off the spikes to get the body out. He cracked his knuckles and stepped in.

Her smell was still sweet, although fading fast. Wren could already taste a hint of decay on his tongue as he gripped Heather's shoulders and pulled her towards him. Her back yanked off the spikes with a wet slosh, and she fell into Wren's arms. He dragged her out.

"Place her on the slab, Wren," said the master. "We need her heart."

The master had already removed Victor from the slab. His corpse tossed to the ground like garbage. The master was staring at the dead and crucified Jennifer hanging above the entrance as Wren dropped Heather's body on the slab then immediately went to work, using the blade he'd used to carve Victor's body. He cut open her shirt, then dipped the knife into her chest bone, sawing through it. He noticed the other victims looked on in disgust as he pried the chest bone apart then dipped his hands in and pulled out her heart, clipping the arteries with his knife. Wren then regarded his master as he took the heart and tossed it into the fire where the flames danced across the organ with a dull roar and an orange glow.

"Should we remove her from the rafters?" Wren stepped to the slab again, looking up at Jennifer.

The master looked over his shoulder at Wren, that deep-seated conniving grin plastered across his lips. "Not at all. Not this one Wren." He turned back to Jennifer. "I like her where she is." He clucked his tongue. "Like an ornament. A mascot for our macabre." And he laughed, chuckled beneath his breath when he gestured to the firepit. "When you took her heart, it was too late. Jennifer's essence had already transformed into the ether. This is why we must take the heart immediately and add it to the fire. But worry not, my Wren. Jennifer now lives in the cemetery ether." He turned to Wren. "Our host, Mr. Saduj, never knew what hit him. He'll be running from her hate filled ghost for the rest of our time here. Which means he won't be able to continue with his little manipulations of his dear beloved Lori. I do believe our host has become more knowledgeable to our dealings than he has let us know." He regarded the other victims. "But we have plenty more hearts to offer."

"What happens to them after the fire devours the heart? Where does the essence go?"

"To Xibalba. An offering to Baphomet. The more hearts we send him, the more he is satisfied." He stared into Wren's eyes. "The more satisfied he is, the better for our cause. Baphomet is our King, Wren. All we do is in his honor. Only Satan himself is above the great Baphomet, but that presence is more of a consciousness than anything physical. An energy existing in polarity with the opposite."

Wren smiled smugly while scanning across the dungeon. He could feel the change in energy and essence. It felt like basking in the glory of hell and damnation. He could feel the evil like a dark seed blossoming in the center of his mind infecting his cells with venom. He welcomed the dark energy. Welcomed it and embraced the driving essence of pure evil. He looked at Heather, lying dead on the slab. Then to Victor, sprawled across the floor.

"What to do with them?" asked Wren. He regarded his master. "Another bonfire."

The master thought and thought, his head craned to the right. He ran his tongue across his lips before looking at Wren and shaking his head. "I don't think so. Not any longer, Wren." He shifted his cane from one hand to the other. "I believe, Wren, that it is time. Time for Sleepy Hollow to capture a glimpse of their future." He paused then, and Wren gritted his teeth in anticipation. "It is time for us to reveal our work. To bring fear to the Hollow." He gestured to the dead bodies. "Bring them to the Hollow, Wren.

314

Albeit strategically placed." He looked up at the ceiling as if looking through the ceiling. "We only have a few hours before twilight beams across Sleepy Hollow. Before I must return to the ether and the privacy of my crypt." He returned his gaze to Wren. "You will need help in your endeavor."

Wren's eyes narrowed. "Help?"

The master grinned and tapped his cane. "Indeed. The ghost demons are uniquely possessive creatures and strong too. They can help you dump good Victor and Heather and will provide aid in our quest. I have expected their role in our venture and will need them to seek out the authority, the council that has maintained my earthly prison for far too long. Those descendants of the faith that bested my dealings so long ago. I do believe it is time to pay them a visit. Once the bodies are discovered the council will undoubtedly conspire against us. It would be best to cut them off before any plan can be put into effect. For this, I have a special task for Marc to complete tomorrow regarding the council. His time for sitting on the sidelines is coming to an end." He locked eyes with Wren. "Over the next few days, he must begin to see the effect of his desperation, and the ghost demons are best suited to aid him in this transition. What better way for us to open the doorway in Marc's mind other than the destruction of the authority?" He gazed over each of his victims. "But who will it be? The ghost demon chooses the host. Who among them will take up the mantel?"

Wren looked around the chamber, regarding his waiting victims. They looked so weary, so tired and petrified all at the same time. Wren understood that after a few days in shackles while standing up had brought a profound weakness to their bones. Dehydrated and famished, their bones and muscles depleted of strength. He was certain more than a few of them welcomed death.

"But master, do we not need all of them to complete the rituals?"

"There are always more patrons to choose from. It's time we brought our little ruse into the light. Our ghost demons can provide us with what we need. They are uniquely manipulative creatures. Plus…" He gestured to the fissures. "We've done well, Wren. The portal has gained power not even I thought would happen so quickly." He scanned around the dungeon "I believe it is the time period. I notice the fear vibration is stronger now than when I previously walked the earth." He stared into Wren's eyes. "Such essence provides the perfect cocktail for evil deeds."

"As you wish, my master." He looked over at his patrons, then back to the master. "How is it done?"

"So simple, really." He raised his cane then twisted the cap. Left, right, then left, slowly turning until the golden handle clicked into place. "All it takes, Wren. Is free will."

The ghost demons slithered from the cane. Three fog plumes billowed from the golden round top in the shape of faces with tiny red eyes and mouths filled with fangs. They slithered around the chamber, taking an inventory on the potential hosts, wrapping and coiling around them, one by one, leaving a chemtrail around each victim. The essence dissipated a moment after as the ghost demons continued to spiral around the room.

Then stopped. Stopped in front of Sarah with her short auburn hair and emerald eyes. She glared at the smoke in front of her. The other two ghost demons hovered in front of Hal and Andrew.

"Seems our ghost demons have chosen their hosts," said the master. Wren watched as the ghost demons slithered into their nostrils. "It is like a marriage, Wren. A symbiotic relationship. The ghost demon talks to them." He looked at Wren. "Like a voice in their head." Turned back to Sarah when the last vaporous tendril disappeared into her nose. "Choose death or choose union. Welcome the demon with open arms… or breathe your last breath before embracing death."

Then the rattling, as if they were captured in the throes of a seizure. Bodies shook violently; heads whipped from side to side and Wren was certain that if the gags hadn't been in place they'd belt out high-pitched screams. The back of their heads smacked against the stone as if they were gagging on a bone. Then their eyes rolled to the back of their skulls.

"For the host, the marriage is surreal. The ghost demon drains the mind of its conscience, melting away fear, insecurity… and attachment. They will feel powerful, with no recourse to punishment. They will take what is theirs without a moment's pause. And while they live without rules, boundaries, or consequence the ghost demon feeds on their essence, draining them of their lifeforce until all that remains is an empty shell with their souls trapped in Xibalba. But the host must comply." He looked at Wren. "Their agreement allows the ghost demon to occupy the body and control the mind."

"Is that how it is between you and our host, my master?"

The master stepped forward, his stare burrowing into Sarah's soul. "Not at all. It is uniquely different. The ghost demons require the mind to enter. For me, it is Marc's heart. I must devour his essence of love and admiration, leaving the soul in anguish for eternity. With the ghost demons, the host is devoid of empathy but for Marc, his empathy is heightened. All to cause profound suffering to his bleeding heart. And with the ghost demons the host is aware of all that happens around them, but Marc's heart is blind to our dealings. Not that he couldn't know if he chose to know, but it is not Marc's mind we are concerned with, it is his heart. The path to eternal suffering is through the human heart. Because of his suffering. Because of his guilt, Marc closes his mind to our dealings, although his heart feels the effect of our deeds. Feels it through the cemetery's ether but he chooses to remain blind for his own cause. Until recently of course, but the how behind his knowledge is an enigma." He looked down at his body. "This pitiful excuse for a body, this heart, it carries such a cruel, foul, and putrid stank." He looked at Wren. "Love is such a disgusting abomination."

And then, quiet. Calm and quiet as their heads leaned forward. Sarah took a deep gaping inhale while Hal and Andrew examined the dungeon.

"You may release the shackles, Wren. The ghost demons have succeeded."

Wren walked over to Sarah. There was a red glint in her irises. Her veins were prominently displayed across her skin. They looked like a spiderweb crawling from her neck to her cheeks and around her eyes, thick and black with the slightest hint of purple. Wren noticed the same veins in Hal and Andrew. He removed her gag, followed by the restraints. Wren could feel the heat rifling off her skin.

Sarah stepped away from the wall. She scanned around the dungeon, her head moving at a snail's pace, investigating every turn, stone, and victim. Wren removed the restraints from Hal and Andrew. They both stepped forward, gazing over the dungeon with childlike wonder.

"How do you all feel?" the master inquired. "Are you ready to unleash death upon Sleepy Hollow? Are you ready to become gods among these feeble and pathetic humans?"

A smile curled in the corners of their mouths.

They all turned to the master.

Sarah said, "With delight."

"It is our honor to walk beside you again," said Hal, raising his chin in recognition of the master.

And Andrew, with his wide beaming eyes stood with a subtle air of satisfaction. He looked at the master. "Seems our time has finally come." He closed his eyes and bowed. "I am yours to instruct."

The master curled his fingers around his cane. "Once the spell on the portal has been broken, everyone in Sleepy Hollow will be possessed by a ghost demon…

"And my army will rise."

Where desire collides with darkness, every secret bleeds, and love is the most dangerous weapon of all.

The portal is opening. The demon's army is stirring.
Grab your copy of Book Three today at www.pdalleva.com!

Also by PD Alleva

Horror

Golem: A haunting tale of suspense, loss, isolation, contempt, and fear. The Devil is in the details!

Jigglyspot and the Zero Intellect: A satirical cosmic horror fantasy thriller novel. Jigglyspot is a half-human, half-warlock, travelling carnival clown moonlighting as a drug dealing pimp and lackey for a demonic army from Xibalba.

Sci-Fi/Fantasy

The Dark Veil: The Rose Vol 1 & 2: A masterful, dystopian science fiction thriller of telepathic evil greys, mysterious rebellion, martial arts, and Alien Vampires.

Dark Fantasy

Presenting the Marriage of Kelli Anne & Gerri Denemer: One known terrorist. A protest about to erupt. A family on the brink of collapse. Is the bond between husband and wife strong enough to defeat evil?

Purchase these and other fine books of horror, scifi, and psychological thrillers from Chamber Door Publishing today.

www.pdalleva.com

About the Author

PD writes books. Horror, scifi, psychological thrillers, fantasy, and sometimes a literary gem. Good ones, crazy ones, fun books, entertaining books, terrifying books that are absolutely insane, and books with depth and thrills that rip out the heart of humanity then tosses it on a slab to be feasted on. Yeah, that's what he does, he writes books. Any questions?

To learn more or join PD's newsletter visit www.pdalleva.com.